THE
NECKLACE

ALSO BY MATT WITTEN

The Jacob Burns Mystery Series
The Killing Bee
Strange Bedfellows
Grand Delusion
Breakfast at Madeline's

THE
NECKLACE

MATT WITTEN

OCEANVIEW◯PUBLISHING
SARASOTA, FLORIDA

ISBN 978-1-60809-458-5

Published in the United States of America by Oceanview Publishing

Sarasota, Florida

www.oceanviewpub.com

10 9 8 7 6 5 4 3 2 1

PRINTED IN THE UNITED STATES OF AMERICA

For Nancy

ACKNOWLEDGMENTS

THANK YOU TO everyone in my beloved writing group, the Oxnardians: Harley Jane Kozak, Bonnie MacBird, Patricia Smiley, Jonathan Beggs, Jamie Diamond, Andrew Rubin, Linda Burrows, Bob Shayne, and Craig Faustus Buck. Also, thanks to all the other writers who gave me words of wisdom: Lee Goldberg, Danny Greenspan, Elizabeth Wilks, Erinne Dobson, Alia Little, Alexa Darrin, Byron Willinger, Philip de Blasi, Zack Witten, and Jacob Witten. Special thanks to John Henry Davis and Sagit Maier-Schwartz, who gave me key structural suggestions.

Thank you also to Erica Little, Miguel Peralta Canton, Christian Martin, Tiffany Peckenpaugh, Milan Perisic, Sally McDonald, and everyone else who worked at the 18th Street Coffee House in Santa Monica, for their coffee, muffins, and unfailing kindness and good humor as I sat in the corner muttering dialog to myself while I wrote this novel.

Many thanks to the brilliant Josh Getzler and Jon Cobb at HG Literary, and to Pat and Bob Gussin, Lee Randall, Lisa Daily, Kat Daue, and everyone else at Oceanview for their expert editing and marketing.

I'm very grateful to Nancy Seid, who's not only a great wife and girlfriend, but also a darn excellent editor.

Also, many thanks to anyone I might be forgetting! And one final note: I took a couple of small liberties with geographical distances in upstate New York, for dramatic purposes. Sorry, Galwegians!

CHAPTER ONE

"Which do you like better?" Amy asked. "The purple dolphin or the pink duck?"

"Here's the fun part," said Susan, ruffling her daughter's silky hair. "We can get both."

They were at the Soave Faire Craft Store in Glens Falls, picking out beads so Amy could make a necklace like her friend Kate's. These long, leisurely Sunday afternoons together after church were Susan's favorite part of the week.

"Are they expensive?" Amy asked, her big brown eyes open wide.

Susan hated that her seven-year-old went straight to "expensive." "Nope a dope," she said. "Get as many as you want."

So they bought a hundred beads, and as they left the store Amy jumped up and down with excitement. "We got eleven animals and eleven and a half different colors!" she crowed. Susan had been a quiet, shy girl herself, and she thought, *Where did this little bundle of energy come from?* Not that she was complaining.

They went next door to Baskin-Robbins for jamoca almond fudge. "Is it expensive?" Amy asked.

Good grief. "No worries," Susan said. "Let's get double scoops."

Danny hadn't sold a house in two months, and clearly Amy was feeling the tension. But his luck would turn around—it always did. Hopefully today's open house was going well.

After they had every last lick of their gigantic ice cream cones—the teenage girl at the counter, charmed by Amy, had given them extra big scoops—they got into Susan's Dodge Dart and drove back home through the Adirondack foothills. It was early April and the trees were starting to bud.

"Mommy, why do frogs croak?" Amy asked.

"That's how they find girlfriends."

Amy giggled. "No, really."

"I'm serious. That's their way of saying, 'I'm looking for looooove.'" She drew out the word really long, and Amy thought that was hilarious. For the rest of the trip, they tried to outdo each other with how long they could make looooove last.

"I loooooooooove you," Amy said.

"I loooooooooooooove you more than the moon loooooooooooooves the stars," Susan replied.

CHAPTER TWO

BEER IN HAND, Susan watched the crowd two-stepping on the dance floor and thought how strange it was, everybody drinking and partying on a night that was all about a brutal murder. Pink and purple balloons and silver tinsel decorated the old wooden walls and the Stony Creek Boys were playing for free. This was the Crow Bar's biggest night since summer season.

Terri, Susan's best friend and fellow waitress at the diner, touched her shoulder. "Wanna dance?"

Susan started to say no without even thinking, but Terri leaned in closer and said, "Amy would want you to. She loved to dance."

It was true. Amy started dancing to country music when she was a toddler, and she would have loved this party. So finally Susan said, "Okay," and got up out of their booth.

People noticed within seconds. Three young women standing nearby—Amy's old childhood friends—smiled encouragement, and everybody made way for her. Susan honestly couldn't remember the last time she'd been out on a dance floor, and her bones felt stiff. But she told herself nobody would be judging her tonight.

Terri put her arms around Susan as the band turned it up a notch. Susan's feet began searching for the rhythm. She looked around the bar and saw the crowd facing toward her, clapping. Everyone she

knew in the whole town was here, and it felt like they were all dancing with her.

She closed her eyes for a moment and swayed, listening to the
twanging of the guitar. *I should be grateful for this party,* she thought.
After all, the whole thing was for her benefit.

She looked up at the wall behind the bar. There was a huge photo of
Amy from twenty years ago, when she was seven. It was blown up from
a faded Polaroid, so it was a little fuzzy. But Amy's wide, gap-toothed
smile and joyful spirit came through loud and clear. Her light brown
hair fell to her shoulders and she wore a multicolored beaded necklace.
If you got close you could see the individual beads: the purple dolphin,
the pink duck . . .

This was Susan's favorite picture of her daughter. She'd taken it the
week Amy was killed.

Terri whispered in her ear, "Here comes Evan."

Susan saw Evan Mullens dancing closer to her. Evan was fifty-seven,
two years older than she was, and freshly divorced. He'd moved back
to town last year to run the Adirondack Folk School and seemed to
like her. He came by the diner at least once a week and flirted with
her, and Terri always said if Susan encouraged him just a little bit,
he'd ask her out.

He wasn't bad looking, either. But Susan was as out of practice with
that as she was with dancing. So now she looked at Evan's big smile
and red checkered shirt and gave him the briefest of smiles in return,
then looked away.

She found herself facing her mother, sitting in a nearby booth
drinking beer and bobbing her head to the music. Lenora waved to
her, then leaned past her oxygen tank and shouted over the music,
"Nice party, huh?"

Right, nice party. Despite herself, Susan felt a sodden mass of buried
rage rise back to life in her chest. What happened to Amy was her
mom's fault—

No. Don't go there.

The song ended with a bang of drums and smash of guitars, and everybody cheered. Johnny, the long-haired, craggy-faced lead singer, acknowledged the applause by taking off his purple cowboy hat and giving a sweeping bow. He wasn't the world's greatest singer but made up for it with what Lenora called "vim."

He called out, "How's everybody doing this evening?"

The crowd whooped and hollered, and Johnny gave a big grin. But then he put up his hands. "Now, as y'all know," he said, "these festivities ain't just about fun."

The crowd wasn't quite ready to get serious, so they gave Johnny some good-natured boos. "Shut up and sing!" one drunk guy on the dance floor shouted.

Johnny persisted. "We got a higher purpose tonight."

Now everybody turned quiet. The drunk guy started to shout his displeasure, but somebody elbowed him in the side and he stopped in mid-yell.

"In honor of which," Johnny continued, taking the microphone off the stand, "I would like to call Susan Lentigo, Amy's mom, to the stage."

Susan hated speaking in public, but she'd had enough experience since her daughter's murder that she'd gotten okay at it. So now she smoothed her dark brown hair, adjusted her glasses, and took a deep breath to steady herself as she walked up to the small raised bandstand. She wasn't into clothes as she had been years ago, but she was glad she'd let her mom talk her into wearing her nice yellow shirt and putting on some makeup. The crowd clapped respectfully as she climbed the two steps and took the microphone from Johnny's hand.

"Hi, everybody," she said, but her mouth was too close to the mic and there was screeching feedback. She saw her mom wince.

Johnny stepped toward her to help out, but she knew what to do. She held the mic a few inches farther away and started over. "Hi, everybody." This time it worked.

She looked out at the crowd. Some of these people had known her all her life. They'd been here during her childhood, during her marriage, during her tragedy. Many of them had helped her search the woods for Amy.

Now they were helping her again. Every beer the bar sold tonight would help pay her way to the penitentiary in North Dakota next weekend.

"I want to thank each and every one of you for coming tonight," she said. She looked over at Parson Mary Parsons, sitting in a booth with a couple of women, in their sixties now, who had brought Susan casseroles every week for about a year after it happened. "I want to thank everybody from the church . . ."

Parson Parsons nodded solemnly, and one of the women dabbed at her eyes with a Kleenex. Susan looked away. The last thing she wanted right now was to break down herself. She had to finish her speech.

She said, "Also all the beautiful ladies who work with me over at the diner . . ."

Terri, on the dance floor, called out, "We love you, Susan!" Terri had been a teenager when Amy was killed, had babysat for her.

Susan smiled briefly and kept going. "Also, my wonderful neighbors . . ."

At a far booth, Tom and Stacy, who lived in a trailer down the street and chopped wood for Susan, gave her a thumbs-up.

Now she looked over at her mom. She knew her mom had tortured herself over what she had done and didn't deserve the mindless anger Susan sometimes felt. ". . . And my mom, Lenora."

Lenora liked public attention a lot more than Susan did, and she'd had a few drinks. Her face brightened and she gave everybody a wave.

"Most of all," Susan said, "I'd like to thank Amy's best friends, Sherry, Kate, and Sandy, for bringing joy into Amy's life when she was alive and never forgetting her."

The three young women were still standing together by the dance floor, arm in arm. In their late twenties now, they had jobs, husbands, and kids.

They had lives.

They had everything Amy didn't.

Susan could still picture the four of them the summer before Amy died, practicing dance routines to Garth Brooks songs on her front porch. Seeing them here now was both sweet and agonizing. Evidently, they felt the same way, because all three of them began to weep.

Susan turned away from them and looked up at the big photograph of her daughter behind the bar. "I believe Amy is here with us tonight," she said.

In the picture, Amy was missing one of her top front teeth. The tooth fairy had put two dollars under her pillow the very night before she was taken.

Susan turned back to the crowd. "It's been twenty long years. But now, in only seven days, next Saturday at five-thirty p.m., Amy will finally get justice. Thanks to you guys and your kind generosity, I will be there in North Dakota when the fucking Monster"—Susan's voice took on a fierce intensity—"who raped and murdered my daughter is sent to his much-deserved reward, in hell, and my Amy can rest in peace at last."

Susan thought for a moment, realized she didn't have any more to say, and said, "Thank you." She handed the mic back to Johnny, stepped off the stage, and headed back toward her booth.

The adrenalin from speaking to the crowd was still running through her. She couldn't even feel her feet stepping on the cold, dark, wooden floor.

She passed Sherry, Kate, and Sandy, and they all hugged her, one at a time. Slowly but surely, everybody in the bar began applauding. The ones who had been sitting all stood up. Several people held out their hands for a high five, which she felt weird about, but she went ahead and high-fived them. The drunk guy on the dance floor high-fived her so enthusiastically he stumbled and fell over.

Johnny put down the mic so he could clap too. Then he picked it back up and said, "Susan, just make sure you take pictures, 'cause we all wanna see that sick bastard fry."

A woman yelled, "Hell yeah!" and everybody cheered.

Johnny continued, "Now there's about a hundred of us here tonight, and we've all been buying lots of beer—"

"No shit!" the drunk shouted.

"—which means Susan's already raised a lot of money for her trip. But it's a long way out to North Dakota, and I happen to know her old Dodge Dart needs a new set of tires. And then there's hotels and such."

He took off his big cowboy hat. "So even though times are hard for all of us, let's see what else we can do for this brave gal."

He put a twenty-dollar bill in the hat and gave it to the man closest to him. As the hat passed and money went in, the band began playing a slow ballad that Johnny had written last week, just for this occasion.

"*Love of my life, storm of my tears,*" he sang. "*All of my sorrow over the years . . .*"

Finally, Susan allowed herself to cry. She looked through her tears at all these people who cared for her, who had gathered here to help her. She and her mom had less than a hundred dollars to their names, but now she'd be able to make it to the execution. She'd been hoping for this day for so many years, she'd almost forgotten what life was like before it happened.

She had lost not only her daughter but her husband, her soul mate, the only man she had ever loved.

Sometimes Parson Parsons talked to her about forgiveness. But she didn't give a fuck about forgiveness.

Maybe if the Monster—she never called him by his real name, she wouldn't give him that dignity—ever actually *asked* for forgiveness, if he ever quit lying and claiming he didn't kill Amy, then maybe she might feel a little something toward him besides pure red-hot rage.

She balled her hands into fists. The Monster had been there when Amy drew her last breath. Now Susan would be there while he breathed his last. She would put her face up close to the window so the last thing he saw in this life was her, and she would watch him die.

As Susan sat back down in her booth, Lenora walked up, rolling her oxygen tank with one hand and holding up a beer in the other. "Nice speech," she said. "Want another beer?"

God, her mom was so inappropriate. Except come to think of it, she wouldn't mind another beer. "Thanks," she said.

As she drank down a big gulp, she wondered how she'd feel next Saturday night, after the Monster got what he deserved. Would she finally be able to let go of what happened and "move on," as her mom was always telling her to do?

She knew her mom was right. She was only thirty-five when it happened. She could have gotten married again, even started a new family. Sure, she couldn't have her own kids anymore, but she could have adopted or had stepkids. God knows there were plenty of divorced men in Lake Luzerne who had hit on her over the years. Evan was far from the first.

But she couldn't help herself. She sometimes felt there was something stealing the air out of her, like she was chain smoking. Maybe it was just grief and guilt choking her spirit. But somehow, even twenty years later, the story didn't feel finished. She still had a feeling in her bones that she couldn't put her finger on, that didn't make sense, that there was something about her daughter's murder she had missed, and if she had noticed it at the time, she could have prevented it.

But what did she miss? What could she have done?

The psychiatrist down at Albany Hospital had told her it was a common phenomenon: people feeling guilty after a senseless tragedy, trying to come up with some scenario whereby it wasn't just random but something they themselves had somehow caused. For some people, it was better to feel guilty than to feel like they had no control over what happened in their lives.

But even though she heard the psychiatrist's words, it made no difference. She went over the tragedy again and again in her head almost every night.

As Susan drank down her beer, she replayed, once more, her daughter's final week on this earth.

CHAPTER THREE

Susan and Amy got back home from their bead shopping and ice cream expedition a little after five. Danny had beaten them there and he was watching the Celtics on TV.

He got up and said, "Hi, guys!" and Susan could tell right away the open house had been a success. He'd taken off his sport jacket, but he was still wearing his light blue shirt with an open collar, and he flashed her that confident grin, and for the first time in weeks she remembered how sexy he was. She and Danny had been together since his senior year of high school—her sophomore year—when he was both star running back and starting pitcher. On their first date they went swimming at Fourth Lake, and she could still remember feeling short of breath when he took off his T-shirt. Now he stayed fit by working out religiously at the Y in Corinth.

If she did say so herself, they made a good-looking couple. She walked a couple miles a day even in winter, and between that and waitressing at the diner, she'd managed to get back to her pre-baby weight. She had a knack for finding nice clothes at the church thrift store, and she allowed herself one treat: having the ladies at Country Girls color her hair.

Amy ran up to Danny, jumping up and down. "Daddy, we got the best beads. The lady at the store said they had one hundred thousand of them."

"Wow," said Danny, sweeping Amy up and giving her a hug. "That's a very big number."

Amy squirmed out of Danny's grasp so she could lay out her beads on the living room table. Susan kissed him hello. "How'd it go?"

Danny gave a fist pump. "We had fourteen people, including three primo prospects. I'm betting we get at least one offer by tomorrow morning."

"That's terrific! How about I make chicken to celebrate?"

Amy said, "Wanna see my pink duck, Daddy?"

Amy showed him her beads while Susan put dinner together. She baked the chicken thighs with lemon and garlic for slightly over an hour, just the way Danny liked it. The night before her wedding, Lenora had told her, "Men are simple creatures. Just feed them and they're happy." It was the best advice her mom ever gave her.

Their marriage had gone through some tough times. Susan had two miscarriages in her twenties. When Amy, her little miracle, was born, Susan was told her cervix was permanently incompetent and she would never be able to have any more kids.

But the marriage survived her medical problems and the uncertainties of Danny's career. He had days when he'd get depressed by job stuff and feel like he should have gone to law school instead of settling for being a real estate agent, and he'd get snappish at Susan. But she always knew he'd be himself again soon.

And he hung in with her during those terrible months after she lost her babies. He brought her endless pints of jamoca almond fudge and took her snowmobiling to distract her. Sometimes he rode faster than she liked, but the excitement was probably exactly what she needed.

"Dinner's ready!" she called out. Danny and Amy raced each other to see who would sit down at the table first. They all had second helpings of the chicken and potatoes, and Amy regaled her parents with a long, complicated story about a baby hoot owl that liked to eat snakes, but only if they were mean. Susan caught Danny's eye and they smiled.

After dinner, while Susan did the dishes, Danny and Amy played with her dolls and then wrestled each other on the living room floor. "I'm gonna getchou," Danny growled, and Amy squealed with mock fear. Susan loved it that her husband and daughter were so close. *I wish I'd had that with my father*, she thought. Susan's dad had always come home worn out from his job at the paper mill and gone straight to the living room sofa, where he'd kill a few beers and watch a game. He dropped dead of a heart attack when Susan was only ten.

After that, she never had any other real father figures. Her mom went to work as a dental receptionist and began "sowing my wild and crazy oats," as she put it, dating a variety of guys, some married, some not. Susan got that her mom had a right to her own life, but she felt Lenora made some pretty dumb choices, especially when she drank. It was one reason Susan went easy on the drinking herself.

As she scrubbed chicken fat off the baking sheet, she bit her lip and thought about what had happened two nights ago. Lenora was babysitting Amy, and they went out for ice cream with Lenora's latest beau. Amy came home afterwards and declared the guy a "dodohead."

"He kept calling me 'Pretty Baby,'" Amy said. "Like 'Hey, Pretty Baby.' And then he'd touch my hair. Eww!"

Susan needed to have a talk with her mom about that. Amy shouldn't have to spend time with Lenora's boyfriends, especially the ones who made her uncomfortable. Susan had been putting off this argument since Thursday night, but she should get it over with. *I'll call Mom right now,* she thought.

But when she finished the dishes, Danny was in his study with the door closed, sending emails to clients and potential clients and getting on real estate listservs. His being on the internet would tie up the phone line for the next hour, and Susan wouldn't be able to call Lenora after all.

Well, that was okay. This computer stuff was important for Danny's business. Besides, maybe she was better off waiting 'til tomorrow to talk to her mom. Lenora was never at her best on a Sunday night, when the weekend was almost over.

So Susan hung out with Amy at the kitchen table, stringing beads onto the necklace. They could only use about fifty beads for the size necklace Amy wanted, so they spent a lot of time choosing which ones to include.

"The dolphin and the duck should be next to each other, because they're gonna get married," Amy declared.

"That makes sense," Susan said. "What about the blue unicorn?"

"Well, he should have yellow beads on both sides. Or maybe red . . . What do you think, Mommy?" Amy asked, furrowing her brow as if the whole world depended on it.

Susan smiled and smoothed Amy's hair. How lucky was she to be able to bring this beautiful creature onto this earth?

They beaded the necklace together as the sky grew dark.

CHAPTER FOUR

The party at the Crow Bar broke up after midnight. Susan stood outside in the cold Adirondack wind thanking and hugging everybody, feeling their warmth.

But then it was time to go home. Susan got into the ancient Dodge Dart with her mom, and Terri gave her a final goodbye. "Have fun!" Terri called through the window. "Knock 'em dead!"

Susan realized this was a twisted joke about the execution and shook her head, smiling.

Five minutes later, Susan and Lenora were back at their house. It was the same cozy three-bedroom just off 9N that Susan had lived in years ago with Danny and Amy. Lenora wheeled her oxygen tank up the driveway, while Susan carried a big plastic garbage bag full of money from tonight's party.

"Wow, that sure looks heavy," Lenora said. "How much you figure is in there?"

"A lot," Susan said. She stumbled a little on the front steps, feeling wrung out. But the night had definitely been a success, raising way more money than she'd expected.

She unlocked the door and they went in. As they walked through the shag-carpeted living room, Lenora said, "The hell with the execution. You should go to Florida and hang out on the beach."

Not this again. For months now, Lenora had been trying to talk her out of attending the execution. But she knew her mom didn't mean any harm; she was just afraid if Susan saw the Monster in person again, it would bring back old traumas. So she swallowed her annoyance and kept her tone light. "Don't know about Florida, but maybe I'll hit Niagara Falls on the way."

She wasn't sure if she was serious about that idea, but Lenora jumped on it. "You should. And go to Mount Rushmore too. I bet that's really something."

They entered the kitchen, where Susan untied the garbage bag. Lenora moved the duck-shaped coffee creamer and duck-shaped napkin holder off the table to make room for the money. One thing the two of them had always agreed on was commemorating Amy's love of ducks. Whenever Susan or Lenora found a duck at a yard sale, they grabbed it.

Susan dumped the bills onto the table and blinked at them, overwhelmed. She had never seen this much money in her life, not even on a Saturday night at the diner during Fourth of July weekend.

Lenora held up two fat handfuls of bills and brought them to her nose. "God, this money smells good. I just wanna eat it."

Susan picked up a couple of stray bills from the floor. "We should put them in piles."

They began making piles of ones, fives, tens, and the occasional twenties. In the corner by the stove, Rumples, their old gray cat, licked his paws.

"You know, with this much cash," Lenora said, and Susan prepared to get annoyed again, because she knew exactly what was coming, "you could take a plane."

Lenora had gotten obsessed with the fear Susan would get in an accident while driving to North Dakota. Yeah, okay, so she'd never gone on such a long trip by herself before, but still, she was a perfectly decent driver. Her mom needed to relax!

But Susan was pretty sure she understood why Lenora was being so overprotective. Her mom was still trying to make up for not protecting Amy like she should have.

"A plane would cost eight forty round trip," Susan said as patiently as she could.

Lenora pointed at the piles of bills. "You've got more than that right there."

"Yeah, but I need money for the motel in North Dakota—that's ninety a night, plus food money. Plus, I'm leaving you fifty dollars to tide you over for the week."

"I don't need any money. I'll be fine."

Susan didn't answer. They both knew Lenora would have to do another food shopping in a couple days that would cost, if anything, more than fifty.

Lenora said, "Can't you put the airplane on your card?"

Was her mom developing memory problems or just being willfully stubborn? Susan's jaw tightened. "I maxed out, Mom, I told you that." She took rubber bands off the windowsill and wrapped them around the piles of ones and fives. The piles of tens and twenties were smaller, so she'd use paper clips on them.

"I don't like you driving that far north. What if it snows?"

"You're the one who's always saying I should be more adventurous."

"Yeah, but not like this. I don't want you slipping around on the highway. And your leg ain't gonna like driving fifteen hundred miles."

Enough already. Susan sat back down and looked straight at Lenora's face. "Mom, I've been waiting twenty years for that man to die. If my leg bothers me, I'll just cut it off and keep going."

Lenora regarded Susan and shook her head. "You shoulda got married again," she said.

Susan rolled her eyes. "Okay, Mom."

"Don't roll your big brown eyes at me. You're still a very attractive woman. It's not right, you hiding yourself away."

"I said okay."

But Lenora wouldn't quit. "What about that guy Evan? He's handsome, don't you think?"

"Whatever," Susan said, realizing immediately she sounded like a teenager. She got back up from the table and scavenged in the drawers for paper clips.

Maybe it wasn't such a great idea, having Lenora live with her. But she worried about her mom living alone, and anyway they didn't have enough money to keep up two places anymore.

Lenora said, "I could give your hair a little trim. Take some of that gray out."

Susan had to hand it to her mom: she never quit. She paper clipped the twenties and stuffed them way down into the inside pockets of her worn wool coat, alongside the other bills. Then she stood up. "Big day tomorrow. I'm going to bed. You should too."

"Nope. Gotta finish your scarf." Lenora took out her knitting. She was making a bright aqua scarf for Susan to wear when she went out on the road.

"Okay, good night, Mom."

"Good night, baby."

Susan went off to bed, in the same bedroom she once shared with Danny. Her mom slept in Danny's old study, because Amy's bedroom was still full of her stuff. Her two bunnies hugged each other on the pillow, just like they did on the morning she was taken. Susan had made a promise to herself that she wouldn't clean out Amy's room until after her killer was dead. Lenora thought that was stupid, but Susan wouldn't budge.

The next morning, she woke up at five thirty and couldn't get back to sleep. She made some coffee and decided she'd take off early.

In the quiet of dawn, she looked around at the house she'd be leaving soon. Getting milk for her coffee, her eyes fixed on the refrigerator door. It was covered with photographs of Susan, Lenora, and Amy through the years: sledding together at Buttermilk Falls, swimming in the lake, holding up two little pumpkins they'd grown in the back-yard. At eye level was a picture of Susan and Amy on Halloween night, wearing matching princess outfits and mugging for the camera.

There were pictures of Danny too, down toward the bottom of the fridge. Susan always felt a little sad when she looked at them, but they made her smile too: the shots of her and Danny ice fishing together in Lake George—not really her thing, but she'd come to enjoy it—and honeymooning up at Bar Harbor in Maine. And then there was her favorite picture of him, at the hospital the day Amy was born. Susan held Amy in her arms, and Danny kissed the baby's tiny perfect fingers—

"Good morning, honey," Lenora said. Susan watched her mom walk in, rolling her tank and proudly holding up the newly made scarf. "I got this all finished for you."

Two hours later, when Susan was all packed and ready to go, Lenora wrapped the scarf around Susan's neck. She looked at herself in the living room mirror. She had on her old gray coat, a dark blue sweater, faded jeans, and boots that had been new eight years ago. But the bright aqua scarf made her look more cheery.

It made her feel like she was going on a big adventure.

Though it was kind of screwy to think of going to an execution as an adventure.

She watched her mom's bony, veined hands adjusting the scarf, and reminded herself how much her mom had always loved her. Lenora hadn't been perfect, and God knows she had made one terrible mistake. But she'd been a good mother.

"Thanks, Mom. It's beautiful."

Her mom beamed. Then she said, "I fixed you a bag of peanuts and chocolate chips. Also, those sweetened cranberries you like."

Susan kind of wished her mom had saved that money to buy basic groceries for herself this week, but she just said, "Thanks, Mom."

"I put it in your purse. Also, I made you this to take with you." Lenora went over to the fridge and grabbed a small-sized Windex spray bottle from on top of it. The spray bottle was filled with a red liquid. She handed it to Susan.

"What is it?" Susan said, bringing it close to her face.

"Careful! That's pepper spray."

Susan quickly moved the bottle an arm's length away from her. God, her mom was a total nut. "Seriously?"

Lenora nodded. "Extra strength. Red pepper and rubbing alcohol."

Susan raised her eyebrows at her mom, incredulous. Lenora was offended. "Hey, there's a lotta wackadoodles out there."

Susan decided not to argue. After all, what if she did have a car accident and this was the last time she ever saw her mom? Or what if Lenora had a stroke while she was gone? Susan had learned only too well never to take anything for granted. "Thanks," she said, and put the pepper spray in her purse.

Then she rolled her suitcase with the half-broken zipper across the muddy gravel to her car and lifted it into the trunk. She couldn't believe she was finally going on this trip. As her mom wheeled her tank outside and watched, Susan put her purse in the front seat.

Now she was ready to go.

She was beyond ready.

She told Lenora, "I should be back by next Wednesday. I laid out two whole weeks' worth of pills for you."

Lenora asked, "Did you call Danny?"

Susan was about to slam the trunk door shut, but she stopped and looked at her mom. She got the feeling Lenora had been wanting to ask this question for days, but hadn't wanted to upset her.

Lenora thrust out her chin, covering her discomfort with belligerence. "Well, did you?"

Susan shrugged and said, "What for?" She didn't want her mom to know how much she'd been thinking about Danny lately, ever since the Monster's final petition had been rejected by the Supreme Court and his execution was assured at last.

"Amy was Danny's daughter too, you know," Lenora said. "Ain't his fault y'all split up."

"Never said it was."

"He wasn't perfect maybe but he was a good man. You guys just got dealt some shitty cards."

Funny, just a minute ago Susan had been thinking pretty much the same thing about Lenora: she wasn't perfect but didn't deserve her bad luck. Susan's head felt suddenly heavy, even though it was still morning. She didn't want to think about Danny right now. She slammed the trunk shut. "I gotta go."

She stepped closer to her mom and frowned a little, looking at her mom's stooped posture and thinking how frail she'd become. But then Susan smiled.

"What's funny?" Lenora said, ready to get offended again.

"Nothing." Actually, she'd been thinking that, frail though her mom was, she wouldn't be surprised if she brought a guy home some night while Susan was away. "I asked Terri to look in on you."

She bent down and kissed Lenora. Her mom hugged her fiercely. "Honey, if you get tired, pull over."

"I will, Mom. I promise."

She got in the car, took a deep breath, and drove off in a puff of black engine smoke. She saw her mom waving goodbye in her rearview mirror and waved back.

Half a block away, at the corner of 9N, she passed the spot where the Homestead Motel used to be. She was grateful the old haven for small-time crooks and seedy transients had gone out of business. Now it was a collection of small condemned buildings with boarded-up windows and a For Sale sign that had been out front for five years.

She turned left on 9N and drove on. The morning sky was dark gray and every tree that could lose its leaves in winter had already lost them. As she drove, she tried to remember the last time she'd been away from Lake Luzerne for as long as a week and a half. Geez, had it been her honeymoon?

Thinking about that made her depressed. Maybe she really would hit Niagara Falls and Mount Rushmore this week.

She turned onto Mill Street and drove past the tiny library where she and Amy used to sit and read Amelia Bedelia books. She drove past the old bowling alley where she and Danny had their first kiss. It started out as a quick peck on the cheek when he was congratulating her for getting a strike, but by the time it ended, she and Danny were both branded for life.

Then she passed the Presbyterian church, where she sang in the choir every week and tried to believe in God. She did enjoy the music at least. At the center of town, she went past Lake Luzerne Realty, where Danny used to work. Then she pulled into Rozelle's Gas Station and Repairs.

Clarence Rozelle came out to greet her. He was in his late forties, with a long beard and thoughtful eyes. Years ago, Danny had told her Clarence was a great chess player, winning tournaments down in Albany and even New York City. She wondered why he had never done anything else with his life besides run this auto shop.

Maybe he was like her, a guy who couldn't leave home.

"Getting ready for your trip?" he said, wiping his hands on a rag he carried with him.

She nodded. "I'm pretty sure I could use some new tires and an oil change."

Clarence looked down at the tires. "Yeah, these two are looking pretty worn out." He walked around to the other side of the car. "And these two are just about bald. Must be that misalignment we talked about."

"Yeah." The Dodge Dart's carriage had been slightly out of whack for the past fifty thousand miles, but it would have taken three hundred bucks' worth of parts, plus labor, to straighten it out.

"Well, let's get you fixed up."

She sat in the waiting room reading about Hollywood stars in a two-month-old *Us* magazine. She always thought the magazine should be called *Them* instead of *Us,* because she sure as hell had nothing in common with those people.

After half an hour or so Clarence came back. "You're all set," he said.

She reached down into her coat pocket and brought out her paper-clipped collection of twenties. "What do I owe you?"

"Nothing."

She looked at him in disbelief. "No, really."

"Really nothing. I remember your daughter. She was a sweet kid."

Susan's eyes got wet. "Thank you."

"No worries. You think you'll see Danny there?"

"I don't know," she said. It was true, she had no idea if Danny would be at the execution.

But she was really hoping he would be. Whatever this magical thing called closure was, she was afraid she wouldn't feel it unless he was with her. They had suffered this terrible loss together, and they needed to get past it together. It had been nineteen years since she'd seen him, but maybe this weekend could bring them together again, at least as friends—

"Well, if you do see Danny, tell him I said hi. God bless you both."

"Thank you, Clarence."

Susan got back onto 9N and headed out of town. *Fifteen hundred miles to go,* she thought.

She passed the Crow Bar, where the "Amy Lentigo Night" sign was half torn off and flapping in the wind. Three miles later, she rode through Corinth. In the middle of town, she came to Molly's Diner.

Her old memories started to play again. This was where, for Susan, it all began.

CHAPTER FIVE

Susan was in the kitchen, about to drive Amy to school, when Molly called from the diner.

"Oh good, I'm so glad I caught you," Molly said. In her sixties now, she had opened Molly's Diner thirty years back, when the paper mill was still going strong. Somehow she'd kept the place open through all the economic ups and downs—mostly downs—since then. Susan respected the hell out of her.

"Hi, Molly, I'm just on my way out the door."

"Any chance you could take dinner tonight? Nancy and Eileen both have colds, and I'm a little desperate."

Susan did a quick calculation. She loved Friday nights at home with Amy, playing Monopoly or watching a movie. On the other hand, weekend nights were pretty good at the diner and they could use the tips right now, especially since Danny's three leads from the open house hadn't panned out.

As for Danny, he liked having dinner ready when he got home, especially at the end of a long week. But he'd said he would be working 'til seven or eight, prepping a property on Scofield Road for an open house tomorrow. When Danny came home that late, all he really wanted was crackers, cheese, and a beer in front of the TV watching basketball. So he should be okay with her working tonight.

She needed to get Amy taken care of, though. So she told Molly she'd make a quick call and get back to her.

Amy tapped her feet impatiently and whined, "Mommy, we're gonna be late."

Susan said, "How'd you like to hang out with Grandma after school today?"

Amy immediately brightened, clapping her hands. "We can make bracelets!"

"I'm sure Grandma would love that," Susan said, and dialed her mom. They hadn't spoken in three days, ever since she asked her mom to keep her new boyfriend—Frank was his name—away from Amy. Hopefully, Lenora wouldn't still be pissed off.

Her mom lived less than a mile away, in a trailer on 9N. She picked up on the second ring. "Who is this?" she growled in her morning voice.

"Hi, Mom, I didn't wake you, did I?"

Lenora was silent for a couple moments, then finally said, "You beat my alarm by five minutes. What's up? Everything okay?"

Susan sighed inwardly, relieved her mom had decided not to hold a grudge. "I wanted to know if you could take Amy this afternoon."

"Sure, okay. You want me to pick her up at school?"

"That would be great. Thanks, Mom."

"And don't worry, I won't bring Frank. Even though you're totally wrong about him."

"Love you, Mom," Susan said.

As she hung up, Danny walked in, smelling of the aftershave Susan and Amy had bought him for his birthday. She told him, "Molly called. I'm taking dinner tonight, okay? Mom will pick up Amy."

He nodded distractedly and set about making his coffee just the way he liked it. He'd been a little down ever since all his leads fell through. Trying to cheer him up, Susan said, "Come by Molly's tonight. She'll give you a free dinner, and there's a really cute waitress named Susan who'll flirt with you."

Before Danny could respond, Amy tugged on Susan's arm. "Mommy, I'm gonna be really, really late."

Danny turned lively for the first time this morning. "Did the tooth fairy come last night?" he asked.

"Yeah! She gave me two whole dollars!"

"Wow, she must really like you. Have a great day, Amy Shlamy," Danny said.

"Bye, Daddy Shladdy," Amy said. Danny smiled. Amy always made him smile no matter what mood he was in.

Susan and Amy got in the car and rode off to school, passing the Homestead Motel. There were always ten or twenty unfortunate people staying there, and one of them was out front this morning, getting what looked like a toolbox out of his rusty old car and eyeing the Dodge Dart as it drove by. He had a flat, tired face and looked like he'd had a hard life. Amy fingered the blue unicorn on her necklace and said, "You know the coolest thing about unicorns?"

"What's that, honey?"

Amy proceeded to chatter away about unicorns and centaurs, but Susan only half-listened. She was thinking about a conversation she and Danny had in bed last night, about her going back to college.

Susan had gotten her Associate's at Adirondack Community College when she was twenty-one, shortly after they got married. She'd always meant to go back for her B.A. and maybe study nursing. But she didn't really like school, was never very good at it, and working at Molly's was just too comfortable. Then she'd had the pregnancies and miscarriages, and then Amy was born and Susan devoted her life to her.

But now, as she had told Danny last night, "I'm thinking maybe I should start taking some courses again."

"Like what kind of courses?"

"Maybe Anatomy or Human Growth and Development. The courses you need for nursing school."

"I'm all for it, honey," Danny had said, running his hand down her arm. "Let's just save up a little money first. Soon as the market turns around we'll be solid again, and we won't have to take out a loan."

Susan was grateful Danny didn't pressure her to make more money. But at some point, she needed to decide what she wanted to do with the rest of her life.

Amy was still talking. "Mommy?" she said, in an annoyed tone. "Mommy, you're not listening."

Susan turned off 9N into the long school driveway. "I'm sorry, honey, what were you saying?"

"I'm never gonna take this necklace off," Amy said, rubbing her dolphin bead. "Never."

Susan smiled. "Even when you take a bath?"

"Nope."

"Even when you go to sleep?"

Amy gave her head a vigorous shake. "Nope. Not even when I die."

They pulled up in front of the school, a brick building the town had built twenty years ago when it had more money. Amy's three best friends, Sherry, Kate, and Sandy, were on the sidewalk out front.

"I love you, sweetie. Grandma will pick you up at three thirty."

"Love you too, Mommy."

Amy gave her a quick kiss and skipped off with her friends, as Susan drove away.

Most mornings after dropping Amy off, Susan went back home. Danny would leave for work, and she would clean the kitchen and read the *Post-Star* before heading to Molly's. It was her quiet time, all to herself.

But today, since she'd be cooped up all day, she decided to go walking on the River Road next to the Hudson. It was the height of mud season, so she stayed on the road itself. The sun was shining and it had to be at least fifty degrees. It might even make it up to sixty this afternoon.

She enjoyed the river views and the country music station on her Walkman—a lot of Tim McGraw and Faith Hill, Susan's favorite celebrity couple. She waved hi to the drivers of all the cars and trucks that went by. A lot of them she knew personally.

When Susan finished her walk, she drove to Stone's, where she bought kids' toothpaste for Amy, and the IGA, where she got Danny's favorite spaghetti sauce for tomorrow night. Then she headed for Molly's, seven miles away, and got there in plenty of time for the lunch rush.

Not that it was much of a rush. The first customers to straggle in were four elderly women in wool coats who took a corner booth. They came here every Friday and always tipped poorly. But Susan tried not to judge them. She guessed this might be their big social event of the week, the one thing they had enough money for, barely.

Around noon some road repairmen came in, followed by two tables of people from the town hall, but when she added up all her tips, it only came to twenty dollars.

"Tonight'll be better," Molly promised. "And if it isn't, I'll throw in some extra."

"No problem," Susan said, thinking twenty dollars would cover an afternoon movie for her and Amy tomorrow while Danny did his open house. They could see *Mulan* for the third time—Amy loooooooooooooved that movie.

She checked in with Danny around two thirty. He sounded like he was having an average day; not too inspiring but not too discouraging either.

"I'm on my way to the Scofield Road house, see if I can make it presentable," he said. "You still working tonight?"

"Yeah. If you're too tired to come by, you want me to bring you home a hamburger?"

"Sure, thanks. I'll pick up Amy from your mom around seven thirty, when I'm finished at Scofield."

"Okay."

They rang off, and Susan hit the sofa in the back room for a nap. The sofa was saggy and technically nowhere near as comfortable as her bed at home, but somehow she always got her best sleep here. Danny could be a little restless at night. She slept until five and woke up refreshed, ready to work.

Dinner went a lot better than lunch. A full day of spring weather had put people in the mood to go out on the town. The turkey chili special was a big hit tonight, and most of the diners were generous with their tips. Susan worked constantly, and by eight o'clock she had already made forty in tips with more to come.

Then Molly stepped away from the front register and walked up to her as she was picking up an order from the cook. "You got a phone call," Molly said.

"Can you take a message?"

"I think you better get it. It's Danny."

Susan could tell right away from Molly's tone there was a problem. This wasn't just about whether Danny wanted cheese on his burger. She hurried to the register and grabbed the phone.

"Hi, what's up?" she said.

Danny's voice came back. "Do you know where Amy is?"

"She's with Mom."

"I was just at her house. Nobody's there."

Susan didn't get why he was so worried. "They must have gone out somewhere. Maybe they're coming to Molly's."

"I just got home. There's a message on our machine from this morning, from your mom. Saying she's sorry, but she just remembered she's busy tonight, so she can't take Amy."

Susan stared at the phone. Amy wasn't with her mom. She wasn't with Danny. She wasn't with her.

But school ended four hours ago!

Where the hell is Amy?

CHAPTER SIX

SUNDAY, NOVEMBER 28, PRESENT DAY

AS SUSAN LEFT Corinth behind and turned onto Route 29, she thought about that phone call from Danny, and wondered if their marriage was doomed from that moment.

Probably.

She noticed her thumb was playing with her engagement ring as she drove. She still wore it on her right hand because it was the nicest piece of jewelry she owned—a blue sapphire surrounded by tiny diamond chips.

The last time she saw Danny, they were hugging goodbye outside the mediator's office in Saratoga Springs. Then he moved to the small town of Tamarack a few hours to the west, near Lake Erie. From what Susan had heard, it was like Luzerne but a little more upscale and tourist-friendly. He was working as a realtor there.

Sometimes Susan wondered what her life would have been like if she'd never met Danny. But she always shoved that thought out of her head, because that would mean Amy never would have existed.

And also, she and Danny had a lot of good years together. In his own quirky way, he was a romantic. When he proposed, he got down on both knees—and then turned a double somersault before offering her the ring. For her twenty-first birthday he gave her a music box that played "Somewhere Over the Rainbow," which she'd told him was her favorite song in first grade. The birthday card read, *"Susan, Never lose the beautiful child that's inside your heart. Love, Danny."* That card was still at the bottom of one of her dresser drawers.

Danny had lost some of his own childlike spirit as the years and disappointments mounted, but hell, so had she. Hopefully he was doing well now.

She had no idea if Danny even knew about the upcoming execution. She should call him and tell him.

Actually, she *had* called him, at his office, three times in the last two weeks. But he never picked up, probably because he was out showing houses. And she never left him a message, because it just felt too weird after all these years.

Suddenly she thought, *Screw it, I should call right now and leave him a message before I lose my nerve. I should do it.* She checked her mirror and abruptly pulled over to the shoulder, in front of a broken-down barn.

She reached in her pants pocket and took out a piece of paper where she'd written Danny's number at Tamarack Realty. Then she brought out her old Radio Shack flip phone and dialed. Maybe she'd even get lucky and he'd be in on a Sunday, getting ready for an afternoon open house.

The phone rang once, twice, and a third time. Then, just as it had before, Danny's message came on. He sounded young, upbeat. "Hi, you've reached Danny. I'd love to help you find the home you've always dreamed of. Please leave a message and I'll call you back just as soon as I can."

Susan heard the beep. She was about to say something but stopped herself.

Why hadn't he picked up? Why did he *never* pick up?

Is he screening my calls? Does he not want to talk to me?

She didn't blame Danny for leaving her. But still, he *had* left her. And in nineteen years he never reached out to her, beyond the Christmas cards they sent each other every year.

On the Tamarack Realty website, it said Danny had a wife now. And two kids, a son and a daughter. When Susan had read that he had a new daughter, her heart broke a little.

Danny had made it clear long ago that he wanted basically nothing to do with Susan anymore. He wanted to forget his old family, because the memories were just too hard for him to deal with. So why was she calling him? Why did she feel she needed to see him again, needed to be with him at the execution?

She snapped her phone shut without leaving a message.

Fuck him.

Yeah, she had loved him, but she shouldn't make like their marriage was all sweetness and light. He used to have those down days at work when he'd come home and get pissed off if the TV was too loud or the lights in the bedrooms had been left on all day. He'd get on the internet after dinner and wouldn't talk to her and Amy for hours. Sure, it was for work, but still.

Over the years, Susan had begun remembering more things she didn't like about him, that she used to make herself ignore. He should have supported her better after Amy was killed. To leave her less than a year later? That wasn't right.

I'm better off without him, she thought.

She turned her key in the ignition, and after a couple seconds the old Dodge Dart came back to life. She got back onto 29.

But just as she did, some jerk in a big SUV came roaring up behind her, doing eighty at least and coming within ten feet of her car. He hit the horn hard and swerved around her.

What an asshole. Suddenly Susan decided not to take this guy's shit. She slammed her foot on the gas. It took a while, but the car made it up to sixty-five, seventy-five, eighty . . . Now it was up to eighty-five. The old car probably hadn't gone this fast since the 1990s, and maybe not even then. But now she was right behind him. She could feel him wondering what the hell this middle-aged lady was up to.

She swerved into the passing lane and pulled up alongside him. He looked over at her, confusion and fear growing on his face.

She rolled down her window. "Go fuck yourself!" she yelled, and gave him the finger.

Now he was definitely terrified. She roared in front of him as he dropped back.

She laughed to herself, victorious. Ahead of her the dark gray clouds began to lighten. There was even a broad band of blue, which seemed to get bigger as she watched.

This was going to be an adventure.

CHAPTER SEVEN

FRIDAY, APRIL 12, TWENTY YEARS AGO

SUSAN GOT OFF the phone with Danny and told Molly she needed to go home. But she was so distraught, she walked straight into the closed front door of the diner.

Molly took Susan's car keys and said she'd drive her. From the door, she told the customers, "I gotta run. Just leave your money on the counter or pay next time you're here."

On the ride home, Susan repeated "Please, God" over and over, desperately hoping Amy would be home by the time she and Molly got there. When they arrived, three police cars were on the street out front. It made everything even more devastatingly real. She jumped out of the Dodge Dart before it came to a stop. The weather had turned cold again but she didn't feel it. Two cops, men in their forties, sat in one of the cars. The front window was open and Susan could hear police radio sounds.

"Did you find her?" she said breathlessly.

The cops looked up, and she knew their answer even before they spoke. "Not yet," the cop closer to her said.

She ran inside with Molly following. She heard Danny in the kitchen saying to someone, "Maybe she fell somewhere and cracked her head or something." Susan dashed in there and saw two men sitting at the table while Danny paced the floor, eyes wild with fear.

He and Susan looked at each other, unsure whether to hug or what. It was as if their pain was so huge they couldn't afford to touch each other, because that might make things even worse somehow, magnify their terror.

The two men at the table were cops: a crew-cut man in his fifties and a short man in his thirties with a sour expression. Susan recognized the crew-cut man, Michael Lynch. His wife worked at the drugstore. He was sitting ramrod straight, like he was still in the military.

Both cops stood up when Susan entered. Lynch started right in, saying crisply, "Ms. Lentigo, we're sending people out to look for your daughter. We're also contacting the teachers and crossing guard to see if they saw anything when Amy left school."

Susan said, "She probably decided to walk home by herself. We should check the woods between here and the school."

Lynch nodded. "We're doing that. We have people out there."

"It's freezing tonight! We have to find her!"

"We're doing everything we can, Ms. Lentigo. Now if you're okay to talk, we have some questions for you that may help us."

Susan sat on a chair and said, "Okay," nodding her head up and down. She found herself staring at a stray hair on Lynch's nose. She couldn't take her eyes off it for some reason.

Danny sat back down and grabbed at his head. Lynch sat too, and said, "I understand there was a miscommunication with your mom. You thought she was taking care of your daughter."

Finally Susan's eyes snapped away from the hair. "Yeah, that's what she said."

"But then she called to say she couldn't do it."

Susan frowned, confused, and looked around at everybody: the cops, Danny, and Molly, standing by the door. She felt a rushing in her ears. Was this cop accusing her of something? Of being a bad mother? Did Danny think that?

She protested, "I didn't know. Not 'til tonight."

"Let me play you the message," Lynch said. Susan sensed he wasn't a man who spent a lot of time trying to make people feel better.

He stepped over to the phone machine on the counter and hit *play*. They heard a robotic male voice say, "Eight fifty-six a.m." Then Lenora's voice came on: "Honey, I just remembered I have a date tonight. We're going out for dinner, so I can't get Amy from school. Sorry about that. Maybe tomorrow night."

There was a beep, then silence.

"I never heard that," Susan said, defensive. "I've been gone all day. If I knew, I would've picked Amy up myself!"

"That's what I *told* them," Danny said, gesturing angrily at the cops. "I don't know why they're wasting time on this!"

She was relieved Danny didn't seem to be blaming her. Meanwhile Lynch ignored his outburst and said to Susan evenly, "Your husband says he didn't hear it either."

Danny said, "Yeah, I had already left for work when your mom called."

"I don't get it," Susan said to Lynch. "Like Danny says, why are we even talking about this?"

"Exactly!" Danny agreed.

Lynch put up his hand to quiet them. "Please. Is there anyone else who had access to your home today and might've heard this message?"

Susan jumped up. "This is stupid! We should all be out looking for Amy right now!"

Lynch said firmly, "Ma'am, we need to know if somebody learned about this mix-up and decided to take advantage. Maybe they realized they'd have four hours before anyone realized Amy was missing and went searching for her."

Finally she understood what Lynch was going for. A rock of fear rose in her throat.

Four hours.

Four hours for some creep to do whatever he wanted to Amy.

Apparently Danny understood now too, because his face went white.

Lynch asked, "Who else has a key to your house?"

"Just Susan's mom," Danny answered.

"Are there any workmen who come in during the day?"

"No, nobody like that."

Lynch asked Susan, "Is it possible your mother took Amy for some reason?"

What was this cop accusing her mom of? "*Took* her?" Susan said, outraged. "No, of course not!"

But then she had an alarming thought. Lynch must have caught traces of it on her face, because he asked, "What?"

She looked down and shook her head. "What is it?" Lynch persisted.

She looked back up. "My mom is going out with a guy Amy doesn't like. She thinks he's creepy. He called her 'Pretty Baby.'"

Danny stared at her. "What the fuck? Why didn't you tell me?!"

Susan tried to fight her growing shame. "I didn't want to upset you. But I told Mom I didn't want him around Amy anymore."

Danny was still staring, his mouth open. "You should've told me. I'd have kicked his fucking ass!"

Before she could apologize, Lynch asked, "What's his name?"

"Frank something."

"You don't know his last name?"

She racked her brain but came up empty. "My mom never told me."

"Un-fucking-believable," Danny said. Maybe he didn't blame her before, but Susan knew he sure as hell blamed her now.

But that didn't matter. She needed to focus, remember everything she could.

Lynch said, "This guy Frank, is that who your mom had dinner with tonight?"

She desperately searched her memory—*did Mom tell me anything about any upcoming dates?* —but then shook her head in defeat. "I don't know if it was him or somebody else. She's going out with a couple different guys."

"So you don't know where Frank was this evening?"

"No." *Oh God, oh God . . .*

Lynch and the sour-faced cop exchanged a look. She could tell they considered Frank a serious suspect. Lynch asked, "Where does he work?"

Susan squeezed her eyes shut, trying to remember if her mom had ever told her. But once again she had to say, "I don't know."

Lynch's partner spoke for the first time. "What *did* she tell you about him?"

"I think he's from Glens Falls. Amy said he had a beard and a tiny nose. She thought he looked weird."

Danny exploded. "Jesus, Susan, and you never told me?!"

"You and Mom would've gotten in a fight," she said, but knew right away how lame that sounded.

Danny's eyes burst with fury. "This guy may have kidnapped our daughter!"

Susan felt so horrible. But Lynch put up his hand again. "Don't jump to conclusions. Let's just locate this individual as fast as possible."

She tried to pull herself together. "We should call everybody we know and get a search party going."

Still standing by the door, Molly said, "I can start making calls right now."

"I'll do it too," Danny said, and reached for the phone on the counter.

But Lynch stopped him. "Good idea, but call from a neighbor's house so we can keep this phone free." He turned to Susan. "I need you here with me in case I have more questions for you."

Molly gave Susan a hug and said, "Hang in there, sweetie." Susan was grateful that Molly at least didn't hate her, but it didn't change anything. When Amy told her Frank was creepy, she should have done more than just call her mom. She should have called Frank and told him to stay the fuck away from her daughter.

Molly hurried off to a neighbor's trailer down the street. Then Susan turned to Danny, and they looked each other in the eye. But they still didn't touch. If Frank had hurt Amy, Susan would never forgive herself and neither would Danny. They nodded to each other, then he took off.

Susan turned to Lynch and asked, "What do you think happened to her?"

Lynch took out a notepad. "I'd rather not speculate. We need to find your mom so she can help us locate this individual. Every second matters, ma'am."

Susan wrung her hands, then something came to her. *Finally.* The words poured out. "My mom said the next time someone took her to dinner, she'd make him go to Cooper's Cave. She heard they have great lobster."

Lynch immediately got the number for Cooper's Cave from Susan's phone book and called them. He stayed on the line while the restaurant manager searched for a bearded man with a tiny nose or a woman fitting Lenora's description: fifty-six, dyed blonde hair, five-seven with a good figure. Susan waited anxiously, hoping against hope Lenora would come on the phone and it would turn out Amy was right there at the restaurant with her.

But when the manager came back on the line, he told Lynch, with Susan listening, that he hadn't found Lenora. Several women more or less fitting her description had been there earlier tonight, but he didn't know anything more about them.

"Did anyone see a man with a beard and a tiny nose?" Lynch asked.

"Nobody remembers a guy like that."

A chill ran through Susan. *So Mom wasn't with Frank tonight. He was somewhere else—maybe with Amy.*

They better find him—now.

Lynch radioed the Glens Falls PD and asked them to send officers to question all the waitresses at Cooper's Cave. Maybe one of them had heard Lenora and her date say something about where they were going after dinner. Then Lynch asked the Glens Falls cops to send cruisers to all the bars in the area. "And the ice cream places too," Susan said into the radio. "My mom loves ice cream."

She told Lynch everything she could think of about Lenora's colleagues and friends. Maybe somebody would know Frank's last name. Then she told Lynch about all the other guys her mom had gone out with in the past year. Frank wasn't the only questionable boyfriend of hers who'd had contact with Amy.

Lynch radioed back and forth with cops from all the local towns, while Susan took the calls that came in on her phone. Every time it rang, her heart jumped, thinking it was Amy. But each time it was just a concerned friend or neighbor, and her heart broke all over again.

Between calls, Lynch informed her about what was going on. Danny and Molly were out there calling people, who called other people, and within hours over two hundred searchers were hunting the woods in Lake Luzerne, calling Amy's name. They were mainly unorganized, though some of them were given specific missions. They went down to the footpaths along the Hudson. They went up to the lake that gave the town its name and walked the empty campsites. They drove up and down 9N and the intersecting streets and looked into parked cars. They drove into the parking lots of the town hall, the bowling alley, and the video rental store.

Lynch had the cops banging on the doors of known sex offenders. If you included all the different categories, there were a lot of them—almost thirty in the town itself, and a hundred if you included Corinth and Lake George.

Susan set her highest hopes on the search party Danny was leading. He took his big flashlight with him and went to the elementary school, where he was joined by several neighbors and people from church. Together they walked the same shortcut Amy might have used to come home from school: the path above the old tannery. In spots it was treacherous, especially during mud season. Maybe Amy slipped and fell to the stream below and hit her head, and she was still lying there. They checked every bend of the stream, with Danny slipping more than once and cutting his arms badly on the rocks.

Susan was crushed when Danny called in and said they hadn't found her.

But at least he was nicer to her now. "Susan, I was talking to Parson Parsons," he said, "and she told me I was wrong to blame you. So . . . sorry about that."

Susan felt her chest growing warm. Danny was not a guy who apologized or forgave easily. If anything, he tended to be on the rigid side, harboring resentments about screwups that seemed pretty minor in her eyes. So she realized he had worked at this.

"I'm really sorry, honey," she said, sniffling, her eyes getting wet. "I feel like it's all my fault."

"Forget it. We're gonna go search by the river now, so, goodbye."

"I love you!" she said into the phone.

She couldn't sit still anymore, so she went out to the backyard, leaving the door open, and called Amy's name. She looked out at the darkness, toward the woods at the back of the yard and the wetlands beyond them. "Amy!" she called again. A dog barked in the distance and Susan heard what sounded like an owl, but nothing else.

Then the phone rang. She rushed inside and picked it up. "Hello?" she gasped.

"Susan, what the hell is going on?" she heard Lenora say. "I'm at some bar and I heard the police are looking for me. Amy is missing?"

Susan could tell right away her mom didn't know anything about Amy, and her spirits sank. But still, she asked breathlessly, "Yes, have you seen her?"

Lynch stepped closer, listening, as Lenora said, "No. My God, Susan, do they think something happened to her?"

"Were you with Frank tonight?"

"Who?"

Susan ignored the bewilderment in her mom's voice and snapped, "Frank! Your boyfriend!"

Now her mom got defensive. "He's not exactly my boyfriend, and no, I wasn't with him. Why?"

Shit! "What's his last name?"

There was a pause, then her mom said, "Susan, get off this. Frank is not some perverted kidnapper, for chrissake."

"What's his last name?"

"He's married. I don't want to get him in trouble."

Susan had never been so furious at her mom, or maybe anyone, in her whole life. "Tell me his fucking last name!"

Lenora finally said, "Okay, fine, but this is crazy. Frank Simmons."

Susan repeated the name for Lynch's benefit, then asked her mom, "Where's he live?"

"I've never been there, but it's somewhere in South Glens Falls."

Lynch got the phone book and searched for Frank Simmons's address.

Lenora said, "Look, it's probably nothing. She's probably just lost somewhere."

"I hope so, Mom," Susan spit out, not bothering to keep the anger out of her voice.

Thirty minutes later, Lynch was still using Susan's kitchen as a command post when he got a radio call. She could hear the conversation.

"I'm at Frank Simmons's house," the cop on the other end said. "We got him."

Lynch asked, "Is the girl with him?"

Susan gripped the edge of the kitchen table.

"No," the cop said, and Susan moaned with pain.

"How's he acting?" Lynch said.

"Freaked out. He's denying everything."

"Does he have an alibi for this afternoon?"

"We asked him. He said he won't talk without a lawyer."

Susan's eyes widened. He wouldn't talk? This had to be the guy! *What did he do to Amy? Is she still alive?*

Lynch asked, "Did he say why he won't talk?"

"No."

Susan yelled into the radio, "*Make* him talk! Beat the fucking shit out of him!"

The cop said, "We're doing everything we can, ma'am."

CHAPTER EIGHT

Susan drove west on Route 29, leaving Lake Luzerne far behind. The band of blue grew and took over the sky. As the state highway rolled out in front of her, she thought, *what a big world.* She opened her window and breathed in the invigorating cold air.

She turned on the radio, looking for pop or country, but all she could find were sports and political talk. The hell with that. She turned it off and, without thinking, began to sing, *"Ain't nothin' gonna break my stride, nobody's gonna slow me down, oh no . . ."*

She remembered when the song came out: the summer before she started dating Danny, when she was sixteen. Young, free, and filled with hope. She sang louder: *"I'm running and I won't touch ground, oh no, I got to keep on moving . . ."*

As she passed the exit for Galway, another song came to her: "Rock Around the Clock." It was one of her few joyful memories of her father. They'd sing it together after dinner sometimes, during the ten minutes or so when he had some life in him before settling down to TV and sleep. A couple of times she even danced with him.

"We're gonna rock around the clock tonight," she sang. *"We're gonna rock rock rock until broad daylight . . ."*

She checked her odometer. She'd already done fifty miles. Only fourteen fifty to go! She'd make it all the way to Buffalo by this evening, maybe even a couple hours farther. Then she'd get off the highway and look for a cheap motel. She hadn't made any reservations on the internet because she figured she'd just see how far she got each day and count on finding a place then. She could always sleep in her car if she had to.

She tapped out the beat of the song on her dashboard. Tomorrow she'd drive to Niagara Falls, maybe even spend the whole day if it wasn't too expensive. Giving herself a couple extra days for this trip had been a smart idea. And her mom was right: the folks who donated to Amy Lentigo Night wouldn't mind if Susan spent a little of the money taking her first vacation in forever.

She knew it wasn't just about seeing the sights. Amy's killer was about to be dead. It was time, finally, for Susan to be free.

She began singing again, a country hit from one of those American Idol singers. It came out after Amy was killed, and had given Susan great comfort over the years. *"Jesus, take the wheel,"* she sang, *"take it from my hands—"*

Suddenly she heard a horrible grating *screech.* What the hell?! Then the car shook violently under her feet.

She felt it slowing, so she slammed the gas pedal. But nothing happened! *Did the car just die?* In the mirror, she saw a truck bearing down on her—*hard.* Its tires screamed and the driver blared his horn. Now the truck filled her whole mirror.

She didn't have time to check how wide the shoulder was. She swerved right—and smashed into a metal guardrail. Her body got thrown toward the right, as the front of her car veered back onto the road. She tried to get back behind the wheel and straighten out without spinning. The truck roared even closer.

She fought the steering, swerving left and then right. Then, about half an inch from her side mirror, the truck squealed past.

The Dodge Dart slammed to a stop on the shoulder.

Susan sat there, heart pounding. "Holy fucking crap," she said.

Two more cars swooshed by her. Then she tried to start the engine again.

It whined, growled, and screamed. But the car wouldn't move.

I'm such an idiot! Why did I push this old car to eighty-five?

God, it better not be dead.

CHAPTER NINE

Susan stalked back and forth in the kitchen, unable to sit down. Officer Lynch was telling the cop on the other end of the radio call, "Take Frank to the station in Luzerne. And keep asking him where Amy is. Don't let up."

Lynch signed off and radioed several other cops, directing the search of Frank's house, car, and computer. Frank's wife was off in Ohio visiting her mother, so he could have brought Amy back home if he wanted.

What if Amy is in Frank's basement, alive? But twenty-five minutes later, just after midnight, word came over the radio that Amy was nowhere to be found in Frank's house.

Then Susan heard the voice of Lynch's sour-faced partner come crackling over the radio. "Okay, Frank's here. We put him in the box."

"Sill not talking?" Lynch asked.

"No. He used his phone call on some lawyer he knows named Dewey Martin. Ambulance chaser from Saratoga."

"I'll be right there. Over," Lynch said, and got off the radio. He asked Susan to stay home by the phone in case he had any questions for her. Or in case Amy called. Then he took off.

Without the police radio, Susan felt even more cut off from everything that was going on. Fortunately, Molly came back from searching, so she wasn't all alone.

"Let me make you a cup of coffee," Molly said gently. "You need to sit down and catch your breath."

But as soon as Susan sat down, Lenora walked in through the door. Susan jumped back up, fingers curled like talons, ready to rip her mother apart.

"How could you just leave a message?" she yelled. "Why didn't you make sure you reached me?"

Lenora yelled right back, "You always go home after you drop Amy off! How was I supposed to know today would be different?"

"You should have checked!"

Molly said, "Ladies, this isn't helping."

Susan shouted, "Your creepy fucking boyfriend kidnapped my daughter!"

"How can you even think that?"

"Are you fucking kidding me?"

"That's bullshit! Frank would never do that!"

"I know you're both very upset," Molly said, "but please, quiet down."

Susan opened her mouth and let out an ear-splitting, wordless roar. Her mom jumped back, terrified, and put her hands up to protect herself from Susan's rage.

It was three in the morning, almost twelve hours since Amy had disappeared. Susan was afraid she really would hurt her mom, so she went outside and screamed Amy's name to the wind. The hoot owls went quiet for a few moments, then resumed.

She couldn't just stay here with Molly and her goddamn mother and do nothing. She felt like she would spontaneously burst into flames. She jumped in her car and started the engine. Molly and Lenora came out the front door and called to her, but she raced off.

Five minutes later, she was at the police station. The parking lot was full of police vehicles, not just from Lake Luzerne but Corinth,

Lake George, Queensbury, and Glens Falls. There were cops coming and going, searching for Amy, she assumed. She got out of the car, ran up the front steps, and went inside, blinking at the fluorescence. A young woman in a gray V-neck sweater was at the front desk, showing a couple of cops a street map. Susan hurried up to them. "Where is Frank Simmons?"

The woman said, "I'm sorry, I can't tell you that. Who are you?"

"I'm the mother," Susan snapped.

She walked around the woman and opened the door to the hallway. The woman stood up and grabbed her arm. "Ma'am—"

Susan shook free and ran down the hall.

The woman and one of the cops chased her, calling to her to stop, but she ignored them. She looked in all the rooms that were still lit up at this hour of night. She found a big room full of cubicles, with five or six cops inside, and went in.

The woman and the cop were still coming after her, shouting that she couldn't go in there. Another cop got in her way, but she dodged him and kept going. Something told her the man who took her daughter was here somewhere.

And then she found him. Inside a small room with a big plate-glass window. He was in his fifties, balding, with the thick brown beard and tiny snub nose Amy had noticed. He looked terrified. He sat at a small table by himself, banging his fists together to relieve his anxiety.

Susan tried the door. It was unlocked. She hurried into the room and Frank looked up. His face was ugly, pinched and loathsome. What had her mother seen in this creep? She stormed up to him. "Where is my daughter?" she demanded.

Frank sat there with his mouth open.

"What did you do to my daughter?"

She laid into him then, with both fists. He raised his arms to defend himself, but she punched him square in the mouth. She'd never fought anybody before in her life, but she landed blow after blow. He tried to back away from her, but his chair slipped and he fell to the floor. She kicked him and yelled, "Where is Amy? *Where's Amy?*"

Two cops came in and grabbed her arms, but she kept kicking Frank savagely.

Then Lynch ran in and shouted, "Susan!" He pulled her into a rough bear hug and moved her backward so her feet couldn't reach Frank anymore.

Frank sat on the floor bleeding from his split lip and feeling his ribs where she'd kicked him. A middle-aged guy in a leather jacket—Frank's lawyer, Dewey, Susan figured out—ran in and yelled, "What the hell is going on? What did you do to my client!"

Still in Lynch's grasp, Susan turned her head and looked down at Frank. "Please," she begged. "Just tell me. Where is my daughter?"

Finally Frank stood up. "I don't know," he said.

Dewey said, "Don't say a word, Frank."

"I don't need this shit," said Frank. "I don't know where your fucking daughter is. I was out fishing yesterday."

"Shut up, Frank," Dewey said.

Frank pointed a finger at Susan. "You're an even bigger bitch than your mom, you know that?"

Lynch said, "Where were you fishing?"

Dewey warned, "Frank, I'm telling you—"

But Frank ignored Dewey. Susan studied Frank's eyes, trying to figure out if he was telling the truth, as he said, "Schroon River. Just over the bridge past Warrensburg."

Lynch said, "When did you leave there?"

"Sundown, whenever that was. I went home, ate leftover pizza, and went to bed. Slept pretty good too, 'til your goons woke me up in the middle of the night."

"Anybody see you yesterday afternoon or evening?"

"No. I was supposed to go out with this bitch's mother, but she stood me up for some other guy. Now I *am* gonna shut the fuck up. Counselor, this little beatdown I just got, can I sue the cops for it?"

"Hell yes," Dewey said. "It's worth a hundred grand easy."

Frank smiled. "Excellent. Thanks, lady. I'm much obliged."

Susan wanted to rip this guy's balls off. But she let Lynch walk her out of the room. She had no choice.

"What do we do now?" she demanded.

"Well, at least now we have his alibi," Lynch said. "Let's go to my office and cool down for a minute."

"I don't want to cool down! Do you think he's telling the truth?"

"We'll find out. We have people going through his computer, and we're looking for any other places he might have gone. Now why don't you head on home." They were back at his cubicle now—plain metal desk, no decorations—and he reached into a drawer and pulled out a two-thirds-full bottle of Jack Daniels. "Take this with you. Pour yourself a drink when you get home."

Susan knew Lynch was not a touchy-feely guy, so she appreciated the gesture. She took the bottle and drove home. Molly and her mom were still there, and so was Danny. She tried to read Danny's mood. Mainly he just seemed terrified, like her.

"Anything new?" he asked.

"Yeah, I just beat the crap out of Mom's boyfriend."

Lenora sat there, totally thrown, while Susan described how she got Frank to talk. By now Lenora knew better than to object out loud, so she kept her mouth shut.

But Danny gave Susan a half-smile and said, "Good job, honey."

Susan looked in Danny's eyes. And for the first time since they'd gotten the bad news, they touched each other.

It was tentative at first, but then they put their arms around each other and cried.

CHAPTER TEN

DESPITE THE JACK Daniels, Susan didn't sleep that night. Lynch called her throughout the night and the next morning to update her. The police thought if Frank killed Amy, he might have dumped her body at a place he was familiar with. So they got a cadaver dog on loan from Albany and checked fishing spots near Warrensburg, and also a hunting blind somebody said Frank used during deer season.

Every time Lynch called, Susan was petrified he was about to say they'd found Amy's body. She could barely breathe, and if she was standing, which she tried to remember not to do, her legs got wobbly.

But each time, he was only calling to say they'd come up empty.

Around noon, Lynch stopped by to tell them the latest in person. As Susan and Danny listened, they sat close to each other on the living room sofa. If Danny was still mad at her about Frank, he was stuffing it way down inside, at least for now.

"Frank Simmons works at a Xerox store," Lynch said. "But before then, he worked for a locksmith 'til he got fired for being late all the time. Anyway, at the locksmith he learned how to use skeleton keys."

Lynch looked at them above the rim of his coffee cup and waited expectantly. Susan sensed she was supposed to be figuring something out, but she didn't know what. She felt dumb.

But Danny got it. Eyes widening, he said, "You think Frank broke into our house yesterday and heard that message from Susan's mom."

Lynch nodded. "Right. He doesn't have a good alibi for the morning either. He could easily have done it."

Susan grabbed at her hair, trying to think it though.

Last week Frank meets Amy— "Pretty Baby"—and gets obsessed with her, maybe stalks her. Yesterday he waits for Susan and Danny to leave the house, then he breaks in—

She stopped. "Why would he break into our house?"

Lynch said, "If he was a pedophile fixated on Amy, he might've wanted to steal something of hers, like her underwear. Then he hears Lenora's message and decides he'll show up at Amy's school and try to grab her."

Danny frowned, thinking. "He figured since Amy knew him, he could just say, 'Grandma sent me,' and she'd get in his car."

Susan put her hand to her heart. "Has he ever done anything like this before?"

"He's never been arrested for a sexual crime, not exactly. But last year he got busted for indecent exposure—urinating on the street in downtown Glens Falls one Saturday night when he was drunk. He also has two DWIs."

My mom sure knows how to pick 'em, Susan thought.

But did he kill Amy? Did that weasely piece of shit—

Lynch put his coffee down. "I want to ask you guys something. How would you feel about talking to the media?"

Susan pictured it and shuddered. She'd be one of those crying mothers she saw on TV sometimes with microphones in their faces. God, she so did not want to be one of those women!

"Will it help?" she asked.

"It might. You'll have more people on the lookout for Amy."

"Then sure, we'll do it."

The street outside their small house was littered with reporters' cars and TV vans. Three times that day, Lynch led Susan and Danny out to their front yard to speak to the cameras. "Please, if you have our daughter . . ." "Amy was wearing a beaded necklace and a pink Ninja Turtles jacket . . ." "If you know anything, please. Please help us!"

When Susan and Danny weren't parading their pain, they walked through the woods all day long with the other searchers. She called Amy's name so many times she turned hoarse. Danny was a rock, holding her hand and putting up with all her frantic, semi-insane thoughts. The only sort of slightly positive thing about this whole horrible experience was that their shared terror had brought them closer together than they'd been in a long time. Danny had been a little moody the last few months, frustrated by his problems at work. But now both of them were totally focused on their family. They'd gotten out of the habit of touching each other, but now they seemed to be doing it all the time.

But she kept getting crazy thoughts. First she got it into her head that maybe Frank's beard meant he belonged to a cult, and then she wondered if Frank had sold Amy to someone he met on the internet—she'd heard a story about that happening to a girl in Indiana. Or maybe Amy was okay but had amnesia and was wandering around Aviation Mall in Glens Falls, so they should look there.

Danny and Molly tried to get Susan to eat something, offering her mild foods like Saltines or oatmeal or the string cheese Amy liked so much. But she wasn't hungry, even when night came and she hadn't had a thing besides coffee and bourbon since yesterday evening at the diner.

That felt like so long ago now. Like another lifetime.

At one in the morning, Susan and Danny came out of the woods behind the town dump after yet another fruitless search. They turned off their flashlights, got in the car, and headed back home.

The door to Amy's room was open, and for a moment Susan almost expected her daughter to run out and greet her. But nothing had changed inside the room. Amy's two stuffed bunnies still sat on her pillow, exactly where they'd been yesterday morning when she left for school.

"How long will the cops be able to hold Frank?" Susan asked Danny.

"Unless they get more evidence, I think they have to let him go tomorrow. But I'm sure they'll keep an eye on him."

"Maybe he has her hidden away somewhere," Susan said. "Maybe he'll lead the cops to her."

"It's possible."

They finished off the Jack Daniels, and Susan managed to get a few crackers down. But she still didn't sleep much, thrashing violently and waking up repeatedly. At four a.m. she awakened from a dream in which a man with a blank, fuzzed-out face and a long dark coat threw Amy off a bridge into a river.

She couldn't get back to sleep, and by five o'clock she and Danny were back in the Dodge Dart driving toward the nearest bridge over the Hudson. They scoured the area around there, then headed for two more river bridges. After that, they went to Bon's Ice Cream and Miniature Golf, which was still closed for the winter. There were woods out back where the kidnapper could have taken Amy.

It was such a horrific mission, searching day and night for something that you desperately hoped you wouldn't find, that would destroy your life forever if you did find it.

Lenora was riding with them now, in the back seat. Earlier this morning, Susan and Danny had gotten in a big argument about Lenora, and for maybe the first time ever, Danny was on his mother-in-law's side.

"You gotta let it go, Susan," he had said. "Your mom loves Amy."

"She cared more about her idiot boyfriend than her own grand-daughter. My God, Danny!"

"Honey, she made a mistake. Making her feel worse won't help anything."

"I don't care," Susan said petulantly. But she knew he was right. When he asked if he could invite Lenora to search alongside them, she grumbled but said okay.

Now, as they entered the Bon's parking lot, she stole a glance at Lenora in the rearview mirror. Her mom looked back at her, eyebrows sagging over sad, pathetic eyes, like a beaten dog. Susan knew she would have to forgive her.

But not yet. She tightened her jaw and looked away. She could feel her mom's disappointment from the back seat.

Danny parked and they got out. Ellen, one of the church ladies, was over by the closed ice cream window waiting for them. Susan greeted her, then gazed at the miniature golf course and thought about how much Amy loved this course, especially the hole with the big purple shark where it was pretty easy to get a hole in one. Would she ever get to play that hole again?

Lenora and Ellen headed deep into the woods. Susan sensed her mom was keeping a distance from her.

Meanwhile, Susan and Danny split up, her going off to the right and him going left, a routine they'd established in the past twenty-four hours. She took a deep breath, steeling herself, and looked behind a thick oak tree.

No Amy.

She headed to another oak tree, and another, and another.

No Amy.

She looked back toward Danny and saw he was walking with Lenora now. *Maybe this whole thing is bringing them closer too,* she thought. Danny and her mom never exactly fought, but they didn't totally get along either. He got frustrated when she acted flighty, and she thought he could be too controlling, like when he told Susan exactly how he liked his chicken cooked.

But now, in this moment of crisis, they had put aside their differences. Susan felt a sudden warm glow in her heart for both of them.

She looked around and found another oak tree that might be thick enough for a girl's body to be lying behind. *Jesus, this is torture.* She headed for the tree.

But then a police car pulled into the parking lot. Looking closer, she saw Officer Lynch was inside.

Something about the way he parked the car, something she would never be able to explain, terrified her.

Then Lynch stepped out of the car. He saw Susan and took off his police cap.

Literally took it off.

Right then, Susan knew. She knew.

She started to cry. By the time Lynch got to her, she was sitting next to the tree trunk weeping.

"I'm sorry," he said.

She was gasping too hard to speak. He leaned down and touched her shoulder, then just sat down next to her and took her hand.

Danny and Lenora hurried up.

"What happened?" Danny said, and Lenora asked, "Did you find her?"

"I'm afraid so," Lynch said.

Lenora sat down on the ground too. Then so did Danny. The four of them all sank into the cold muddy leaves as Lynch told them what had happened.

Four hours ago, just after dawn, a young newlywed couple was out running with their terrier on the shores of the Mettawee River near Granville, an hour's drive to the east. The dog went off the path and began barking loudly. The couple called him but he wouldn't come, so they went to where he was.

They saw a little girl's body. She was lying on her back, half-covered by leaves, with a bloody gash on her forehead. Her neck was bruised, and though Lynch would wait for confirmation from the medical examiner, he was pretty sure she'd been strangled.

Susan rocked back and forth on the ground. "Are you positive it's Amy?"

"I'm afraid so. I just came back from there, and there's no doubt. I can show you a Polaroid, if you want."

Susan didn't answer. She just screamed. She screamed so loud people coming out of the church heard it almost a quarter mile away.

Danny grabbed her and held her. She stopped screaming but stayed rigid in his arms.

Through her pain, she sensed her mom wanted to hold her too, but was afraid Susan would push her away.

Lynch said they didn't have to look at the photograph now. One of them could look anytime they were ready, or if they preferred, they could view the body and identify it.

"Where is she?" Lenora said.

"She's being transported to the police morgue down in Albany," Lynch said. "She was found across the border in Vermont, so the FBI is getting involved. They asked that the body be taken to Albany because it's closer to both Lake Luzerne and Granville."

Susan couldn't make sense of what Lynch was saying. She could barely hear him. She didn't care about the FBI or anything like that. All she knew was that her baby was dead.

She didn't care about revenge. She wasn't even thinking about it.

Not yet.

CHAPTER ELEVEN

Susan sat in her immobilized Dodge Dart on the shoulder of the highway and told herself not to panic. Maybe she'd get lucky and the car would just need minor repairs.

She waited for a pickup truck to pass by, then got out of the car and eyed the right front bumper where she'd banged into the guardrail. It was bashed in, alright, but didn't look like something that would keep her off the road.

Then she opened up the hood. She figured Clarence back at Rozelle's wouldn't have let her take this trip without topping out all the fluid levels, and she was right. There was plenty of transmission fluid. The problem was bigger than that.

She checked for detached cables or wires, then called Clarence and described what had happened. "What do you think it is?"

"I'm not sure. Could be some kind of transmission problem."

"Will it be expensive?"

"That depends. Sounds like you'll need to get it towed. Where are you?"

"Just west of Galway."

"Okay, I know a guy out there who'll give you a good price."

Clarence gave her a name, Louie Paterno, and a number, and she called it. Louie said he'd be there in forty-five minutes, maybe an hour.

It turned out to be more like an hour and a half, but Louie did give her a nice price: only seventy dollars. He took her to an auto repair shop in Galway that he said was the cheapest garage in the area. It was run by a woman in her forties named Tina with beefy arms and a heavy way of walking.

"We're booked pretty solid today," Tina said. "My guys can get to your car in forty-five minutes, maybe an hour." Susan wondered if that meant an hour and a half too. She could forget about making it to Buffalo tonight.

She walked several blocks to a nearby diner, where she got grilled cheese with fries. It was okay, but not nearly as good as the food at Molly's. She waited until a little over an hour had gone by, then walked back to the repair shop to hear the verdict. Whatever was wrong with her car, hopefully Tina would give her a break like Louie did.

Tina was standing by the Dodge Dart talking to a mechanic when Susan walked up. "Hey," Susan said.

Tina looked at her and sighed, and Susan's heart fell. That sigh couldn't mean good news. Sure enough, Tina said, "I'm afraid your transmission is totally shot. You'll need a new transmission box, everything."

"How much will that cost?"

"I'm afraid the best I can do for you is about two thousand dollars."

Susan had gotten nine hundred eighty-nine dollars from the fundraiser. She'd decided to leave a hundred bucks for her mom, not fifty; and she'd spent that seventy bucks on towing.

"I only have eight hundred," she said.

Tina gave her a sympathetic nod. "I hear you." She put her hand on the repainted but still rusty car roof. "Well, at least you got two hundred fifty thousand miles out of this car. That's nothing to sneeze at."

"I'm kind of in a bind," Susan said.

Tina folded her thick arms, obviously preparing herself to hear yet another sob story. Susan continued, undaunted. "I need to make it to North Dakota by Saturday. Is there any way you can help me out?"

"Not twelve hundred dollars' worth."

"Can you get the transmission secondhand?"

Tina shook her head. "They haven't been making these cars for twenty, twenty-five years. That's why the parts are so expensive."

Susan chewed on her thumbnail. "Is there any way to keep it together with paper clips and duct tape for a little while?"

"I'm afraid not."

Susan knew Tina was right. She'd heard that screech. Her old Dodge Dart was dead.

But what should she do? She still had to get to North Dakota. She couldn't just go back home.

"How much can you pay me for the car?" she said.

"Honestly, ma'am, it'll cost me money to tow it to the junkyard. There's nothing in here anybody's gonna want."

"I got all new tires today."

Tina looked down at them. "Okay, I can give you a hundred dollars for that."

Susan nodded. She looked down at the damaged bumper, then put her hand on the car's dark green hood and rubbed it gently. It felt ice cold. "Poor Juliette," she said.

Tina looked at her questioningly.

"That's what my daughter called this car. I drove her to school in this car the day she died."

Tina searched for words, then finally said, "I'm sorry. Maybe it's good you're getting rid of it. Bad memories."

"No. Best memories of my life."

Susan reached in her pocket for the car key, then remembered she'd given it to Tina. She was feeling scattered, her emotions all in a jumble. "You got the key?"

Tina handed it to her, and she opened the trunk. She took out her old suitcase.

She couldn't afford the eight forty for a plane, even after she got a hundred for the tires. She'd have zero money left for food or anything else. And how would she even make it down to the Albany airport from here?

"Where's the nearest bus station?" she asked.

Tina hesitated, considering. "Probably Gloversville."

Susan remembered passing a sign that said Gloversville was twenty-five miles away. *Well, what choice do I have?* she thought, as she expanded the suitcase handle.

Tina watched her and said, "I'd ask one of my guys to give you a ride, but we really are booked solid."

"No worries. I can hitch."

Between hitchhiking and taking the bus, she should still be able to make it.

I have to make it.

Tina reached in her pocket for a wad of bills and pulled off five twenties. "Here."

"Thanks. Appreciate it."

Then Susan reached out and gave the hood of her car a love tap. "So long, Juliette." She nodded goodbye to Tina and started rolling her suitcase down the driveway out of the shop.

The wind was blowing in from the north now, and the blue in the western sky had gone back to gray. Susan wrapped the aqua scarf her mom had knitted for her more tightly around her neck. It was maybe a quarter mile back to Route 29. She'd stand at the intersection and put out her thumb.

Okay, so maybe she wouldn't be able to make it to Niagara Falls. But she'd sure as shit get to North Dakota.

Behind her, she heard Tina mutter, "Oh hell," probably to herself. Then Tina called out, "Hold up!"

Susan turned and saw Tina heading toward her. Less than three minutes later, she was climbing into the front seat of Tina's Ford pickup, getting a ride to the Gloversville bus station.

As they pulled onto the road, Susan said, "I really appreciate this."

"So why are you so fired up to get to North Dakota?" Tina asked.

Susan told her. Tina was so appalled she took her eye off the road and almost crashed into a lumber truck.

After Tina got back into her lane, she said, "Guys like that, who mess with little girls, we oughta skin 'em alive and leave 'em in the desert for the coyotes to eat."

Susan nodded. She looked out the window at a lonely stand of cattails bordering a small pond on their right, and thought about the Monster.

Some nights she lay in bed and it was like the Monster was right there in the room with her. She would see his face the way it looked on the opening day of the trial, when he walked into the courtroom for the first time and gazed up at her. Their eyes met, and his eyes had been so goddamn puzzling. They seemed so sad, even sympathetic, not angry or sneering as she had expected.

"I want to ask him why he did it," Susan said.

"'Cause he's a fucking psycho, that's why."

"But why'd he pick my daughter? Why her?"

Tina frowned, confused. "I thought you said he confessed."

"He did. I mean, then he tried to take it back and claim he didn't do it after all, but, yeah, he confessed."

"So didn't he say in the confession why he picked her?"

Susan tugged at her ear. "He said it was because he liked Amy's necklace. But that didn't really make sense. How could he even see the necklace from across the street?"

It was something that hadn't occurred to her at the trial. The Monster's lawyer never brought it up.

But then two years after the murder, one Monday morning in April, Susan was driving past the elementary school. She did that almost every day, because if she tried to avoid that stretch of 9N, it would take her fifteen minutes longer to get to work and another two dollars' worth of gas. She was a block past the school when it suddenly hit her.

In the Monster's confession, he said he was parked across 9N from the school when he saw Amy and her necklace. He talked for, like, a paragraph about the necklace, and how that afternoon was the first time he ever noticed it.

But could he actually have *seen* the necklace from that far away?

Susan did a U-turn and pulled up at the spot where the Monster said he'd parked that afternoon. She looked across the two-lane road and the stretch of grass on the other side to the pavement where Amy would have been standing.

It would be very hard to see a necklace from here. Maybe impossible.

Sometimes, driving home from the lunch shift, she would pull up at that same spot and wait for kids to come out of school. She'd watch them, to see if she would have spotted a necklace if they were wearing one.

She wondered if maybe the Monster got it wrong and he was waiting on the other side of 9N, closer to the school. But he had been so clear about where he was parked.

Maybe he was lying about seeing Amy's necklace for the first time right then. But why would he lie about that, when he was telling the truth about everything else? It was strange.

Tina broke into her thoughts. "Shit happens," she said. "It just happens."

Susan had heard this many times before, from both her mom and Molly. She looked out the window again. She still missed Molly, even though it had been seven years now since she passed away.

Tina said, "My advice? Don't even talk to the fuckhead. Just spit in his face."

"He took her necklace for a souvenir," Susan said. "I'm hoping he'll tell me where he put it."

She touched the aqua scarf on her neck.

"I'd like to put the necklace on Amy's grave."

CHAPTER TWELVE

Susan needed to see Amy's body. She wasn't sure why, but she had to. So Danny drove her and Lenora down to the police morgue in Albany.

"Fucking motherfucker," Danny said, his fists tightening on the steering wheel. "Fucking Frank Simmons! And they let him out of prison, can you believe it? I don't give a shit if they don't have evidence, fucking lock him up!"

It clearly hadn't taken Danny long to get into revenge mode. Susan was still numb, not saying a word. Lenora, in back, wasn't talking much either.

Susan knew her mom was tearing herself apart, but so what? They still didn't know for sure Frank was the killer, but it seemed certain that her mom's failure to tell Susan she wasn't picking up Amy resulted in her death. Somebody spotted Amy waiting outside and grabbed her.

Susan shut her eyes tight, trying to squeeze that image out of her head.

When they got down to Albany Police headquarters, shared by the Albany cops and the New York State Police, Lynch was waiting for them in the parking lot. He walked them to the front desk and showed his badge to the desk cop, who had just come on duty a couple minutes ago.

"I'm Officer Lynch from Lake Luzerne. I have the victim's family with me."

"Which victim?" the desk cop asked.

Susan snapped out of her shock when she heard that. God, she loathed this cop! Loathed him like he was a piece of dogshit stuck to her shoe. She wanted to reach across the desk, grab his head, and smash it against the wall behind him, over and over. *Smash. Smash. Smash.*

"Her name is Amy Lentigo," Susan snarled at the cop through gritted teeth. "She's seven years old. Here's her picture." She shoved her photo of Amy, gap-toothed and smiling, in the cop's face.

He blinked. "I'm sorry, ma'am. She's downstairs." To Lynch he said, "Just follow the signs."

"Thank you, Officer," Lynch said, and he took Susan, Danny, and Lenora down to the basement.

Susan was expecting to look at her daughter's body through a window, like on *Law & Order,* which she and Danny watched on Wednesday nights after Amy went to bed. But instead, Lynch opened the door and led them right into the morgue. It was cold. There were two long, stainless steel tables in the center of the room. A tall cabinet with big metal drawers lined one wall.

To their left was a closed office door. Lynch knocked, and a woman in her early thirties with thick black hair and heavy purple earrings, the morgue attendant, opened up.

She looked them over. "Can I help you?"

Lynch said, "These are the victim's parents and grandmother."

Susan was ready to kill her if she asked, "Which victim?" But the morgue attendant nodded solemnly and said, "Okay." She stepped out of the office and asked Lynch, "Can you give me a hand?"

Lynch and the morgue attendant pulled the handles on one of the drawers and a long tray rolled out. There was a girl's body on it, with a white sheet draped over her.

The morgue attendant removed the sheet.

It was Amy.

My poor baby.

"That motherfucker," Danny said.

Lenora moaned, "Oh . . ." and stumbled backwards.

The morgue attendant put an arm around Lenora's back to stop her from falling.

Susan ignored everything else in the room. She put a hand to her heart and stepped closer to Amy.

Her daughter's eyes were wide open. They looked terrified.

Her forehead had a big bloody gash. Dried blood ran down her pale white face onto her neck.

Her neck was bruised, like Lynch had said. Susan could see the purple and yellow under the blood.

There was some kind of pattern in the blood. Susan fixated on it, and realized what it was: imprints of the necklace beads.

Amy was wearing her necklace when the killer strangled her. The beautiful necklace she never wanted to take off. She only got to wear it for one week.

"Where is it? Where's the necklace?" Susan said.

"It's missing," Lynch said.

Susan frowned in bewilderment, then figured it out.

The killer had taken the necklace, for a souvenir.

He enjoyed killing Amy so much, he saved a keepsake.

In that moment, a passionate desire to make that man suffer overwhelmed Susan's heart and soul.

CHAPTER THIRTEEN

Tina and Susan pulled into the tiny one-room bus station in Gloversville at two thirty. Tina opened the back of her pickup and brought out Susan's suitcase.

"Thank you," Susan said.

Tina gave her a hug, enfolding her in her strong arms. "Good luck, honey."

As Susan waved goodbye, she resolved to remember that really, the world was full of good people.

Then she rolled her suitcase into the bus station. The place smelled of wood varnish and felt cozy. There was only one customer, a young bearded guy sitting in a far corner. He was munching lazily on French fries while he listened to music on his iPhone.

From behind the counter, the ticket agent, a guy in his sixties with a thick gray walrus mustache that was beautifully combed and cared for, greeted her. "Afternoon, young lady. What can I do you for?"

Susan stepped up to the window. "Hi. I'd like a ticket to Hodge Hills, North Dakota."

The ticket agent raised his eyebrows, which were thick like his mustache. "Hodge Hills, North Dakota, huh?" he said doubtfully. "Well, let's see what we got for ya."

He typed away on his computer, humming an old pop song that Susan almost but couldn't quite place. In the corner, the bearded young man bobbed his head to whatever song was on his phone.

"Well," the ticket agent said, scanning his computer screen, "you can take an Adirondack Trailways to Buffalo, then we'll put you on a Greyhound to Toledo, Midwest Trailways up to Chicago, another Greyhound to Minneapolis, Windstar to Fargo, then up to Hodge Hills on a Dakota Northern." He looked up at her. "Sure you don't want to take a plane?"

"How long will it take?"

"You got a few layovers, as you can imagine. It'd take you three days."

"It gets in on Wednesday?"

"That's right."

So if she took the bus straight to North Dakota, she'd be there three days early. "Wednesday's fine. What'll it cost?"

The ticket agent looked dubious, but he said, "Three hundred nineteen dollars and forty-six cents."

"Okay," Susan said. If she managed her money really carefully, maybe she'd even have enough for the return trip. Or she could call Terri or somebody and ask them to send her a couple hundred dollars. They'd figure out how to do it.

Well, she couldn't think about that now. She reached in her coat pocket and decided to start with one-dollar bills, because they made up the bulkiest stacks. She'd tied them up with three rubber bands, which she removed now. She laid the bills down one by one in front of the ticket agent and started counting out loud.

"One, two, three, four, five . . ."

The ticket agent and the bearded young man both stared at her, clearly wondering if she was actually going to count out three hundred nineteen dollars, one by one.

"Six, seven, eight . . ."

Five minutes later, she was done, and her coat felt a lot less heavy.

"Impressive," the ticket agent said. "May I ask where you got that money?"

Susan didn't want to go through the whole "my daughter was raped and killed and I'm going to the execution" thing again. "I won a bar raffle," she said.

The ticket taker smiled. "Lucky you!"

"Yup. When does the bus leave?"

"Six thirty tonight. About four hours. You want me to recommend some of the local sights?"

Susan looked over at an old wooden bench across the room. "Actually, could you just wake me up when it's time to leave? I'm exhausted."

"That's what you get for living the high life. Sure, I'll wake you up."

*   *   *

Susan lay down on the bench and closed her eyes. Before she knew it, the ticket agent was gently shaking her shoulder. "Young lady," he said.

She opened her eyes and sat up. Outside the sky was darkening, and through the front window she saw an Adirondack Trailways bus.

"Your chariot awaits," the ticket agent said.

"Thanks."

She reached for her suitcase but he beat her to it. "I'll get that."

He rolled the suitcase outside and stowed it in the luggage compartment at the bottom of the bus, while Susan pulled her coat and scarf tighter against the wind. She showed her ticket to the bus driver, a chubby man in his forties.

"Farewell, my lady," the ticket agent said, and despite his corniness, Susan wondered what it would be like to kiss a man with a thick mustache like that. Then she gave herself a surprised little smile. She usually didn't have those kinds of thoughts anymore. Getting out of Luzerne and having an adventure, going someplace when she wasn't even sure how she'd make it back, must be bringing out that side of her.

She got on the bus, joining the nine or ten people who were already there. Most of them were traveling alone and spread themselves out so they occupied two seats at once. Susan sat in an empty seat in the middle of the bus and spread out too. There was plenty of room for her arms and legs. *This isn't so bad,* she thought. *I can take three days of this.*

The bus pulled out into the late November night and headed west on the winding, two-lane county highway. She looked out at the rolling hills and her mind started to drift.

She wondered what the Monster looked like now. Was his hair turning gray, like hers? Probably. She wondered what his life in prison had been like.

She thought back to the very last time she saw him, twenty years ago, after he got convicted. Now that the trial was over, he was no longer trying to act sympathetic. He allowed his anger to burn brightly on his sneering face.

The Monster sits at the defense table with his lawyer. His eyes are pure, black hatred.

"Ms. Lentigo?" the judge says.

It's time for her to give her victim impact statement. Danny squeezes her hand. She walks to the front of the courtroom on shaky knees, each step feeling like a mile. She's wearing a pink and purple wool sweater, because those were Amy's favorite colors.

She looks down at the sheet of paper in her hand, where her speech is all typed up. But then her eyes blur over and she can't read a word.

She looks up and sees the Monster's hostile glare. Her eyes suddenly clear. She steadies, her rage overriding her nerves. She doesn't need this paper. She's been practicing this speech in her mind ever since the moment the Monster was caught. When she speaks, her voice rings strong.

"You're not even human," she says. "You raped my seven-year-old daughter while she was lying there bleeding."

The Monster interrupts her. "You fucking idiot—"

The judge slams his gavel. "Shut up or I'll have you gagged."

Susan spits out furiously, "You took her tiny neck in your big hands and you strangled her."

The Monster interrupts again. "That's not what happened—"

The judge is about to bang his gavel down even harder, but Susan doesn't need him. She moves closer to the Monster and her look of cold dead hate, a thousand times more powerful than his, like it's been summoned by the demons of hell, silences him. She hisses, "I hope you get raped in prison."

Then she turns to the judge. "But life in prison isn't enough for this man. I demand that he be sentenced to death!"

She turns back to the Monster and says, "And I pray your execution will be slow and painful."

The Monster glowers back at her, but can't work up the nerve to say anything.

She goes back to her seat, and Danny puts his arm around her. She doesn't want to cry but can't help it.

Danny holds her close.

Now, twenty years later, Susan wondered if the Monster had been raped in prison, and whether she would really want that. She decided if she was being honest the answer was probably yes.

The bus was slowing down, and Susan watched the two-lane highway become the main street of a small town. The air brakes wheezed as the bus stopped in front of a place called the Canajoharie Diner. The greyhound on the roof showed it doubled as diner and bus station.

"Canajoharie. Canajoharie, New York," the driver said. He stood up and faced the passengers. "Okay, people, I'm taking a little break. Feel free to get off the bus and wash up, just be back here in fifteen minutes. And if you're hungry, may I recommend Sylvia's apple pie. Homemade and delicious."

Susan got up, stretched, and followed him off the bus. So did most of the other passengers, at least the ones who weren't asleep.

Inside the diner, with its cheerful waitresses and comfy-looking booths, Susan smelled fresh-baked apple pie and newly brewed coffee. She thought it was the most amazing combination of smells she'd ever encountered in her life. She went to the bathroom—freshly cleaned, she noticed—and then got in line at the counter with three of her fellow passengers. The pie underneath the glass cover had a golden crust and a glistening apple filling.

This was one of the few diners she'd ever been in that was as good as Molly's. Maybe even better!

When it was her turn, she smiled to the middle-aged woman in the Canajoharie Canaries baseball cap, presumably Sylvia, who was taking their orders. "That apple pie looks absolutely amazing."

The woman smiled. "Fresh out of the oven, hon."

"I'd love a piece, and a cup of coffee too."

"That'll be two fifty," the woman said, as she brought out the pie.

Susan reached into her coat for one of her wads of bills. She'd used up almost all of her ones at the Gloversville bus station. She decided she'd pay with a five—

What the fuck? Her coat pocket was empty!

She reached deeper. *Nothing.*

She reached into her other inside pocket, on the other side of her coat. *Nothing.*

Was she going crazy? She tried them both again. Then she reached into her outside pockets.

Nothing.

"Hon?" the woman behind the counter said, holding out a slice of pie on a paper plate. "Are you okay?"

Susan stood there, mouth open. She had the money when she got on the bus, right? She was positive she did.

"Excuse me," she said, and ran outside. The driver was just coming back from his break and he was at the open door of the bus, about to go in. She intercepted him, out of breath. "Somebody stole my money."

The driver stopped. "I'm sorry, what?"

"I had four hundred seventy dollars inside my coat. One of your passengers stole it."

She was speaking loudly, and she sensed the passengers inside the bus could hear her. She saw two teenagers in the front, a boy and a girl, frowning at her.

Well, screw them. They might be the ones who did it!

The driver asked, "How do you know it was a passenger?"

"Because the money was inside my coat when I got on the bus. You need to search them," she said, shifting her eyes to glare at the teenage couple.

"Are you sure you didn't just misplace it somewhere?"

"I'm positive. It'll be easy to find. It's big wads of ones and fives and tens and twenties."

"Have you looked in your purse?"

Inside the bus, the teenage girl giggled. Susan was furious. *What the hell is funny about this?* "I don't have to look in my purse," she snapped. "One of these people took my money."

The driver held up his hands placatingly. "I'm just saying, it might help if you look in your purse. That usually solves the problem."

"You look."

She thrust her purse at him. Now the teenage boy laughed too.

The driver said, "Ma'am, you've had your coat on ever since we left Gloversville. And nobody came up to you while you were sitting on the bus."

"I was sleeping!"

"I wasn't. If somebody was to reach inside your coat, I would've seen it in the mirror."

"Well, somehow you missed it."

The driver turned away from her and put his hand on the railing of the bus door, ready to go in. "I'm sorry about the money, ma'am, but we need to get going now. Maybe it'll turn up in your suitcase."

"Only way it'll turn up is if you search these people!"

Now everybody on the whole bus was watching them. The driver said, "I'm not doing that. For one thing, it's illegal. Now if you want to keep riding, get on the bus."

He got on. Susan stayed outside, seething.

"Suit yourself," the driver said, and started to shut the door. But before he did, Susan got on too.

She stood at the front and faced the passengers: the smirking teenagers, the sleazy-looking man with the pockmarked face, the lady with too much makeup who spoke some weird language on her phone.

"People," she said, "my name is Susan Lentigo."

The driver said, "Ma'am—"

"Twenty years ago, my seven-year-old daughter, Amy—"

"You need to sit down—"

"—was brutally murdered."

The driver stood like he was about to escort her off the bus, but then he paused and listened to her. The teenage boy was still smirking, but the girl looked at him and he stopped.

"I'm on my way to North Dakota to witness the killer's execution. I only have four hundred seventy dollars to my name, and I need it for food and lodging. One of you took this money from me. Please give it back and I will be grateful. I won't press charges and I will even pray for you. Please. Give it back to me."

Everybody on the bus stared at her. Then they cast sidelong glances at each other, waiting to see if someone would raise their hand and stand up and return the money.

But nobody moved.

"Please," Susan said, "I beg of you."

Nobody moved.

"If you don't give it back, my dead daughter's curse will be upon you."

Nobody moved.

Susan gave them all a look she hadn't used since that day she confronted the Monster in the courtroom and sat down.

It wasn't until hours later, just as they were about to hit Buffalo, that Susan had a sudden flash of memory: *the bearded young guy eating fries at the Gloversville bus station. Watching me pull bills out of my coat.*

Did he steal my money?

Did I get it all wrong?

CHAPTER FOURTEEN

Officer Lynch opened the door for Susan, Danny, and Lenora, and they stepped out of the morgue. Susan was shell-shocked, whipsawing from the horror of seeing her dead daughter to feeling the power of this new fury raging through her.

A tall man in his early forties, in a blue suit, walked up the fluorescently lit hallway toward them. "Hello, you must be the Lentigo family," he said, a little formally.

Lynch responded, "Yes, and I'm Officer Lynch. May I help you?"

"I'm Special Agent Robert Pappas," the man said, shaking Lynch's hand and then turning to Susan and the others. "I am so terribly sorry for your loss. I want you to know, we'll be working day and night for as long as it takes until we catch the man who did this. Kidnapping across state lines is a federal crime. We have several more agents coming within the hour, and we'll work closely with the local police"—he nodded toward Lynch—"as well."

Susan belatedly realized *special agent* meant FBI. She looked into the man's eyes to see if she could trust him and found herself getting hypnotized by his dark irises. She shook her head to clear it.

Standing beside her, Danny solemnly shook Agent Pappas's hand and said, "Thank you."

Lenora asked, "What did this fuckhead do to her? Did he rape her?"

Pappas said, "Why don't we go to the conference room and have some coffee."

Susan knew that meant the answer was yes.

Why? Why my daughter? Why little Amy?

Her fists tightened and she started punching the cement wall, just like she'd punched Frank yesterday. She couldn't feel any pain in her hands, couldn't feel anything except a rush of blood in her ears. It was like her soul had left her body and left behind nothing but rage.

Lenora shouted, "Susan!" and Danny yelled, "Honey, stop!" Pappas grabbed one of her fists and Lynch grabbed the other. She kept trying to throw punches at the wall, but finally she gave up. She heard her fast, shallow breathing growing more regular. She felt weak.

Danny put his arm around her as they walked upstairs to a conference room. She looked down at her knuckles. They were bleeding.

Pappas noticed them too. On their way up the hall, he asked a passing Albany cop to look for Band-Aids.

Inside the large conference room, a pot of coffee sat on a side table. Lynch poured for them all as Pappas began talking. Susan looked closely at his mouth. His bottom teeth were crooked, but they were white.

"Ms. Lentigo, I'm afraid there was a sexual assault," Pappas said. "There was physical trauma in her vaginal area."

Danny shook his head, appalled. "How could somebody even . . . ? I mean, she was a kid."

Pappas shifted in his seat. "We'll run further tests to determine exactly what happened."

Susan understood he was saying they'd look for semen. She had followed the O.J. trial a few years before, so she knew about DNA matching. She sat there with her mouth open in horror, unable to speak.

Lenora asked, "Do you think it was Frank?"

"We don't know yet."

"Oh, good God," Lenora said, agonized. Susan felt her now familiar urges: she wanted to both scream at her mom and comfort her.

Danny put his hands on top of his head like he was trying to keep it from exploding. "Why did somebody drive Amy all the way to Vermont, to that river? Why there?"

"That's one of the things we'll explore. It's an important clue."

Susan finally found her voice. "When did she die?"

"Nothing is official until the autopsy. But based on the state of rigor mortis and other factors, we're safe in saying she's been dead for quite a while. I believe she was killed on Friday evening, shortly after she was abducted."

Susan gave a small sigh of relief. This was the first "good" news she'd heard since Danny called her that night at Molly's Diner. At least Amy's suffering had been relatively short.

But Danny wasn't mollified. He said, once again, "Fucking motherfucker." Then he wiped his eyes with his sleeve.

Pappas said, "I know the three of you have already talked to the Luzerne police, and some of what you said has been relayed to me. But I'd like to hear it again from you personally. There's always the chance I'll pick up on something another law enforcement agency missed." He looked at Susan as he asked, "Do you feel able to talk?"

Susan, Lenora, and Danny all nodded. Susan found herself looking into this man's eyes again. She decided she liked him. Nothing against Officer Lynch, who was solid, but this FBI agent seemed more caring.

Hopefully, he'd also be really good at his job. She wanted Frank or whoever thrown in prison *today*—and fried as soon as possible.

Pappas put his hand on the table. "Okay, I'd like to speak with you one at a time."

Susan frowned, confused. Lynch hadn't done that. "Why one at a time?"

"It's the best way to get accurate memories. Otherwise, you might influence each other."

"Whatever you say, Agent Pappas," Danny said.

"Thank you. Who'd like to go first?"

Susan immediately said, "I want to get it over with." What she really wanted, she realized, was a break from Lenora and Danny. She was sick of her mom and she couldn't bear looking in Danny's eyes. Now that they knew for sure Amy was dead, Susan's discomfort at being with Danny had resurfaced. It had been their job to keep their daughter safe, and they'd failed.

Lynch stood up and told Danny and Lenora, "I'd be happy to take you down to the break room."

But Lenora didn't move. She clearly had something to get off her chest. "We'll talk all you want," she said, "but I think the killer was someone we don't even know. A total stranger."

"We told her not to talk to strangers," Danny said, sounding pissed off. *How can he be mad at Amy?!* Susan wondered, then realized he was just being defensive. "We told her all the time."

Lenora said, "But she was such a nice, polite girl. It would be hard for her to just *ignore* somebody."

"You may be right," Pappas said. "We'll definitely investigate that possibility."

Lenora nodded vigorously, glad that Pappas seemed to be agreeing with her. "He was probably some sicko waiting outside the school, stalking the kids. He saw Amy standing by herself too close to the street and he got the urge to grab her. He didn't even know we weren't coming to pick her up, he just got lucky."

Susan knew her mom was desperate for it to be a stranger and not Frank. She'd feel a lot less guilty.

But even if it is a stranger, Susan thought bitterly, *it's still Mom's fault.* If she'd done the right thing, Susan would have been there two days ago outside the school. Amy would still be alive.

Pappas said to Lenora, "Again, what you're suggesting is very possible. It's far more common for kids to be abducted by someone they know, but of course there are plenty of exceptions. Now if you'd like to go downstairs with Officer Lynch, I'll be with you soon."

Finally Lenora let herself be led away by Lynch. At the door, she took one last look back at her daughter. Susan knew Lenora was hoping for forgiveness, kindness, at least the hint of a smile. She sighed, irritated, and looked away. She couldn't deal with Lenora right now. She needed to do everything she could to help this FBI agent.

Danny nodded goodbye to Susan, avoiding her eyes the same way she was avoiding his, and left the room too. Susan took a deep breath and Pappas turned toward her.

"Let's take this from the beginning," he said.

She so did not want to relive this past week one more time, but she bit her lip and steeled herself. "Okay."

Pappas seemed to know what she was feeling. "Anytime you want a break, just let me know. Would you like me to get you a sandwich?"

"No thanks. I'm not hungry."

"You sure? How about a chocolate bar? You need to keep your energy up."

She almost smiled at his solicitousness. "Okay, a chocolate bar."

Pappas went out to a vending machine somewhere and came back with two Kit Kats. Susan discovered she was actually starved and ate them voraciously.

Then she told Pappas everything, from the beginning: how Frank creeped Amy out and Susan told Lenora that, and how Lenora left that phone message, and how Frank knew about picking locks. "I keep picturing in my mind the way Frank acted at the police station," she said. "I can't tell if he was acting guilty or not."

Pappas nodded. "Is there anybody else you think we should look into besides Frank?"

Susan said bitterly, "My mom has an active social life. Frank isn't the only guy I wasn't wild about."

"Who were the others?"

"Mark Lyman from Warrensburg and a guy named Ray Clarke from Lake George. We told Officer Lynch and he checked them out, but like you say, maybe he missed something."

"Right. We'll look at them again and also talk with your mom about any other men she might know." Pappas shifted in his seat. "Now I hate to ask, but, what about you?"

Susan was confused. "What about me?"

Pappas's eyes hardened for a moment. "Are you seeing any other men?"

She stared at him, embarrassed and annoyed. "Agent Pappas, I'm not seeing any men besides my husband."

He put up his hands to placate her. "I'm sorry to offend you, but I have to ask."

She shook her head and let out a breath. "Yeah, I guess you do. But the answer's no."

Pappas nodded, then said, "Also, let me review your situation on Friday. You were at Molly's the whole afternoon?"

Oh my God, he's thinking I *could have hurt her?* "Yes."

"And she'll verify that?"

"Yeah, of course." Susan tried to remind herself these stupid questions were just part of the process. This guy with the caring eyes knew what he was doing.

"What about your husband?"

"Danny's a real estate agent. He was in the office 'til around two thirty, then he went to a property that was having an open house the next day. He had to clean it up and get it ready."

Pappas frowned, looking puzzled. "Isn't that the homeowner's job?"

"She's in Florida, and Danny says she kind of has her head up her ass. There was a lot of mouse crap in the house, stuff like that."

Pappas nodded. "So how long was he there?"

"'Til around seven thirty. Then he went to my mom's house, looking for Amy."

"Can anybody verify he was there that whole time?"

Susan could feel herself getting impatient again. "I'm sure his car was in the driveway, so if anyone went by, they saw it. But that house is at the top of the street, and it's a little off in the woods, so . . ." She shrugged.

Pappas raised his eyebrows slightly. "So your husband was up there by himself that whole time?"

Susan had had enough. She put her hand on Pappas's wrist. Immediately she felt funny, because it seemed like a very intimate gesture with just the two of them in the room. But still, she kept her hand there. "Officer, please don't waste any more time. I promise you, my husband did not rape and kill our seven-year-old daughter. You need to find the man who did this."

Pappas looked at Susan and his eyes softened. She removed her hand from his wrist.

"Ma'am," he said, "my wife and I have two daughters. They're six and eight years old."

He covered Susan's hand with his own. "I'll find that piece of shit scumbag or die trying."

CHAPTER FIFTEEN

As the bus pulled into the Buffalo station at one in the morning, Susan's head buzzed with weariness and confusion. Thinking back, she was pretty sure now that the bearded guy at the Gloversville station had stolen her money. Maybe she should apologize for falsely accusing her fellow passengers.

But she was too embarrassed, so she didn't say anything to the driver or the other passengers as she got off the bus and retrieved her suitcase. They all looked at her furtively, not wanting to engage.

She rolled the suitcase into the station and looked around. The bright lights assaulted her eyes and the place smelled of cleaning fluid. Hopeless-looking people of every age, race, and body type sat in the molded plastic chairs and waited. Lounging against the walls, in the corners, were several men with sharp, angular faces who looked as if they were hunting for prey. One guy with a big Adam's apple watched Susan intently like he was coming up with a plan for what to do with her.

She went up to the ticket area and saw a big poster that listed all the cities in New York that Greyhound serviced. Her eyes lit on "Tamarack." But then she turned away, willing herself to forget about Danny.

She found the schedule for the westbound bus, and saw it wouldn't leave until nine a.m. *Eight hours! What do I do 'til then?* She had nowhere to go and she wasn't just tired but starved. All she had to eat was the little baggie of peanuts, chocolate chips, and sweetened cranberries her mom had packed for her. She was dead broke except for maybe three dollars of loose change in her purse—

"Excuse me," a woman's voice said behind her.

She turned. It was a young woman from the bus with brown bangs almost down to her eyes, carrying a sleeping baby girl in her arms.

"When's your bus coming?" the woman said. She couldn't be older than twenty.

"Nine o'clock."

"Need a place to crash? I'm only five blocks from here."

Susan looked at her holding her baby and decided she trusted her. More or less. "Thank you."

As they walked toward the young woman's apartment, Susan learned her name, Marla, and her baby's name, Sophie. It turned out Marla worked at a diner too, just like Susan. After several blocks, they arrived at a strip club with a flashing red neon "Girls Girls Girls" sign.

"Home sweet home," Marla said. "I'm upstairs."

Susan wasn't so sure she'd made the right move coming to this sleazy place with this girl. But she didn't want to walk back to the bus station alone. They opened the front door and entered the club. Music was playing, some hip-hop hit Susan vaguely recognized, and a heavyset, big-breasted woman danced onstage, or at least swayed. The music woke Sophie up and she started to cry.

There were only eight or nine customers this late on a Monday night. A big Filipino bouncer waved hi to Marla, then ignored her and Susan as they walked past the stripper and through the club. They headed into a dark back hallway and up a creaky flight of stairs, with

Susan hauling her suitcase and Marla carrying her crying baby. "It's okay, sweetie," she cooed. "We're almost home."

Marla unlocked the door and led Susan into a small studio apartment. As the red neon light flashed on and off through the window, Marla took Sophie straight into the kitchen area for milk and cookies. Soon the baby was quiet and cheerful. Watching them together, Susan decided maybe Marla and Sophie didn't have such a bad life, despite where they were living.

"Are you hungry too?" Marla asked.

"Well . . ."

Marla smiled. "That's a yes, right? I'm starved. We've got Cheerios and raisins, if you're good with that."

"Cheerios sounds great," Susan said.

The three of them settled around the table wolfing down cereal, raisins, and milk. Susan had never enjoyed a meal this much in her whole life.

After Sophie's initial hunger was sated, she began staring at Susan's neck.

"I think she likes your scarf," Marla said.

Susan took off the bright aqua scarf her mom had made and hid her face behind it. Then she lifted the scarf. "Peekaboo!"

Sophie laughed, so Susan did it again. "Peekaboo!" Sophie laughed even harder.

Susan wrapped the scarf around her head like a babushka and made a funny face, scrunching up her nose. Sophie gurgled with laughter.

"She's so cute," Susan said.

"You're good with her."

Susan made another silly face for Sophie, getting more laughter. She enjoyed being with babies. It was hard for her being around girls who were older, like six or seven, but babies brought back sweet memories.

"I'm a little worried she's not talking yet," Marla said.

"How old is she?"

"Fourteen months."

Susan waved her arm. "Oh relax, my girl didn't talk 'til she was two. Then I couldn't shut her up." She said to the baby, "Aw, you sweet thing."

Sophie smiled happily. Marla said, "I feel like she understands what people are saying."

"You can tell she's a smart girl. Look at those eyes—and these cute little fingers!" Susan said, taking Sophie's hand.

Marla watched Susan playing with the baby's fingers. "Do you have any other kids?"

Susan shook her head. "No. I couldn't." She left it at that, not wanting to burden Marla with the whole miscarriage story, and let Sophie grab her thumb.

Marla said, "I can't imagine what that would feel like, to . . ."

"Don't try. You and your daughter will have very good lives. I can feel it."

Marla put some raisins on a little plate for Sophie. "It's hard right now. My boyfriend left town last month, and I haven't heard from him yet."

"He sounds like a jerk. Maybe it's better he's gone."

Marla nodded uncertainly. "I just feel like people should be together." She held out the box of raisins to Susan. "Do you have a boyfriend?"

"Not really." She put more raisins into her bowl. "I kinda don't care."

"Are you still in love with your ex?"

Susan gave a dubious laugh. She definitely had confused emotions about Danny, but she was pretty sure she wasn't in love with him anymore. "He only lives a little bit west of here, but I haven't seen him in years. I don't know if he even knows about the execution." She ate a spoonful of cereal. "The government was supposed to contact me, but they forgot. I just found out from googling."

"You should call him and tell him. He should be there with you."

Susan felt a sudden tightness in her chest. She shrugged noncommittally, not wanting to admit she'd called Danny but hadn't had the . . . the what, the courage? . . . to leave him a message. She ate another spoonful. "Oh my God, I totally forgot how delicious Cheerios and raisins are."

Susan, Marla, and Sophie all "got the sleepies," as Marla put it, about five minutes later. Marla set her phone alarm for 8:20 for Susan's benefit and put blankets on the sofa. "I hope this'll be okay," she said. "It's a little lumpy."

"I'm good," Susan said, and meant it.

"I wish I had some money to give you."

Susan waved that off. "No worries. You've done enough."

"But how will you survive 'til Saturday?"

Susan was too tired to worry about that now. "I'll figure it out later." She fell asleep almost as soon as she lay down.

When she woke up, she didn't remember where she was. She could tell she was lying on a sofa, so she thought she was in the back room at Molly's. But then she looked over at the double bed where Marla and her baby were sleeping soundly, and she remembered everything.

Marla lay on her back, with Sophie on her side facing her. They looked angelic together. Susan smiled, then looked up at the digital clock above the stove.

8:47? What the hell happened to that phone alarm?!

"Shit," Susan said, and jumped up. She didn't go to the bathroom, instead threw on her coat, scarf, and boots and grabbed her suitcase and purse. She looked back at Marla and Sophie, wanting to wake Marla up and say goodbye.

But she didn't have time. The bus left in thirteen minutes.

She carried her suitcase to the door instead of rolling it, to make less noise. Then she quietly opened the door and started out.

But she didn't feel right. So she came back in, took off her aqua scarf, and laid it down on the kitchen table.

Then she rushed out again, closing the door quietly behind her. She ran the five blocks to the bus station, dragging the suitcase and hoping she wouldn't break the handle. When she got there, the clock on the wall said 9:01.

Almost crashing into a man in a wheelchair, she raced to the passenger loading area. There were a lot of buses there. *Which is the right one?* But none of them looked like they were about to leave.

Then she saw another bus already pulling out of the station. *That has to be it!* "Wait!" she yelled. She ran toward the bus as it went down the driveway and turned right, heading away from her. "Stop!"

The bus kept moving, about to go through a green light and take off. *"Stop!"* she screamed louder, towing her suitcase and running.

The light turned yellow. Would the bus stop? Then the light turned red and the bus's brake lights came on. *Thank God!* She raced up and banged on the front door.

The driver, a skinny guy wearing a Hawaiian shirt under his uniform jacket, eyed her skeptically. At last he opened the door.

"I have a ticket," Susan said, gasping for breath. "I have a ticket."

A minute later, her suitcase was stashed and she was on the bus as it headed west.

Eleven hundred miles to go.

CHAPTER SIXTEEN

SUNDAY, APRIL 14, TWENTY YEARS AGO

AFTER SUSAN ANSWERED all of Agent Pappas's questions, she went to a bar down the street and had a burger and a couple of cheap happy-hour beers while some baseball game played on TV. Mainly she didn't want to be alone with her mom in the break room while Pappas questioned Danny.

The alcohol and the finality of her daughter's death exhausted her. When Danny and Lenora picked her up at the bar at dusk and they all drove home, Susan was too drained to join in their conversation. She looked silently out at the trees lining the Northway. They were beginning to turn green again after the long winter, promising renewal. Rebirth.

What a goddamn joke. She pictured Amy running through these woods, screaming.

Lenora was complaining to Danny about how Pappas had questioned her for over an hour and wasn't at all nice about it. "I don't know what you're telling these cops," she said, "but I wish to hell they'd quit harassing all the guys I go out with."

Susan turned away from the window and focused on Lenora. "You think I care about that, Mom?"

Lenora knew enough to shut up, but Susan was on a roll. "You think I give half a flying fuck about your dickhead boyfriends?"

Danny stepped in, telling Lenora, "At least nobody's saying *you* killed Amy. Pappas practically accused me to my face. Asking all these questions about my alibi."

Their whole marriage, Susan had tried to downplay it whenever she got mad at Danny. She'd make nice or go in another room and wait for her anger to pass. But now she was at the end of her rope. "Why don't both of you shut the fuck up," she snapped.

Danny looked at her in surprise. She turned back to the window.

By the time they got home it was dark. Molly and Parson Parsons were there, along with several neighbors. Susan found Molly way more comforting than anybody else. She fell into her arms and sobbed until she had no more tears left inside her.

Her neighbors had made macaroni and cheese and hot cocoa, but Susan skipped all that and drank from another bottle of Jack Daniels that one of her regular diner customers had brought over. Within fifteen minutes, she was nodding off at the kitchen table.

Molly and Lenora took her off to the bedroom. Molly pulled back the blankets while Lenora removed her coat and shoes. Susan had a flash where she remembered she was furious at her mom, but she was too tired to scream at her. She was asleep before she was lying down.

When she woke up in the middle of the night, four hours later, at first she didn't remember anything that had happened in the last two days. She felt a thickness in her head and wondered what it was about. Then she felt a tangy bourbon aftertaste on her gums.

And then she remembered everything.

She sat bolt upright and saw Danny lying on his side of the bed, his body turned away from her, asleep. She suddenly hated him. How could he be sleeping? Their daughter was dead!

She pummeled his back with her fists and screamed, a long wordless scream. He woke up and shouted, "Hey!" and as she rained down blows on him, he managed to break free and roll out of bed. She glowered at him and thought, *He doesn't care! He doesn't care Amy is dead!*

"Susan, calm down," he said, and through the haze of her hatred she could see he was terrified of her. Then she realized how totally irrational she was acting.

She breathed heavily and started to cry. God, she had to stop *punching* people. Danny came back into bed and put his arms around her.

She pulled him to her fiercely, digging her fingernails into his back. She could feel him flinch from the pain, but then he held her tight.

I love this man, she thought.

They had been together for nineteen years now, since she was sixteen. Danny was her first love. Her only love.

She pulled back from him and looked in his eyes, as moonlight eased in through the window. *Will we survive this?*

She couldn't imagine life without him.

But she hadn't been able to imagine life without Amy, either.

"I love you, Danny," she said.

"I love you too, Susan," he said, and held her.

CHAPTER SEVENTEEN

THE FIRST THING Susan did after getting on the bus was hit the restroom. She wished she could brush her teeth, but her toothbrush was in her suitcase inside the luggage compartment, so that would have to wait.

She went back to her seat as the bus left Buffalo behind and got onto the cold, barren I-90 heading west. While it chugged up a long gray hill, Susan opened her purse, moved the pepper spray bottle out of the way, and took out her baggie of food. She figured she better ration it, so she only ate two handfuls before putting it away. At some point she'd probably have to call Terri for money, but she didn't want to do it yet. Terri had already done so much for her, organizing that whole fundraiser at the Crow Bar. She felt guilty she'd lost all the money from it.

Running to catch the bus hadn't done her right leg any good, and it started bothering her like it did sometimes. Susan had never gone to a doctor about the leg, hadn't wanted to spend the money, but she suspected it was some kind of muscle pull. It helped to massage it, and that's what she did now, kneading the back of her leg from her knee down to her ankle.

She didn't have anything to read, so she looked around her. This bus was twice as full as yesterday's, and she'd been lucky to get a seat to herself. Several of the other passengers were talking on their cells, but she hated hearing just half of a conversation so she tried to tune them out. She gazed out the window at the bare trees and occasional billboards and thought about what would happen this Saturday at five-thirty p.m.

From reading up on executions, she knew the condemned man gets to say some final words. She wondered what the Monster would say.

Would he finally admit he had done it? Would he ask for Susan's forgiveness, and tell her where he had hidden Amy's necklace?

She almost hoped he wouldn't. That way she wouldn't have to decide whether to forgive him. She was used to hating him and wanted to hate him forever, no matter what Parson Parsons said.

As she daydreamed about watching the Monster's last breath, and how that would feel, a girl's voice said, "Daddy, which do you think is cooler: singing kangaroos or dancing turtles?"

It was the little girl on the other side of the aisle, who had been quietly reading Magic Tree House books for the whole trip. She was talking to her father, a guy with serious eyes and black-rimmed glass who looked like a high school teacher or professor.

He smiled at her and stroked his chin thoughtfully. "Boy, that's a tough one."

"I think dancing turtles 'cause they're taller. But Zoey thinks singing kangaroos because they can be either pink or blue."

"But dancing turtles can be purple, right?" the dad said earnestly.

So sweet, Susan thought. Except moments like this always came with a desperate pang. The girl was wearing a pink dress with ruffled sleeves, just like Amy's old dress. Susan closed her eyes and remembered a spring afternoon about two weeks before Amy died, when she and her dad were playing basketball in the driveway. The snow had barely melted and it couldn't have been more than forty-five degrees out, but Amy insisted on playing without her coat. She had on the pink dress, which she'd worn to school that day.

Susan came out the front door to tell them dinner was ready and stood there watching them. Danny had bought a hoop low enough for Amy. She could already shoot layups into it, and in a few years, she'd be tall enough to dunk. She couldn't wait.

Susan remembered feeling so happy that afternoon.

Amy dribbling toward the basket, saying, "Daddy, I wanna dunk! Lift me up!"

Danny swoops her up and holds her high in the air.

Amy slam dunks the ball. "Monster jam!" she shouts, and starts to giggle.

"Hurray for Amy!" Danny says, lifting her even higher.

"Daddy, let me down!"

Danny lets her down and Amy goes running after the ball.

Sitting in the bus with her eyes closed, Susan could hear her younger self calling, "Danny and Amy, time for dinner!" She had an odd feeling there was something else to the memory too, but she couldn't quite put her finger on what.

Before she could focus on it any more, she heard the air brakes and felt the bus shudder to a halt. She opened her eyes and saw they'd come to a red light outside some small town. Behind her, a woman answered her ringing phone and said, "Hi, honey, I'm almost home."

She looked out the window and saw a sign advertising a Cumberland Farms convenience store, next to another sign advertising a Stewart's. Funny, there was an intersection right outside Lake Luzerne with the exact same two signs. It was like she hadn't even left home.

Then she saw another sign behind those two, a green road sign. It had an arrow pointing to the right and it said, "TAMARACK 2."

Susan sat bolt upright. *We're two miles from Tamarack?* She'd known it was west of Buffalo, but she had no idea it was right off I-90.

The light turned green and the bus turned right.

Toward Tamarack.

Susan looked out the window, in shock. She half expected to see Danny out there, walking down the sidewalk in one of those navy-blue blazers he used to wear to work.

They were riding up Main Street now. Tamarack looked the way she had pictured it: a small tourist town, like Luzerne but nicer, with a town green and stores that called themselves shoppes. But it was too far away from Boston or New York to be overly fancy.

The bus station was right on Main, in the middle of town. They pulled up out front, and the driver with the Hawaiian shirt called out in a bored voice, "Tamarack. Tamarack, New York."

As the doors opened for two disembarking passengers, Susan looked through the opening and saw a storefront with a sign that read: "TAMARACK REALTY."

Holy shit.

It was almost like God was sending her a sign. *This* sign.

There weren't any passengers waiting to get on the bus, so the driver shut the door and got ready to take off. Susan made a decision. She jumped out of her seat and hurried up to the front.

"Excuse me," she said. "If I get off the bus here, can I get back on later with the same ticket?"

The driver looked her over. "Yeah, but the next bus west isn't for twenty-four hours."

She hesitated. The driver put his foot on the gas and prepared to drive on, positive she'd decide to stay on the bus.

But hell, she could get off here and still make it to North Dakota by Thursday. She said, "I want to get out."

The driver lifted his eyebrows. "Whatever you say, lady." He opened the door.

"My suitcase is down there," she said, pointing at the luggage compartment.

The driver helped her get it. "Have fun in lovely downtown Tamarack," he said, like it was highly unlikely. Then he got back in the bus and started off.

Susan was tempted to wave her arms and get him to stop. She would tell him she had changed her mind, and she would leave Tamarack and Danny behind. She'd go on to North Dakota alone.

This was so not like her, to stop in a strange town with zero money to see an ex-husband who didn't even answer her phone calls. It was nuts.

But before she could make up her mind to wave at the driver, the bus turned a corner and was out of sight.

She got her suitcase and headed for Tamarack Realty.

When she reached the storefront, she immediately got another jolt. There was a big picture on the window of a smiling Danny, fifty-seven now but still handsome, his hair still dark and full, flanked by two women realtors. Danny looked like he hadn't gained a single pound since she last saw him. She had gained twenty.

The picture was captioned, "Tamarack Realty Supports the Police Athletic League." Danny and the two women were holding up a huge, outsized five-thousand-dollar check made out to the police league. Susan stood there and gazed at Danny, at the man he was now. His smile was so open and friendly. She looked for traces of the trauma he had been through twenty years ago, but didn't see any.

Then she remembered how good he had always been at hiding his feelings with a smile. Sometimes they'd be eating dinner together and she would think they were having a perfectly friendly conversation, and he would blow up about something he'd been stewing over all day.

She touched the picture of Danny's face. What would it be like to see him again?

I'm right to be here, she thought. *I need to do this.*

She wiped her glasses with a tissue, straightened her shoulders, and walked inside.

CHAPTER EIGHTEEN

THEY COULDN'T HAVE a funeral because the FBI wasn't releasing the body yet. But the well-wishers and casseroles kept coming.

Susan had no idea what to do with herself. She couldn't focus on anything for longer than a couple minutes. She'd go to her bedroom for something and forget why she was there. She'd turn on the stove and ten minutes later the pot would burn and set off the smoke alarm.

During that first week, she called Agent Pappas at least five times a day. He was still optimistic, but Susan began to fear they would never catch Amy's killer. The FBI continued to suspect Frank, but they didn't have enough evidence to pick him up again.

Pappas asked her all kinds of questions: "Have you had any negative interactions with customers at Molly's?" "Who do you know that has ties to Granville?" "Have you had any problems with other parents at Amy's school?"

One morning Pappas asked, "Do you know anybody who likes to camp out in lean-tos?" This question perplexed her, until he explained they'd discovered Amy's fingerprints on an empty soda bottle inside a lean-to forty yards from where her body was found. The FBI speculated Amy was assaulted there and tried to fight off her attacker with the soda bottle. Then she ran, trying to escape. The FBI had found two sets of shoe prints, from Amy's shoes and a grown-up's shoes.

Susan, on the phone in the kitchen with Danny listening in, got excited about that. "If you have shoe prints, you can figure out what kind of shoe he was wearing!"

"I'm afraid the prints are too indistinct for that."

Danny took the phone from Susan. "At least you'll know his shoe size, right?"

"All we know is it's somewhere between 9 and 11," Pappas said, and the remnants of Susan's excitement disappeared.

Pappas continued, "We're starting to piece together the crime. We think Amy tripped and hit her forehead against a sharp rock fifteen yards away from the lean-to. That's what caused the cut. Then the killer strangled her, probably right near the rock, and dragged her body off into the woods. He was trying to hide it, at least for a while."

Images flooded Susan's mind, unbidden: *Amy, fighting back with nothing but a soda bottle. Running through the woods, looking over her shoulder and screaming, then tripping and falling, lying on the ground. Blood from the gash in her forehead streaming down her face and neck, covering her necklace beads in red. Holding up her little hands to try and fight off her attacker.*

After Pappas told her the details of her daughter's murder, she couldn't get these pictures out of her head. It got harder to be alone. She needed people around to distract her.

But being with Danny didn't help much, because the pain in his eyes made her feel her own anguish even more acutely. Being with Lenora had pretty much the same effect, plus there were all the layers of guilt and anger to deal with.

The visits from friends and neighbors helped a little at first, except nobody knew what to say, not really. They repeated the same things over and over, like "I can't imagine how you must feel," and "Amy's in a better place." She started to think they were all just stupid clichés, and that made her feel even worse.

Once somebody from the church said, "God doesn't give you more than you can handle," and Susan started screaming about what a dumbass he was. There were several other people in the house at the time, but she didn't care. "You think God doesn't give you more than you can handle?" she shouted at him. "Are you fucking insane?"

Danny dealt with his grief by going fishing, usually by himself. He'd always needed a fair amount of alone time, especially when he was under stress. Also, she knew he wasn't enjoying being around her now, the same way she found it hard being with him.

Lenora still came by Susan's house, but she spent most of her time in the living room drinking, while Susan stayed in the kitchen. Finally, on Wednesday, three days after Amy was found, Susan called Molly and asked if she could come in to work.

"Are you sure you're ready, honey?"

"I need to."

So she came in for the lunch shift. But as soon as somebody asked for French fries she began to cry, remembering how much Amy had loved them. Molly took her into the back room and put her on the sofa, where she was able to cry all she wanted without worrying about disturbing the customers.

That sofa turned out to be the best place for her. She lay there all day for two days, hearing sounds from the diner and knowing she wasn't all alone in the world, but she wouldn't have to actually interact with people. Molly brought her tea and chocolate chip cookies, which was one of the few things she liked eating right now.

Then on Friday evening, as she was listening to the dinner shift, one week after Amy was taken, there was a knock on the door. "Come in," Susan said, thinking it was Molly. But Agent Pappas walked in, followed by Danny. She sat up on the sofa.

Her eyes darted back and forth between them. "What's going on?"

Danny sat down beside her. It was the closest they had been to each other in days. Susan had taken to sleeping in Amy's room, both comforted and tortured by her smells.

"Agent Pappas picked me up at the office," Danny said. He had just gone in to work today for the first time. "He has something to show us."

Pappas brought over a folding chair and sat across from them. "I want to show you a picture of someone. Tell me if you recognize him."

He reached inside a pocket of his blue sport jacket and took out a photograph. A mugshot, Susan realized. It showed a man around forty years old with a flat face, thick lips, and surly eyes that glowered at the camera.

Susan and Danny both stared at the man. Susan rubbed her head and thought hard, trying to place him. He did look a little familiar somehow, but maybe it was just wishful thinking. She said, "I don't know."

Danny shook his head slowly. "I don't recognize him."

Susan said, "Why are you asking about him?"

"Let me show you another picture," Pappas said.

He pulled out another mugshot of the same man, in profile. Susan noticed a scar on his cheek just beneath his ragged sideburns. She didn't recall seeing that scar before.

Danny said, "I'm sorry, I'm just not . . ."

Susan eyed the profile, blinking rapidly. It was so strange to think this random person she'd never met might be the man who had destroyed her life. "Is he the guy?"

Pappas said, "We don't know yet."

Danny said hopefully, "But you think he might be?"

Suddenly something flashed in Susan's mind. "Show me that first picture again," she said.

Pappas held it up, and this time it all came back to her: *The morning of the murder. Susan and Amy getting in the Dodge Dart and riding off, passing the Homestead Motel on the corner. Out front, a man gets a toolbox out of his car. He looks up and eyes the Dodge Dart as it goes by. He has a flat, tired face—*

This face. Susan was sure of it. She leaned forward and pointed at the mugshot, excited. "That guy was staying at the Homestead Motel. He watched me and Amy drive off to school that morning."

Pappas raised his eyebrow. "That same morning?"

"Yes."

"That's very helpful to know. You're right, he was staying at the Homestead. We got his name from their register."

"Does he have an alibi?" Danny asked.

"Not from two o'clock on."

Susan's heart was pounding. She stared down at the mugshot. "Who is he?"

"His name is Curt Jansen. He's a drifter type, in and out of trouble." Pappas tapped the mugshot. "This is from Philadelphia, three months ago. He was trying to steal coins from a parking meter. Last month his ex-girlfriend in Worcester, Massachusetts, took out a protection order against him."

Danny said, "I still don't get why you think it's him. I mean, besides that he doesn't have an alibi."

Pappas set the mugshot down on the table next to the sofa. He leaned back, twining his fingers together, and said, "We went to see him at the motel today. He has scabs on his left hand that are consistent with a child-sized mouth, missing one tooth, biting down on it hard. We didn't find any foreign blood in Amy's mouth, but she may have swallowed it."

Oh God. Susan pictured it: *His hands reach up to strangle Amy. She bites down so hard she draws blood . . .*

She grabbed the mugshot off the table and stared. *So this is him. This is the piece of shit who did it.* "Where is he?"

"He's in custody at the FBI office in Schenectady. I'm on my way down there."

Danny looked just as stunned as she was. "When did this guy come to the Homestead?" he asked.

"Last Wednesday. His window faced out onto the backyard."

Danny said, "Right near our driveway. So he watched Amy playing basketball..."

"Dancing on the porch..." Susan said.

"And going to school every morning. He got obsessed by her."

"I'll let you know what we find out," Pappas said grimly, and stood up. "If he's the one who did this to Amy..." His voice tightened. "...we'll get him to talk."

CHAPTER NINETEEN

Susan waited all that night and the next morning without getting any more news. Agent Pappas didn't return her calls.

Then, while she was at her customary station on Molly's sofa, curled up in a ball and listening to the lunch rush through the walls, there was a knock she recognized from the day before. "Come in," she said.

Pappas walked in. Susan waited.

He said, "Curt Jansen confessed."

She started to cry. She wasn't sure why.

Pappas found a napkin and handed it to her. Then he sat down on a folding chair and brought it close to the sofa.

She wiped her eyes and blew her nose. "I'm sorry I didn't get back to you sooner," he said. "It took us all night. We had to question him for about ten hours before he finally broke."

She steeled herself, not sure she wanted to hear the answer to this. "What did he say?"

Pappas put his hands through his hair, clearly not relishing this part of his job. "I don't know how to put it."

"Just tell me."

Pappas sighed and forced himself to get down to it. "He said he likes young girls. He claims he never did anything like this before, he always controlled himself. He would park across the street from elementary schools during recess or when school let out, and he'd get drunk and, you know, fantasize. So last Friday he was out there doing that, and he saw Amy, by herself, wearing the necklace. For some reason, he got stuck on that necklace. He says his mom used to abuse him. I got the feeling she wore a necklace when she was doing it, and that became part of his sickness."

Susan's mouth hung open. Pappas's words were so horrible she had trouble taking in what he was saying.

"You don't need to hear the rest of this."

Susan set her jaw, determined. "Tell me."

"It's not important—"

She needed to get this over with and know the truth once and for all. It couldn't be any worse than what she imagined. She gripped his arm. "*Tell me.*"

Pappas shook his head but continued. "He said his fantasies finally got the best of him. He drove up and told Amy he was supposed to pick her up. She said something about Grandma, and he said Grandma sent him. So she got in the car and he took her to Vermont. He'd been in that lean-to before and he'd had fantasies about bringing a girl there. So he did what he did, and I'm *not* going into the details. She fought back and bit him and tried to run away. He got mad and strangled her."

Susan sat there, in shock. She kept thinking how the necklace she and Amy made together had caused all this.

Pappas said gently, "If you want, I can drive you home, or to your mom's house—"

Susan shut her eyes tight. She could picture it: *the purple dolphin, the pink duck, the blue unicorn . . .* "Where is it?"

Pappas looked puzzled. "What?"

"Where's the necklace?"

He said, "I don't know. That's the one thing he won't say."

She hit her forehead with her knuckles. "It makes no sense! A fucking plastic necklace with ducks on it—that's what made this guy horny?"

He said, "It's weird, I know. But guys get into all kinds of weird things."

For a brief moment, Susan couldn't help wondering if Pappas was into weird things too. Then she thought about Danny. Sure, he had his quirky fantasies, but nothing even in the same galaxy as this.

Pappas reached out and touched her lightly on her shoulder. "Listen, in every case there's a couple loose ends we never fully understand. But we got the guy. Susan, *it's over.*"

And it was.

Or so it seemed—for about twenty hours.

Susan went home for dinner that night, another casserole, and shared it with Danny, Lenora, and Molly. They were all still grieving and weary, but relieved the killer had apparently been caught. In the middle of dinner, Lenora went to the bathroom and stayed there for about ten minutes. When she came back, she said, "Sorry, I smelled up your bathroom. I was constipated this whole week, but ever since that guy confessed, I've been crapping all day."

Lenora gave a little laugh. No doubt learning her boyfriend was not the man who raped and killed Amy made her feel a lot less guilty.

But Susan still blamed her mom for not being at the school picking up Amy. And though she knew it was crazy, she blamed herself, too, for making the necklace that got Amy killed.

The rational part of her knew the real blame didn't lie with herself or her mom, it belonged to that monster Curt Jansen. Maybe one day she would get herself to fully believe that.

Meanwhile, despite everything, she did feel a little better now, and so did Danny. That night, when Susan got into bed beside him, he was watching basketball on TV for the first time since Amy went missing. She rested her head on his shoulder and said, "Thank God they caught him."

Danny laughed. She stared at him and asked, "What's funny?"

He put his arm around her. "I'm sorry, honey, I'm just relieved the FBI will quit hassling me now. I know life will never be normal for us again, but at least . . ."

His voice trailed off and he kissed her. She fell asleep in his arms, and that night she managed to sleep for five hours straight.

The next morning she went to the refrigerator to get milk for her coffee. But then suddenly she stood there rooted to the spot. She looked at all the pictures of Lenora on the refrigerator door. *God, I've been such a bitch to my mom,* she thought.

She grabbed a plate of chocolate chip cookies one of the church ladies had brought over, got in her car, and drove to Lenora's trailer. She knocked on the door and her mom opened it, still wearing her pink nightgown.

"Thought you might like some cookies for breakfast," Susan said, thrusting them forward.

Her mom's lips quivered. Finally she was able to say, "Forget about the cookies, let's have a drink." For the first time in God knows how long, Susan actually laughed. She felt like a huge weight had been lifted off her.

But five minutes later, while they were drinking coffee and kahlua, the phone rang. It was Danny.

"Agent Pappas is here," he said. "Curt Jansen just recanted his confession."

CHAPTER TWENTY

TAMARACK REALTY TRIED hard to look upscale and mostly succeeded. There were leatherish sofas, low glass tables laden with art books, and framed photographs of the lakes and hills of western New York.

Susan walked inside and took it all in. So this was where Danny worked now.

She had the feeling he didn't live in poverty like she did. Maybe she should have been a little more careful with that divorce mediation.

Two attractive, impeccably made-up women in their late thirties, dressed in business suits, looked Susan over as she entered. She assumed they were realtors too. She recognized one of them, the perky redhead, from the picture in the store window.

She knew exactly what they were thinking: this woman in her fifties with the old coat and beat-up suitcase is not the world's most exciting real estate prospect. But the redhead did her professional best to summon enthusiasm. She gave Susan a smile and said, "Good afternoon, may I help you?"

Susan took a quick breath and said, "Yes. I'm looking for Danny Lentigo."

"Of course. Do you have an appointment?"

No, he didn't answer my damn calls, she thought. She saw a row of private offices toward the rear. "Is he back there?"

The redhead's bright blue eyes got nervous, and Susan knew she'd guessed right. Leaving her suitcase behind so she could move faster, she headed toward the back.

"Ma'am, excuse me," the redhead said, following after her. "Ma'am!"

Susan ignored her. She looked into one office and saw a woman behind the desk. She looked in a second office: empty. She looked in a third.

There was Danny.

He looked handsome and younger than fifty-seven, just like he did on that picture in the window. He was on his computer. She flashed back to him sitting at the computer in their house twenty years ago, with the dial-up internet that made that horrible noise when it connected.

She stepped into his office. He heard her coming in and looked up. Seeing a stranger standing there, his face transformed in a split second into a realtor's smile.

A second later, he recognized her. His smile turned to shock and then dismay.

But she kept up a brave front. "Hi, Danny."

"What are you doing here?" he said.

Fuck, I'm such an idiot! Why did I come? I just upset him, he hates me. She wished she'd brushed her teeth before coming in.

The redhead appeared at Danny's door, ready to intervene.

Well, now that Susan was here in his office, she had to go through with it. She said, "The Monster is getting executed in five days. Thought you'd want to know."

Danny's jaw dropped. He waved off the bewildered redhead, then looked back at Susan.

He said, "You could've emailed me."

She looked at him. *What a jerk!* she thought. *Even if I do upset him, he has no right to treat me like this, does he?* "I called four times. You didn't pick up."

Danny leaned back in his chair. "So he's getting executed."

She nodded. "Yeah."

"How do they do it?"

"Lethal injection."

Danny looked up at her. "They should fucking electrocute him."

Susan looked back at him and at last felt the connection she had craved. The connection she'd come here for.

She and Danny were in this together. They always had been.

"Can't have everything," she said.

He nodded and scratched his neck. He looked like he didn't know what to say.

She sat down across the desk from him. "I'm going to the execution. It's in North Dakota."

He looked impressed. "Long drive."

"I'm taking a bus." Then she gathered her courage and asked, "You wanna come too?"

He blinked at her.

"I know we've grown apart, Danny, but I feel like this is something we should do together." She paused. "Amy would want that."

"I don't think my wife would like me spending a week with you."

From Danny's profile on the Tamarack Realty website, Susan knew he was married, or at least had been. Now she knew his marriage was still ongoing. She wasn't sure how she felt about that. Had she been hoping for something different?

But the hell with all that. Only one thing mattered: Amy was their daughter. She said, "You can bring your wife along."

"I have two children now and I'm not bringing them."

She had been so focused on Danny, she hadn't even noticed the photograph in the small silver frame at the edge of his desk. Now she picked it up.

It showed Danny with his arm around his wife, a woman in her forties with shoulder-length blonde hair who looked, Susan recognized instantly, like a younger version of herself back when she used to dye her hair blonde. It wasn't just the woman's hair. Her friendly, maybe slightly mousy smile was just like Susan's years ago.

That was disturbing enough. But even worse, there were two sweet-looking kids standing in front of Danny, a boy of about ten and a girl who was six or seven. Danny's hand rested on the little girl's shoulder.

He really did move on. He has new children now, and he loves them.

The girl was cute and gap-toothed and looked like Amy. Danny had replaced everything, except better, because he had a boy now too.

A boy Susan should have had, except she miscarried.

She said, "Nice-looking kids."

"Thank you."

"What are their names?"

"David and Emily."

Emily. It sounded just like Amy. Danny had done all he possibly could to replace her. Susan put the photo down. A wave of fury swept through her. She wasn't sure it was rational, but she didn't care.

"You shouldn't have forgotten Amy."

"I didn't forget her. I moved on."

Susan shook her head in disgust. "Yeah, you sure did."

Danny pouted his lips. It was an expression she'd forgotten, but the meaning came back to her now full force. He used to look like that when he was about to say something hurtful.

"Susan, I couldn't be with you after Amy died. The way you were, it was just too much for me. I couldn't handle it."

She looked down. He was right. Her depression must've been really hard to deal with. He continued, "I thought you and me would both be better off if we tried to forget about our life together. That's why I didn't pick up when you called."

Despite all her shame about having driven him away, her anger returned. "That is such bullshit. We were married once. How could you not pick up?" *Was he always this big of an asshole and I just didn't notice?*

Danny shook his head, pissed, and his lips curled—another facial expression she was remembering now. Why had she felt a need to forget these things about him? He said, "'Cause I knew you'd give me shit about something."

"For God's sake—"

His voice rose. "I don't want to see Curt Jansen's execution. I don't even want to think about him." He slammed his hand on the desk. "Goddamn it, you shouldn't have come here!"

She looked at him and said quietly, "I almost forgot about your temper."

He closed his eyes and sighed, frustrated. "I didn't mean that." *Sure you did,* she thought. "I'm sorry, Susan, that was stupid. It's good to see you looking good."

She just nodded. "Well, now I've told you, so do what you gotta do."

She turned to go. Danny ran his hands through his hair. "I wish you all the happiness in the world, Susan, I really do."

For a brief moment she thought about asking him for a loan to cover her trip. But she shook that off and started for the door. As she headed out, she saw more photos of Danny and his family on his bookshelf. There were pictures of him and his new wife getting married, him rock climbing on some Adirondack peak, him and his son playing catch, his new daughter standing by a lake—

Wait a minute. Susan stopped in her tracks and stared at the photo of Danny's daughter.

The girl was wearing a multicolored beaded necklace—*and it looked exactly the same as Amy's old necklace.*

There's the purple dolphin and the pink duck!

But how can that be Amy's necklace? It can't!

What the hell?!

CHAPTER TWENTY-ONE

April–September, Twenty Years Ago

Susan was alarmed. *Curt Jansen recanted his confession?*

"It's just standard B.S.," Agent Pappas assured her when she rushed back home from her mom's house. "These guys get lawyers and the first thing they do is try to take back everything they said. Don't worry about it. This case will be a slam dunk."

"Sure," Susan said, but she didn't believe it. After Amy's death, her faith that the world had some kind of order to it was shattered. God either didn't exist or He was a shithead. She began gnawing at her fingers so much they started bleeding. She didn't know what she would do if the man who had done this to her daughter went free.

The trial was scheduled for September. Every night that whole spring and summer, she had terrible nightmares. *The Monster's hands circling Amy's throat. Her eyes bulging. He rips off her necklace and tosses it up in the air. Susan reaches for it desperately as it floats just out of reach. The Monster laughs loudly—*

And Susan would wake up, his derision ringing in her ears.

Danny went back to work and even had luck selling houses. Susan sensed some buyers were throwing business his way because they felt bad for him.

But she couldn't work. She couldn't do anything really. She spent most of her time curled up on Molly's sofa.

She didn't cook for Danny anymore. She didn't have the energy.

He began getting impatient with her dark cloud. "Susan, we still have lives," he would say as gently as he could, but she could tell he was working hard not to get mad at her. "Amy wouldn't want us to roll over and die."

Susan didn't blame him for being upset. She knew how much pain he was in. She hoped that after the trial things would get better for both of them.

But that would only happen if the Monster was convicted.

The trial began on a rainy Tuesday after Labor Day. It would have been Amy's first day back at school. The courtroom, in a federal courthouse down in Albany, was packed. There were a lot of reporters and they all wanted to talk to the bereaved parents. Susan was glad to have Danny do most of the talking; she felt too shaky.

She was sitting in the wooden pews of the spectators' gallery, with Danny on one side and her mom on the other, when the marshals brought Jansen in. He was still in jail, hadn't raised money for the huge bail the judge set. But he'd been allowed to change into a suit for the occasion. He was freshly shaved with a haircut and looked a lot better than he did in the mug shots. He still had the same thick lips and square face, but his eyes weren't surly and he didn't look thuggish anymore. If she didn't know what he'd done to her daughter, Susan might think Jansen looked like a regular-guy construction worker. Some women might even think he was handsome.

Hopefully none of the women on the jury would feel that way.

She stared at Jansen, unable to turn away. This was the man who enjoyed sticking his penis into little girls so much that he killed Amy so he could do it.

Or maybe killing her made it extra fun for him.

Blood rushed to Susan's head. She wanted to jump over the seats and slam his face with one of the heavy wooden chairs.

Lenora squeezed her hand. Danny took her other hand.

She watched as Jansen waved to a woman sitting in the second row of the gallery. The woman waved back and gave him a smile, but Susan could see she was in agony. Her eyes were red-rimmed and puffy, like she'd been crying. Other than that, she was attractive with an open face and long curly brown hair. She wore a conservative dark blue suit and looked a few years younger than Jansen, maybe thirty-five, about Susan's age.

"Who's that woman?" she asked Danny.

"I think it's his sister, Lisa."

Susan couldn't imagine how that must feel, to love somebody who's a monster. She thought Lisa must have known in some way that her brother was evil, even if she didn't know she knew it.

Jansen looked away from Lisa, and his eyes wandered the courtroom. He saw Susan and stopped.

She was paralyzed at first. Then she threw him a fierce scowl, putting every ounce of her hatred into it. She wanted this piece of shit to know she would never rest until he was dead.

Jansen looked back at her with the sad eyes she would always remember. She blinked, confused. She had expected him to sneer angrily or act hateful in some way.

What was behind his sad eyes? Did a part of him feel bad he had killed Amy?

Well fuck him, who cares how he feels. This piece of shit needs to die.

The judge pounded his gavel and jury selection began.

And then the trial.

It was seven days of pure torture. First the autopsy photos. Then the M.E.'s testimony detailing what was done to Amy. The spermicide evidence, indicating her assailant used a condom. The photos of Jansen's left hand with the small scabs, and an analysis of how Amy's bite caused them. Agent Pappas testifying about Jansen's confession and then reading it aloud, including his graphic description of the rape and murder.

Susan broke down again and again. Danny and Lenora both told her she didn't have to do this—why sit through the whole trial and relive her daughter's pain?

But she insisted. The jury had to *see* her. The two middle-aged ladies in the back row, the two younger women in the front, and all the other jurors needed to look in her eyes and know how much she was depending on them.

The prosecutor was a slender young guy named John Hodgman with an expensive dark suit, long thin nose, and confident manner. This was his first big case, according to Agent Pappas, and she worried about him at first; but as far as she could tell, he was kicking ass. The jury didn't seem to find him too cocky. As he walked the jurors through the evidence, she would often look over at them. She sensed they were connecting with both Hodgman and her.

Then on the fifth day, Hodgman rested his case. The defense lawyer, a woman in her forties named Bobbi Reid who wore her hair in a bun, stood up.

Reid had a small law firm in Schenectady that contracted with the public defenders' office. Susan didn't understand how any woman could possibly defend a guy who had raped and killed a child. She didn't care how many times people told her it was an important part of the criminal justice system. It was sick.

Reid acted businesslike, never cracking a smile or showing any emotion really. She began by calling her own expert witness, a retired medical examiner named John Sunderland, to testify about the scabs on Jansen's hand. Sunderland was a little rumpled looking, his tie slightly askew, but he had a strong, resonant voice.

"Those scabs could have been caused by any number of things, not just being bitten by someone," he proclaimed from the stand.

"You could easily get them while doing construction work. And you could *definitely* get them if you had a drunken fall from the second floor of a house onto the sidewalk." That's what Jansen was claiming now.

Susan was afraid Reid and her deep-voiced witness were making an impact on the jury. She watched them but couldn't tell what they were thinking. None of the jurors looked back at her.

Then Hodgman stood up and began his cross-examination. "Mr. Sunderland," he said crisply, "when is the last time you worked as a medical examiner?"

That very first question landed.

"Primarily I've been doing consulting for the past few years," Sunderland said.

Hodgman repeated firmly, "When is the last time you worked as a medical examiner?"

Sunderland finally admitted he hadn't been a medical examiner for fifteen years.

"What periodicals in the field have you read during the past year?" Hodgman asked.

"Well . . ." Sunderland began hesitantly.

Under Hodgman's detailed, withering questions about what Sunderland read, or didn't read, and what conferences he attended, or didn't attend, it became apparent he hadn't kept up on the new developments in forensics during these past fifteen years.

Then Hodgman asked, in a silky, almost loving tone, "Tell me, Mr. Sunderland, why did you leave your last job?"

Reid objected, but the judge overruled her. Sunderland tried to dance around the answer, but then it came. He was fired because he was addicted to prescription drugs and fell asleep in the middle of an autopsy.

Susan exchanged an incredulous look with Danny. *This is the best the defense could come up with?* Either they had zero money to hire a real expert or Bobbi Reid had completely screwed up.

Or maybe she couldn't find a real expert who would agree to back up Jansen's tale about some drunken fall causing the scabs.

It was obvious the jury was not impressed by the old ex-medical examiner's testimony. When he finally retreated from the witness stand in red-faced defeat, the two middle-aged women jurors looked over at Susan and smiled.

But then Reid called Curt Jansen to the stand.

Susan knew this was the make-or-break testimony. The entire courtroom turned utterly silent as Jansen settled in at the stand. He sat up extra straight, as if his lawyer had told him to do that. He put his hand on the Bible and swore in an unwavering voice to tell the truth.

Susan watched the jury watching him intently. The two young women in the front row seemed intrigued by him. It would be just her luck if these two were attracted to bad boys.

Reid started with the basics, getting Jansen's full name, age—forty—and occupation—construction worker. Susan was afraid he would be on the stand for hours, and she'd be forced to listen to it all. But Reid didn't waste time. Within three minutes she was already asking the key questions.

"Mr. Jansen, what were you doing in Lake Luzerne?"

"Drywalling. This contractor I knew from before called me up and hired me for a couple weeks. Put me up at the Homestead Motel."

"And where were you on the day of Amy Lentigo's murder?"

"I got off work about one thirty, 'cause the next apartment I was supposed to be doing wasn't ready yet. So I bought a couple six-packs and started my weekend early." He lifted his shoulders. "Ain't proud of it, but I went back to my room at the Homestead and just drank for the rest of the day."

"Did anybody see you?"

Jansen shook his head. "No, I wasn't into being social. See, this girl I was going out with in Massachusetts broke up with me the week before, so I was pretty much down in the dumps. My room was on the far end, and there wasn't too many people at the motel 'cause it was mud season, so I didn't really see nobody."

Susan watched the jury's faces. Were they buying this crap?

Reid sipped from a glass of water and cleared her throat. "Now, Mr. Jansen," she said. "You heard your written confession read aloud in this courtroom."

Jansen shifted in his seat behind the podium. "Yeah, I heard it."

"Did you say those words?"

"Yeah. But they were all lies. Every one of 'em."

"So you didn't kill Amy Lentigo?"

Jansen shook his head vigorously. "No. Hell no. I never even met her."

If only, Susan thought bitterly.

"Could you tell us the circumstances behind your confession?"

Hodgman stood up. "Objection. That's overly general, Your Honor."

"Please break it down, Ms. Reid," said the judge, a jowly man in his fifties with some kind of southern accent Susan had never heard before except maybe on TV.

Reid said, "What were you doing when the FBI came and picked you up?"

"I was back in my motel room again. Got to admit I was doing some more drinking." Jansen gave the jury a crooked, self-deprecating smile, and Susan worried how it would affect those two young women. "I'd been working six days straight, putting up sheetrock, and I had one day off while the crew did some framing. So I was watching some old sit-com on TV when somebody knocks at the door."

Jansen raised his arm and pointed at Pappas, sitting in the third row of the gallery, where he'd been ever since he finished testifying. Pappas gazed back stonily. "It's this guy here. He says he's FBI and starts asking me all these crazy questions. I know enough not to say anything, so he tells his partner to take me to FBI headquarters. Just a couple miles from this courtroom here."

"What time was it when you got there?"

"Five or six."

"Did they ever tell you that you had the right to a lawyer?"

"If they did, I don't remember it. I'd been hitting the vodka pretty good all day."

Susan hoped his emphasis on drinking would work against him. Maybe the jury would decide he was so drunk he couldn't control his disgusting urges.

"So what happened after you got to FBI headquarters?"

"Nothing. They left me sitting in this tiny room. My head was hurting and they wouldn't give me anything to eat or drink. For a long time they wouldn't let me go to the bathroom either."

"When did Agent Pappas return?"

Susan glanced toward Pappas. He gave her a reassuring look, letting her know he was confident that nothing Jansen could say would hurt them.

Jansen said, "Around ten o'clock. He comes in and starts yapping at me. I tell him, 'Screw you, I didn't do anything.' He says, 'I know it's you. We found your fingerprints in the victim's blood.' Which I knew was bullshit, excuse my language, 'cause like I said, I never met her."

Hodgman stood up. "Objection. Not responsive to the question."

"Sustained."

Reid asked, "Mr. Jansen, what happened during the course of your conversation with Agent Pappas?"

Hodgman rose again. "That's awfully general again, Your Honor."

"Let's see how it goes," the judge said. He nodded to Jansen. "You may answer."

Jansen jumped right in, speaking quickly, like he'd been dying to explain himself for months. "This guy Pappas spends the whole night jumping down my throat, then he acts nice, then he comes at me again. I'm hungry and hung over and all I want to do is go to sleep. But every time I put my head down, he bangs the table." Jansen slammed his podium to demonstrate. "So now it's been like, ten hours, and it's never gonna stop. They'll never let me sleep! So finally I just say, 'Yeah, I did it.' 'Cause I know for sure it's all a mistake and they'll realize they got it wrong as soon as they check those damn fingerprints—see, I didn't know they didn't even have any fingerprints and that was all a lie." He pounded the podium again. "I just want to go to sleep. I never been so fuck—freaking tired in my life. So I go, 'Yeah, whatever. I'll sign whatever you want me to sign.'"

Susan looked at the jury. The two young women sat with their lips parted, entranced. The two middle-aged women she relied on for encouraging nods or smiles weren't looking at her. One of them was actually giving a little smile to Lisa, Jansen's sister. Susan had read quotes from Lisa in the paper, where she claimed her brother was innocent. Maybe the jurors had read the quotes too.

She wanted to throw up. *What if it all falls apart?*

And then she had to listen to her daughter's killer testify for another full hour. It was just lies upon lies.

Finally, Reid sat down. Hodgman stood up to begin his cross-examination.

"Please, God," Susan whispered quietly to the God she didn't believe in anymore, "don't let this rapist murderer win."

Hodgman straightened his sport jacket and stepped toward the witness stand. "Mr. Jansen," he began, "you say you never met Amy. Did you ever *see* her?"

"No, not 'til I was arrested and they showed me pictures of her."

"So you never saw her, even though the window of your motel room looked out onto the Lentigos' driveway?"

"Mainly I was just drinking and watching TV."

"Even though Amy was playing basketball out there? Dancing on the porch?"

"I didn't pay attention to any of that."

"Even with all the noise, the bouncing basketball, the country music . . ." Hodgman gave a little shimmy, as if he was dancing. ". . . Amy's girlfriends coming around and working on their routines?"

Reid stood up. "He's answered the question, Your Honor."

The judge said, "Please move on, Mr. Hodgman."

Hodgman, seeming undaunted, stepped even closer to Jansen. "Do you think little girls look cute when they're dancing?"

Jansen glared at Hodgman and shook his head. "Not sexy cute, if that's what you mean."

"Mr. Jansen, did you tell FBI Agent Robert Pappas, and I'm quoting from your signed confession, 'I saw her necklace on her tiny little neck and it gave me a hard-on.'"

Susan winced. But she liked how Hodgman was getting straight to the point with no screwing around. It seemed like good strategy.

Jansen winced too. *What an actor,* Susan thought angrily. Then he spoke. "Like I said, I was pissed off, hung over, and tired. I was trying to give Pappas whatever he wanted so he'd let me go to sleep."

"So the answer's yes?"

Jansen shifted in his seat. "I just wanted to go to sleep. When you're that tired and somebody's shouting at you for ten hours straight, it's like a million times crazier than being stoned."

"So that's a yes."

"Yeah, whatever," Jansen said, irritated. Then he took a deep breath, obviously trying to calm himself in front of the jury. "Look, I lied. It was a lie."

"You sure you're not lying now?"

"I'm not."

"Did you say, 'I took her necklace so I could jerk off later'?"

Jansen's face reddened. "You don't understand. This FBI agent was putting words in my mouth."

"Agent Pappas told you to say, 'I took her necklace so I could jerk off later'?"

"He wanted details," Jansen said. He turned to the jury, pleading for them to understand. "He wouldn't let me go to sleep until I said exactly what I did—or *supposedly* did. So I'd say, 'Yeah, I raped her, whatever,' and he'd say, 'You'll feel better if you tell us the whole truth.' So I go, 'I don't remember,' and he'd say, 'Don't lie to me.' So finally I made up all kinds of shit just to get him off my back. And yeah, it's disgusting, but I wanted to make it extra disgusting 'cause I was mad at him. I wanted to gross him out."

What bullshit! Susan thought. *The jury can see that, can't they?*

"So these details all came out of your own imagination."

"Yeah, that's right."

"You have a pretty interesting imagination, don't you?"

Jansen wiped sweat off his forehead. "Look, I'm not proud of anything I might've said that night."

Hodgman moved closer to Jansen. "Did you say, 'She screamed when I put my dick in'?"

Jansen looked at the jury and his voice turned desperate. "I would never do that to any woman and certainly not a girl."

Hodgman said sharply, "Did you say, 'She screamed when I—'"

Jansen snapped his head back at Hodgman and said loudly, "Yeah, I said it!"

"Did you say, 'It felt so good, squeezing that tiny neck 'til her pulse stopped'?"

Jansen stood up and shouted, furious, "*I just wanted to go to sleep!*"

Hodgman stayed quiet, letting the jurors observe Jansen. His face was bright red, a big vein pulsed on his forehead, and when he breathed, it made rasping sounds. He looked about to jump off the witness stand and attack somebody—Hodgman, the judge, the jury, whoever, it didn't matter. Three marshals stepped closer so they'd be ready to stop him.

Hodgman said softly, "You have a little trouble controlling your temper, don't you, Mr. Jansen?"

Jansen didn't answer. Everybody in the courtroom listened to his breathing. Finally, he sat back down. But the damage was done. The jury had seen the rage inside him.

Whatever chance he had of winning the case, he had just lost it.

Danny leaned over to Susan and whispered, "He's dead meat." The two middle-aged women in the jury nodded to Susan. The two young women smiled at her.

The next day, it only took the jury forty-eight minutes to find the Monster guilty on all counts.

The day after that, Susan demanded the death penalty, and the judge obliged.

CHAPTER TWENTY-TWO

Behind her, Danny said, "Is there anything else?"

It was lucky Susan's back was to him, so he couldn't see the utter shock on her face as she stared at the necklace Emily was wearing in her picture.

I'm not imagining this, am I?

She started to lean in toward Emily's picture so she could examine it more closely. *The purple dolphin, the pink duck . . .* But then she stopped. She tilted her face away from the photo, so Danny wouldn't realize what she was staring at.

What in God's name was she thinking? *That isn't Amy's necklace. It can't be!*

Or if it is, there must be some—

From behind his desk, Danny said, "Susan?" in a puzzled, irritated voice.

She turned back around and looked at him. Her mouth was so dry she could barely make words come out.

"Goodbye," she said. Then she walked out the door.

As she made her way toward the front of the real estate office, she looked back through the glass window at him.

He was sitting there shaking his head at her flightiness, watching her go.

She struggled to stay upright and act normal as she walked past the two realtors. It was obvious they were both curious as hell.

"Have a nice day," the redhead said. "I hope you got what you needed."

Susan managed a nod and picked up her suitcase. She opened the front door, stepped out onto Main Street, and reeled half-blind past the picture of Danny on the window.

Two men in suits came toward her from the other direction and she almost crashed into them. She took the first side street and staggered toward a wooden bench half a block away.

As she sat down, her fingers fumbled in her purse for her wallet. She took out a small photo of Amy—the same faded photo that had been blown up and displayed at the Crow Bar. It showed cute, gap-toothed Amy wearing the necklace.

There was no question. It looked the exact same.

"No," Susan said to herself, breathing heavily. "No. Jesus, Susan, come on."

But she couldn't stop her brain from racing. Maybe it didn't just *look* the same—*maybe it was the exact same*!

But how could that be? *How could Danny have gotten hold of it?* There was only one way she could think of. But that was insane. There was no way Danny could've—he was a good man! A good father!

But then the thought came to her, irresistibly: *It's true, he never did have a good alibi—*

She shook her head violently, trying to clear it. *What am I thinking? What the fuck am I thinking?! I'm not thinking that, it's stupid!* "It's insane," Susan said to herself out loud. "He loved Amy!"

But that necklace—That necklace—It makes no sense—

She heard a tapping sound on the sidewalk and quickly looked up. She felt so guilty about her thoughts, she was afraid Danny might be coming after her.

But it was a blind woman, using her cane to walk down the sidewalk past her.

Susan watched the woman walk by a Tamarack Library sign and realized she was sitting in front of the library. Slowly an idea formed in her mind. *This is a small town. The elementary school can't be too far.* She checked her watch: 11:55. She got to her feet and hurried up the library's front steps, lifting her suitcase.

This place was a lot bigger than the Lake Luzerne Library. The man at the front counter was helping a mother with a toddler check out books, so Susan went up to the reference librarian, a woman in her late twenties who was busy texting. "Excuse me," Susan said. Her voice sounded strange to her, high and nervous.

The reference librarian looked up, annoyed at the interruption.

Susan cleared her throat. "How many elementary schools are there in this town?" she asked, sounding a little more normal to her ears.

"Just one."

"Where is it?"

"It's by the high school," the librarian said, with an air of finality. Then she went back to her texting.

Susan had an urge to slap this woman's face. Instead she put a hand on top of the woman's phone. She pulled her arm away, startled.

Susan smiled sweetly, but she was sure the woman could see her anger underneath. "Can you tell me where that is?"

A minute later, Susan was rolling her suitcase several blocks toward Beekman Street, where the elementary and high schools were located across from each other. She heard a bell ring and picked up her pace, not sure which school the sound was coming from.

She told herself that when she saw the necklace up close, she'd realize it was different. Or she'd get a chance to talk to Emily, and there'd be an innocent explanation. Some reason she could instantly forget her idiotic suspicions. She'd be able to laugh at them.

She made it to the elementary school just as a security guard with a gun on his hip stepped out the front door. He was followed by three other grown-ups who looked like teachers or administrators, and then an avalanche of loud, excited kids.

It was recess.

She watched the kids pour out of the school. They immediately started running all over the place, shouting gleefully and playing tag, soccer, and four square.

Then, in the side yard, Susan saw a bunch of kids at the handball court. One of them was Emily. She stood against the wall, waiting for her turn to play.

From this distance, Susan couldn't tell if Emily was wearing the necklace. That reminded her of the question that had dogged her all these years: How could Curt Jansen have seen Amy's necklace from all the way across 9N?

Suddenly she wondered why this question had so obsessed her. Had she always had some secret doubt about whether Jansen was really Amy's killer?

No. No way. She had always *hated* the Monster. At night she dreamed of him dying in horrible ways.

So why was she feeling doubts now? *Am I really, seriously doubting if the Monster is guilty?*

I can't be.

She moved closer to the handball court. Emily turned toward her, watching a classmate run after the ball.

The necklace was right there on Emily's neck.

She needed to talk to this girl. But the security guard was standing in the yard, arms folded, watching.

Susan stood her suitcase behind the trunk of an old oak. Then she reached up and smoothed her hair and straightened her back. Assuming a brisk walk, like she was a busy teacher or social worker, she headed across the street and onto the sidewalk. Then she stepped onto the playground.

The security guard noticed her immediately. She knew the last thing she should do was make eye contact. Trying to shut down her nerves, she began checking her purse like she was looking for something important.

When she peeked over the purse a few moments later, she saw the guard had looked away. She breathed a sigh of relief and kept going toward the side yard and the handball court.

The ball the kids were using was as big as a dodge ball. Susan didn't remember Amy ever playing this game. Emily still stood by the wall, waiting her turn. Susan walked up to her.

"Hi there," Susan said. *Oh my God. Purple dolphin, pink duck, yellow, green, an orange cat . . . Amy and I sat at the kitchen table and strung beads just like these.* "What a beautiful necklace."

Emily looked up at her shyly. Susan thought she saw Amy in the almond-like shape of Emily's eyes, the tilt of her eyebrows.

"I might buy a necklace like that for my daughter. Where did you get it?"

Maybe Danny made it for her. He got these beads off the internet. That's what Emily will say—

"My daddy found it," Emily said. Then she looked back at the handball game, watching the ball bounce back and forth.

Susan's mouth opened wide with shock. She was too overwhelmed to speak.

Finally she got out, "You mean he made it?"

"No, he found it," Emily said without a trace of doubt.

"Where?"

The game ended and Emily jumped up. It was her turn to play. "I don't know," she said to Susan, and ran onto the court.

Susan watched her go, her heart filling with horror.

"He found it."

CHAPTER TWENTY-THREE

SUSAN HAD A burst of energy after the Monster was sentenced to death. She went home and cleaned the house that very night, though she left Amy's room alone. Then she cleaned the house a second time.

I'm going to start over. Danny's right. Amy would want me to be happy.

She cooked gourmet dinners every night for a week. She worked every lunch shift at Molly's. She ran five miles on the River Road every day, until she was gasping for breath.

I can do this. I can find a way to live with the pain.

But then she crashed, all at once. She was in the middle of making a new blueberry tart recipe Molly had given her, and before she knew it she found herself sitting on the kitchen floor. She couldn't move. She couldn't think. She'd see Amy in her mind and everything would shut down.

She had no idea how long she'd been there on the floor when Danny came home. She felt him carry her into bed. Then she sensed he was lying down next to her. She heard his voice but couldn't focus on the words. She couldn't open her eyes to look at him, and she couldn't speak.

She stayed in bed for what she later learned was three days, only getting up to go to the bathroom. She vaguely sensed that sometimes Danny was with her and sometimes Lenora.

Danny wasn't a big believer in therapy, but he drove Susan to the Glens Falls Public Health Clinic, which had therapist interns who saw patients on a sliding scale. Susan would remember nothing about the woman who saw her, but according to Danny, she was young and just barely out of social work school. When she came out to talk to him after the intake session, she looked pale and shaken. She strongly recommended that Susan be committed to the mental health wing of the Albany Public Hospital. *Immediately.*

So that's where Susan went, for the next three weeks, even though insurance only covered eighty percent. Gradually her psychotic break dissipated and she began to come back into the world. She could tell her nurses apart now, even knew some of their names, and she asked for extra salt for her French fries. When Danny came to visit, she noticed his aftershave.

The aftershave she and Amy had given him for his birthday.

She didn't think much of this hospital ward she found herself in. She knew the psychiatrists and nurses meant well, but she was grieving. Including her miscarriages, she had now lost three children. How could talking help her? They diagnosed her with acute depression and prescribed Prozac, but she thought that was just stupid.

There's nothing wrong with me except my babies keep dying. A thousand Prozac pills won't cure that. If I want to try and forget my pain, I'll just drink Jack Daniels.

Eventually, she left the hospital and lay around at home or in Molly's back room. She told Danny she was taking her pills even though she wasn't. She spent a lot of time looking out windows at the rain and snow. She lay in bed with Danny at night when he was sleeping and cried quietly, trying not to wake him.

Danny started going to work seven days a week, then coming home and making dinner and watching endless basketball games on TV while Susan lay around in the bedroom. When they did talk with each other, he began to get more impatient. He would flare up and yell at her.

It came to a head one Saturday night when he came home from work and discovered she hadn't gotten out of bed the whole day.

"What the fuck is the matter with you? Stop this!" he shouted.

"Don't yell at me."

"You need to get your shit together!" He leaned over the bed and grabbed her shoulders and started shaking her. *Hard*. It hurt her neck. She screamed with pain and shock. But that just made him shake her even harder. "Get your fucking shit together!" he yelled.

Now she was really scared he'd do some damage to her neck. "Stop it!" she shouted. "Get off me!"

He let go of her, mortified, and his eyes got teary. She was freaked out, seeing a side of him she'd never seen before. He had a temper, sure, especially when his job wasn't going well and he was stressed, but in all the years they'd been together, he had never hit her or physically hurt her.

Danny apologized for the next hour. For the next couple weeks, he tried hard to be patient again. For years he'd gone deer hunting every November, usually not bagging a deer but still finding it restful to spend a week by himself in the woods. This year, though, he canceled his trip and stayed by Susan's side, extra attentive.

But they were both wary with each other.

Then one night in January, four months after the trial, they were sitting at the kitchen table together eating another silent dinner. He put down his chicken drumstick and told Susan, "We need to talk."

She nodded listlessly, feeling hopeless, moving around the instant mashed potatoes with her fork.

"I can't keep living in this house, with Amy's room still the way it was."

She shrugged. "Go ahead, get rid of her stuff. I can't do it."

"I can't keep living in this town."

Susan looked up from her plate. She started to realize there was something different about this conversation.

"Everything here reminds me of Amy," he said. "The school, when I pass it every day. The miniature golf course. Her friends, when I see them on the street."

She blinked. "You want to move? What about your job?"

"I'll find a job somewhere else."

"What about my mom? Our friends?"

"I need to leave. Maybe it's just for a while. But I need to get out of here."

Finally, Susan got it. "It's me you need to leave."

"That's not true."

"I remind you of Amy."

"I just need a break."

They made love that night, their first time since back in September when the Monster had just been sentenced to death. Susan clung to him fiercely, grasping the last remainder of their life together, of the life she used to share with Danny and Amy.

For the next two weeks she made an effort. She went back to work at Molly's and managed to make it through her shifts without breaking into tears or dropping any dishes. She went to church both Sundays and rejoined the choir.

But it was too late.

Danny was gone by the end of January.

CHAPTER TWENTY-FOUR

SUSAN GOT OFF the playground before the security guard could get interested in her again. But she wasn't sure where to go next or what to do. She felt lost and bewildered, her soul reeling.

The Monster killed Amy. He confessed. The jury found him guilty. That question had been answered twenty years ago.

But . . .

"He found it."

Five minutes later, she found herself back in the library at one of the public computers, googling "Amy Lentigo."

The top website was from two days ago, an AP story headlined, "Condemned Man Still Claims Innocence." It had a photo of Jansen, the way he looked now. His hair was going gray, as she'd imagined. His face seemed a little grayish too, maybe from lack of sun for the past twenty years. But the thing that hit her was his eyes. They looked sad, like she remembered them from the very first time she saw Jansen in person. They had lines on each side of them now. It made him look sort of . . . thoughtful.

She read what he'd said to the reporter. "False confession . . . ten hours . . . drunk and exhausted, just wanted to sleep . . . they didn't have any real evidence . . ."

It was nothing she hadn't heard before, both during the trial and whenever he filed an appeal. During the first few years, Agent Pappas called her several times to assure her the appeals would never go anywhere. The judge had conducted the trial with scrupulous fairness, and there was plenty of evidence: Amy's bite marks on Jansen's hand, the complete absence of any alibi, and above all, his confession.

Susan grabbed at her head. Again she told herself there was a simple explanation for Emily's necklace that she just wasn't seeing. *Danny could never have done that to Amy. It's impossible. I'm an idiot.*

Maybe Danny contacted Jansen in prison and got him to reveal where the necklace was. And he never told Susan because he didn't want to bring up bad memories.

That must be the answer. Susan felt comforted for a few moments.

But then she thought, *That makes no sense.* Danny wanted to forget about Amy. There was no way he would've contacted Jansen. And if Jansen contacted him, he would have told Jansen to go to Susan instead.

At least I think that's what he would have done.

She hit the back arrow on the computer screen and clicked on a *Post-Star* article from twenty years ago. There was a picture of her and Danny standing in front of the courthouse addressing the media. Agent Pappas was off to the side.

She thought back to that time. She remembered how Pappas briefly suspected Danny before focusing on Frank and then Jansen. Danny's alibi was almost as weak as Jansen's, but he never had any marks on his hands or arms, what Pappas called "defensive wounds"—

She gave a start. *That's not really true.* When Danny went down to the stream below the tannery searching for Amy, he slipped and fell and cut himself.

At least that's what he said. And she always believed that's where those cuts on his arms and wrists came from.

But what if . . . *What if . . .*

She was too upset to even finish the sentence. She looked down at the computer screen, but her eyes stopped focusing. She was picturing the night after Curt Jansen was arrested, when she had gotten into bed with Danny and said, "Thank God they caught him."

He'd laughed.

And now that twenty-year-old laugh came back to her, ringing in her head. *Maybe he was laughing at the FBI.*

At his own private joke.

Sitting at the computer, Susan chewed on her thumbnail and wondered: *What other things did I forget?*

Or make myself forget?

She started to have trouble breathing, and she felt like the library, big though it was, was closing in on her. She got up from the computer and practically ran out of there.

She'd had a mental breakdown twenty years ago. Was she having another one? Was that what this was all about?

Once outside, she could breathe again. But there was nowhere to run, no one to talk to. On an impulse, which she knew immediately she might regret, she took out her flip phone and made a call.

Two rings later, she heard her mom's voice coming over the phone. "Susan! Everything okay?"

Susan could picture her mom standing at the kitchen counter, talking into their ancient telephone/fax machine that Danny had bought for them in the mid-'90s. The fax machine had broken years ago, but the phone still worked.

"I'm fine, Mom," she said.

Her mom said, "Oh good. I just found the cutest towel rack at the thrift store. You're gonna love it."

"Mom—"

"You hang the towel on a duck's tail—"

"I'm in Tamarack. I went to see Danny."

There was a pause, then Lenora said cautiously, "Well, isn't that nice. How is he?"

Susan felt a need to keep moving. She walked away from the library, and away from Main Street. "I met his daughter, Emily. How well do you remember Amy's necklace?"

"Pretty damn well, there's a picture of it right here on the fridge. Why?"

Susan took a deep breath. "Emily is wearing a beaded necklace with a purple dolphin, a pink duck, and all the same exact beads Amy had."

"Huh. So he made another necklace just like Amy's. That's sweet."

Susan had already considered that possibility and rejected it. "There's no way he did that," she said emphatically. "Danny never made anything in his life. He's the least crafty person I ever met."

"So he had somebody else make it. Why are you so riled up?"

"Because what if it's not a copy?" Susan stopped in the middle of the sidewalk. "Danny's daughter told me her dad *found* the necklace."

"He did what?"

"He *found* it."

"You must've heard her wrong."

"No. I didn't."

"How could Danny have found where Curt Jansen hid it? You're not making sense."

"What if . . ." She stopped. She still couldn't say the rest of it out loud, couldn't even finish it in her head.

"What if what?"

She steeled herself. "*What if Danny hid the necklace himself?*"

Her mom was silent for a few moments, probably trying to figure out if she understood Susan right. Susan was about to say something more, but then Lenora's voice, utterly appalled, came over the line. "What the hell are you saying?!"

The words poured out. "Mom, he never had an alibi—"

"Danny is not some psycho child killer! For chrissake, Susan!"

Susan gripped her phone so hard she was afraid she'd break it. "I know it sounds crazy, but there's so many things I'm remembering now! Like…"

A long-submerged image flashed into her mind:

Danny, in their bedroom, giving her a surprise present, a big gift-wrapped box with a pink ribbon. Susan, excited, unties the ribbon and opens the box, expecting maybe a nice dress, like the one she pointed out to him the last time they were in Saratoga.

"There were things Danny wanted me to do …" Susan hesitated, embarrassed. "In bed, that I never told you about."

She could see it so vividly now: *Inside the box she finds a Catholic schoolgirl uniform, with white blouse and pink plaid skirt.*

She looks up at Danny, bewildered. He wants her to wear this—when? When they're … ?

He gazes steadily back at her—

For one brief moment, Susan wonders who is this man that she married.

Then Danny gives her a smile, and her feeling passes.

But now, twenty years later, she was questioning her marriage all over again. She said to her mom, "I didn't think it meant anything. And then Curt Jansen confessed—"

"Yeah, *exactly*. He confessed."

"But then he recanted."

"That was bullshit, you know that."

"I don't want to believe it either, Mom, but maybe this is why I couldn't move on all these years! I could feel something was wrong!"

She was yelling into the phone, and a couple teenage boys walking past on the sidewalk gave her a wide berth. She needed to be more quiet. What if Danny came by?

Her mom said, "You need to come home. This whole execution is too much for you."

Susan shook her head, upset. "I don't know who to talk to about this—"

"Nobody. Get in your car."

If only.

"Get out of that town and quit imagining things. I never should've let you go off to North Dakota—"

"Okay, Mom," Susan said with a sigh. God, her mom was so useless sometimes.

"What do you mean, okay?"

"I don't know, just take care of yourself. Don't forget your pills."

She shut her phone and just stood there. A middle-aged couple walked past holding hands, talking about where they'd go for dinner tonight. What she would give to be the woman in that couple!

Her phone rang again. Her mom calling back, no doubt. She put the phone in her purse and let it ring.

I don't think I'm having a breakdown. This felt totally different from how she felt twenty years ago. *I really think it's the same necklace.*

She suddenly realized she was starving. All she'd eaten today were a couple handfuls of peanuts, chocolate chips, and cranberries. She got the baggie out of her purse and had three more handfuls.

She needed to *do* something. She needed a plan.

First of all, she needed to talk to somebody besides her mother. But everyone she knew back in Lake Luzerne would agree with her mom that she was crazy. Even Terri would think that. Back when Terri used to babysit for them, she had a little crush on Danny.

Officer Lynch might have listened to her—maybe. But he'd been a victim of the meth violence that swept through the lower Adirondacks ten years ago.

What about the police here in Tamarack? But Danny was a respected local real estate agent, giving five-thousand-dollar checks to the Police Athletic League. She was just a middle-aged woman in an old, worn coat passing through town with a battered suitcase and a wild story. If she wanted the cops to listen to her, she needed more than just a story—

Wait a minute. All at once, Susan realized what she had to do.

It meant returning to Emily's school, so she grabbed her suitcase and hurried the fifteen blocks back there. Her right knee throbbed.

But when she got to the school, she was too late to do what she'd planned. The school had already let out, and Emily and the other kids had gone home.

Standing on the sidewalk, Susan resolved to come back here first thing tomorrow.

Maybe she *was* crazy. She sort of hoped she was. But she needed to know the truth.

Tomorrow morning, she'd come to the school and get evidence the cops would *have* to listen to.

They would have no choice.

CHAPTER TWENTY-FIVE

Monday, November 29, Present Day

But before tomorrow morning came, Susan needed to make it through tonight. It was growing colder by the minute and her hunger wasn't getting any less.

She went back to the library to warm up and counted all the loose change in her purse: three dollars and eighty-two cents. *How will I ever last 'til Saturday?*

No, don't think about that now, just keep going.

She had never asked for a free meal in her life and she hated doing it now. But she walked up to the reference librarian, who was on her cell phone once again. Susan cleared her throat, and the woman looked up, annoyed.

"May I help you?"

"Yes, please. Are there any churches in town where someone without money can get dinner?"

The librarian pinched her lips and said through a frown, "I don't really know. No one's ever asked me that question."

Susan wanted to throttle this woman. "Do you think I *wanted* to ask it?"

"I'm just saying—"

"Why don't you find out the answer so you can help the next person who asks, you bitch."

The woman's jaw dropped. Susan wondered if she had overreacted, then decided she didn't care. She went back to the computer and searched for free dinners in Tamarack. She didn't find any, but there was an Alcoholics Anonymous meeting at five thirty at a nearby church. Maybe they'd have coffee and cookies or something.

At the meeting, she struck gold. Not only did they have coffee and cookies, there was spaghetti with butter and salad. She sat down and had two helpings as she listened to everybody share their problems. She wanted to tell them hers but felt like she probably shouldn't speak.

She'd do her speaking as soon as she got the evidence she needed.

When the meeting ended, she headed outside and wandered. Around seven o'clock she came to an all-night coffee shop. They sold coffee in pretty big mugs for a buck twenty-five, so she ordered some. She sat there nursing her drink, getting refills, and thinking about her life. She couldn't wait for morning to come so she could quit obsessing and get moving.

At nine o'clock the counterman, a hard-faced guy in his forties with a shaved head and thick scruffy beard who looked like a biker, came over. "Anything else I can get you?"

"Just another refill, please."

But the counterman didn't take her cup this time. "I can't let you stay here all night drinking one cup of coffee."

Susan didn't feel like getting up out of this warm place just yet. There was a small bag of chips above the counter that couldn't be too expensive. "How much are those chips?"

"They cost a buck."

"I'll have a bag."

She rooted around in her purse for another dollar in coins. The counterman watched her, then looked down at her worn suitcase. "Where you headed anyway?"

"North Dakota." She handed him a bunch of nickels and pennies. "This is a dollar even."

Susan could see he wanted to count her money, but he decided to be polite instead and just put it away in the drawer. "You visiting family?" he said.

"Long story."

"We got time, seeing as it looks like you'll be here awhile."

She gave him a smile, her thanks that he wasn't kicking her out. Somehow she seemed to have turned a corner with this guy. Maybe watching her fish for pennies had awoken a little compassion in him.

Then she scratched her head, thinking about how to answer him. What *was* her "long story"? She wasn't sure anymore.

"I'm going to see the execution of the man who . . ." She paused.

"The man who what?"

"Might've raped and murdered my daughter."

The counterman blinked. "*Might've?*"

She saw a skinny Tamarack phone book on the shelf behind him. It gave her an idea of something better to do than just sit around all night.

"Can I borrow your phone book?"

His eyes widened, taken aback by her abrupt change of subject, but he said, "Sure," and handed it to her.

She opened it up and found a listing for "Daniel Lentigo." He lived on 89 Ash Street. She'd walked by Ash earlier; it was only five or six blocks away.

"Who are you looking for?" the counterman asked.

She thought about not answering him. But she figured the chances of him having a conversation with Danny before tomorrow morning were tiny. So she said, "Another guy who might've raped and murdered my daughter."

The counterman stared at her, clearly trying to figure how nuts she was, as she grabbed her suitcase and headed out the door. Then he called out, "You forgot your chips."

"Keep 'em."

Ash Street turned out to be pretty long, and 89 Ash was almost a mile away. So it took twenty minutes or so before Susan got there, rolling her suitcase.

Danny's front yard was dark, and she hid behind some bushes at the foot of the driveway. She wasn't totally sure why she'd come here but felt it was important somehow.

Danny's new home in Tamarack was nicer than the house in Luzerne, and she couldn't help feeling a pang of envy. Like most of the other houses on this street, it was a '50s-style ranch, not that big but with a good-sized yard. There was a tetherball pole out front and a basketball hoop in the driveway low enough for a ten-year-old boy and a six-year-old girl.

Susan looked up at the hoop, remembering again that spring afternoon when Amy, in her pink dress, played basketball with Danny. It was a tiny moment in time that had somehow lodged in her memory all these years like a fish bone.

Susan on the front steps, content, watching her husband and daughter play together.

"Daddy, I wanna dunk! Lift me up!"

Danny lifts her high in the air above him, and Amy dunks the ball. She shouts, "Monster jam!" Giggling.

Danny says, "Hurray for Amy!" Lifting her up even higher.

Amy calls out, "Daddy, let me down!"

Susan watches from the steps as Danny lets her down—

No, wait a minute.

There was something else stuck deep inside this memory, tucked way down, that she'd never quite been able to grab hold of. Maybe she hadn't allowed herself to.

But now she did.

Danny doesn't let Amy down. Not right away.

The memory poured into her.

Susan on the steps, watching.

Danny says, "How high can you go?" Lifting Amy still higher.

Amy yells, "Let me down!"

Danny looks up at Amy . . . looks . . .

Susan stands there, mouth open, thinking: Is he looking up her dress?!

Now, standing outside Danny's house, Susan gasped for breath. She felt like she was choking. How could she ever have forgotten that?

She must have made herself forget. She pulled at her hair, remembering.

Amy yells, "Daddy, stop!" Danny finally lets her back down to the ground.

Susan blinks, upset.

Danny sees her standing there. "Hi honey," he says.

She's so confused. She decides she must have imagined the whole thing. She calls them in to dinner. They have a nice meal—

But now Susan replayed that moment when she saw Danny's face gazing intently up at Amy as he held her above him. *Oh my God,* she thought, *what if I didn't imagine it?*

She looked toward Danny's house. The lights were on in the living room and a couple of back rooms that were probably bedrooms. All at once, the living room had a burst of movement. Emily raced in, wearing pink pajamas, with Danny right behind, chasing her around the sofa. Her long brown hair flew behind her and it looked like she was laughing.

No question, Danny could be Fun Dad sometimes.

Susan wanted to see more, so she snuck up the dark driveway, rolling her suitcase on the grass alongside so it wouldn't make noise.

Inside the house, Danny held Emily by her legs and whirled her around in circles. From this distance, Susan could see she was wearing the necklace.

Danny put her down on the rug and tickled her feet. Susan could tell the girl was giggling. She was saying something Susan couldn't hear. He kept tickling her.

And then Emily's face changed.

It looked like she was still sort of laughing, but now she was upset—*panicky, even*—trying to pull her feet away from her father.

But Danny kept on tickling. Emily yelled, loud enough that Susan could hear, "Stop! Daddy, stop!"

Suddenly Susan remembered Danny and Amy wrestling on the living room floor. Sometimes she thought he played a little too rough.

Had he been even rougher than she realized?

Emily yelled "Stop!" even louder and Susan watched, more and more horrified. Then she couldn't see Emily anymore, because the sofa blocked her view. *What is Danny doing to her?* She moved forward for a better look.

But as she did, she bumped into the handle of her suitcase. It fell over and landed on the driveway with a thump. The noise brought a large gray dog, a German shepherd mix, running into the living room. He stood at the window and barked loudly. Danny let go of Emily and stepped to the window too.

Susan grabbed her suitcase and got the hell out of there as fast as she could.

She headed back to Main Street. The wind picked up and she shivered.

Maybe it's true. Maybe he really . . .
And if he hurt Amy . . .
Then he'll hurt Emily.
Unless I stop him.

CHAPTER TWENTY-SIX

At seven o'clock the next morning, Susan paced the sidewalk outside the Village Apothecary on Main waiting for it to open. She'd had a long night, split between a motel lobby before they kicked her out and then the all-night diner again. She got maybe two hours of sleep, all while sitting up. Now she was beyond eager to get started on her plan.

The first thing she needed to do was get hold of a disposable camera at the drugstore. She was hoping to trade her engagement ring for one—it had to be worth at least forty or fifty dollars, and the fact it came from Danny was making her sick now anyway. If she couldn't unload the ring, maybe she could trade her watch. She'd splurged and spent seventy dollars on it a couple years ago.

The lights came on inside the store and a woman walked in from the back room. She was in her forties with stylish auburn hair and a purposeful stride. Susan thought she was probably the store owner, which meant she'd be able to do a trade if she wanted. *Good.*

Susan smoothed her hair. She'd washed it in the bathroom sink at the diner, using liquid soap. The night counterman had still been on duty, and he gave her a fresh towel to dry herself off. She'd put on a little lipstick too.

The woman unlocked the front door and held it open. "Good morning," she said with a businesslike smile. "Awfully cold out there."

"Yes, it is." Susan walked in with her suitcase. She didn't have time to waste. "I'm looking for an inexpensive camera."

The woman gave an apologetic frown. "I'm afraid we don't sell cameras anymore."

Susan stopped and looked at her in surprise. Stone's Pharmacy back in Luzerne still carried cheap cameras; her mom had wanted one for the Crow Bar party. "Not even one of those disposable cameras?"

"I'm sorry, ma'am. With cell phones, who needs them?"

What about people with flip phones? she wanted to say. Her face fell.

"Is there anything else I can help you with?"

"No thanks," Susan said, and left the store, her heart beating frantically. *Shit, Emily will be getting to school in less than an hour.* Susan wasn't sure of the exact time. *What the hell do I do now? I need a camera!*

Then she remembered the elementary school was right across the street from the high school. And the high school would be full of kids with cell phones. *Cell phones with cameras.*

She walked the ten blocks there as fast as she could while dragging her suitcase. She asked the crossing guard, an elderly man with cheeks reddened by the cold, "What time does school start this morning?"

"High school is seven forty, elementary school is eight o'clock."

It was seven twenty now. She hurried to the high school, a sprawling brick building. She hid her suitcase behind a tree so she wouldn't be conspicuous and waited for the kids to come. "I can do this," she whispered out loud, trying to convince herself.

Soon throngs of teenagers started arriving by car, bus, and on foot. She figured her best shot was to catch a kid walking by himself, but most of them were in groups of two, three, or four. Or they were getting dropped off right in front of the school, where a security guard stood. Susan didn't want to risk getting kicked off school property.

Finally, a good prospect came along: a nerdy-looking boy with a shiny, light green parka. She stepped up to him and said, "Excuse me."

He looked at her, a little startled at being accosted.

She continued, "How would you like to earn a quick twenty dollars?" She would have said fifty, but she figured with a small number the kid wouldn't get too pissed off when she eventually had to admit she'd been lying about giving him money.

But the kid just looked at her and started walking faster. Did he think she was a loony? *Geez.*

The next kid she went up to, a tall, pretty Asian girl, gave her the brush-off too, and so did a third kid, an overweight boy carrying a guitar case. It was already seven thirty-five.

She looked up the sidewalk and saw a girl who looked about sixteen, with a half-shaved head and multiple tattoos. She walked heavily in big wafflestomper boots and had a don't-fuck-with-me attitude, softened only slightly by her dreamcatcher necklace. She was busy on her phone, which made rapid high-pitched noises; probably she was playing some kind of game. Susan decided it would be a waste of time to even bother with her.

She looked across the street for more prospects and saw three teenage boys loping toward her—no, they were heading for the girl. They got in her way, forcing her to stop. They were all big guys with short hair—football players, Susan figured. The guy in the middle with a jutting chin and a swagger acted like their leader, like he was the star quarterback.

He said to the girl, in an aggressive, bullying voice, "Hey, Kyra, whatcha doing tonight?"

Susan watched as the girl—Kyra—looked up at his jeering face.

"I'd love to suck your dick," she said. "It's so teeny weeny, it makes me laugh."

Then she shoved right past him.

His two friends immediately began howling and making fun of him, jabbing him in the shoulder. "Oh, you got hosed!" one of them said.

Kyra ignored them and kept walking, going back to her game. On an impulse, Susan stepped in her way. "Excuse me."

Kyra looked up and frowned at her, clearly wondering what the hell this lady wanted.

Susan said, "How would you like to earn a quick twenty dollars?"

Kyra lifted her eyebrows. "Doing what?"

"All you have to do is take a picture."

The girl's eyes flickered curiously, and Susan knew she had her.

A couple minutes later, they were on the other side of the street behind an SUV, watching cars and buses pull up to the elementary school. Susan's suitcase was next to a nearby fire hydrant, because she didn't like having it out of sight for too long.

Susan had told Kyra their mission in only the broadest outline, and now Kyra wanted details. "How come you want pictures of this necklace?"

Susan didn't want to say anything that might give this girl a reason to reconsider, so she said, "I'll explain later." Kids were pouring out of the cars and buses, and Susan's eyes darted around, searching for Emily. "I don't know if she's taking a bus or getting a ride."

Kyra said, "You sure you're not some crazy fucking stalker?"

"Do I look like a crazy stalker?"

Kyra looked down at Susan's old suitcase. "Kind of."

The last few kids came out of the bus on the far left. One of them had long brown hair—*Emily.*

"There she is," Susan said. "She's got the necklace. Let's go!"

She hurried toward Emily. But then she turned and saw Kyra wasn't following her. The armed security guard who'd been here yesterday was standing on the school's front steps surveying everybody, and Kyra was eyeing him warily.

"Come on, hurry!" Susan called.

"Fuck that," Kyra said. "I can't get busted again."

Susan walked quickly back to her. "Please," she said. But the girl folded her arms stubbornly.

So she played the one card she had. "*This girl may be in danger.*"

"Of what?" Kyra said dubiously.

"Getting raped and killed."

Kyra stared at Susan, then held out her phone. "Fine, you do it."

"I don't know how! I have a flip phone!"

Emily was lining up with the other kids at the front door, about to go inside. Ten more seconds and it would be too late. Susan grabbed Kyra by the elbow. "Come on. *Help me!*"

The line of kids was entering the school now. Finally, Kyra let Susan pull her toward there. "*Hurry!*" Susan said.

Kyra sped up, and they ran toward Emily just as she was about to go through the door. Her foot was already on the top step.

"Emily!" Susan called.

The girl turned. Her coat was open so the necklace hung down onto her sweater, totally visible. *Perfect. Now don't button up your coat.*

"You forgot your lunch," Susan said. She held out a small brown bag she'd found in a garbage can outside the high school. She'd half-filled the bag with leaves and stones so it would look like it had a lunch inside. If the guard opened that bag, she would be in trouble.

Standing next to her, Kyra held up her phone and took pictures of Emily's necklace. Susan prayed Kyra was doing a good job.

Emily looked back and forth between the two of them. "I have my lunch. Who are you?"

The guard came over from the other side of the steps. Susan could feel Kyra stiffening beside her. She gave an apologetic smile. "Oh, sorry. Wrong girl."

The guard put his hand protectively on Emily's shoulder and opened his mouth to say something. Susan preempted him. "Have a great day!" she said, and she and Kyra walked away.

Luckily the guard didn't call after them.

Once Susan and Kyra made it across the street and felt safe again, Susan said, "Let me see the pictures."

Kyra brought them up on her phone. "I totally don't get this. What does this necklace have to do with getting raped and murdered?"

Susan looked over Kyra's shoulder at her pictures. In one of them, you could see *every single bead* on the front of Emily's necklace.

"Great, this one's *perfect*. Now I need you to email me this. My address is susanlentigo@aol—"

"Uh . . . the twenty dollars?"

"In a minute. Just—"

"Do you *have* twenty dollars?"

Oh shit. "Can I give you my watch instead?"

Kyra's lips curled with irritation. "I don't wear a watch."

"How about this ring? These are real diamonds—"

"Lady, just tell me what the fuck you're up to. I'm already late for homeroom."

It was so exasperating, having this teenage girl hold the picture hostage. Susan wished she had gotten her own damn smartphone years ago, no matter how much they cost. She told Kyra the whole story as quickly and convincingly as she could, trying to get the girl on her side. She showed Kyra the picture of Amy wearing what sure as hell looked like the exact same necklace.

Kyra looked down at the picture, then back up at Susan with wide eyes. "You really *are* nuts."

Susan's heart sank. "That's why I didn't tell you. I was afraid you'd think that and you wouldn't help me."

A bell rang in the high school. They were standing on the sidewalk, which was almost empty now. Kyra rubbed her half-shaved head and said, "I don't get it. If he's the killer, why would he give his new daughter the same necklace? That would be so fucking dangerous."

During the long night, Susan had been puzzling about that herself. "Maybe he gets off on danger. He always loved rock climbing and snowmobiling really fast." She felt Kyra's skeptical eyes on her and threw up her hands, frustrated. "Hey, I don't know how psychopaths think!"

Kyra eyed her. "You were married to him. If he was like that, wouldn't you have known?"

Susan hesitated. A school bus pulled away from the elementary school and came her way. She felt a sudden desperate wish that the bus would veer onto the sidewalk and run her over. She had an image of herself crushed beneath the heavy wheels.

Then the bus rolled by. She turned back to Kyra. "You're right. I should have known."

She gave her whole body a shake, trying to get rid of her dark thoughts. "But it's too late now. I need to let the cops figure it out. I don't suppose you're friendly with any cops around here?"

Kyra said, "My mom didn't know either."

Susan frowned, confused. "What?"

"What her boyfriend was doing to me."

Susan looked at Kyra and took in what the girl was telling her. She saw the pain in the girl's eyes, underneath her eyebrow rings. "I'm sorry. That's really messed up."

Kyra nodded, then said, "I can send you the picture, but I don't think it'll do any good. The cops around here are all fucking assholes."

"I'll show them my picture of Amy's necklace too, so they start an investigation."

"Good luck with that." As Susan shot her a look, Kyra put up her hands. "Hey, rooting for you, I'm just saying. When I went to the cops about that fucking dickhead, they acted like I was full of shit. You really think they'll take you serious? They'd rather sit around the station eating whatever they can get for free from Starbucks and talking about how women are such a pain in the ass."

Susan ran her hand through her hair. She felt again her lack of a shower and wondered if she smelled, despite all her efforts in the diner bathroom. *What if Kyra's right and the cops blow me off?* "Well, I gotta tell *somebody*. Before Saturday."

"The cops'll probably tell your ex-husband, and he'll throw the necklace away. Then you'll have nothing."

Susan started to say something, but then stopped. All of a sudden it hit her. She knew who she should call.

Agent Pappas.

He'll listen to me.

Won't he?

CHAPTER TWENTY-SEVEN

Kyra emailed Susan the photo, wished her luck, and headed inside the school just before the bell rang. Susan picked up her suitcase and headed off down the street.

This early in the morning the library would still be closed, so she couldn't use the computer there. Instead she called directory information, even though she knew from bitter experience that would add two dollars and ninety-five cents to her cell phone bill. She got the number for the Albany Field Office of the FBI.

She sat on a bench on a side street, on the other side of Main from Danny's house and real estate office. She didn't want to risk running into him, not that he would have any idea what she was up to.

She called the FBI and didn't get an answer, so she called at least twice a minute until nine fifteen. Finally, a woman, presumably a receptionist, picked up. "Albany Field Office, may I help you?" She had the weary sound of someone who'd been doing this job for way too many years.

Susan tried to sound bright and chipper, to make up for the other woman's utter lack of energy. "Hi, my name is Susan Lentigo. I'd like to talk to Special Agent Robert Pappas."

"I'm afraid Mr. Pappas retired from the FBI two years ago."

Damn. It didn't shock her—Pappas must be in his early- to mid-sixties by now—but it was a blow. She'd been hoping for good luck for once. "Do you have his number?"

"I'm not permitted to give that out."

Susan bit her lip, frustrated. "Then I need to talk to another Special Agent, please."

"May I ask what this is in reference to?"

She decided to lay it all on the line. Maybe she could shake this deadbeat woman into getting off her ass. "Agent Pappas was the lead investigator on my daughter Amy's murder case. He arrested a man named Curt Jansen who's gonna be executed this Saturday."

Susan waited a couple moments before the receptionist spoke. She was probably searching for the right thing to say. "I'm glad justice is finally being served."

"Well, there's a problem. I've just discovered evidence he may be innocent."

Now she waited even longer while the receptionist didn't speak. Finally, Susan said, "Hello?"

"Could you hold, please, while I transfer you."

She waited a full five minutes this time. Cold seeped into her, sitting on the bench. She went over in her mind what she'd say to whoever she talked to next.

At last another voice came over the phone, a man with some sort of New York City accent. "Hello, Ms. Lentigo, this is Special Agent Edward Hernandez. How can I help you?"

"Thank you for taking my call, Agent Hernandez."

"Of course."

"I'm calling about the murder of my daughter, Amy Lentigo."

"Yes, I have the file up on my screen. I'm sorry about your loss."

"Agent Hernandez, I believe we may have made a terrible mistake."

"I'm listening, ma'am."

Susan poured her heart out, telling him everything: her husband's lack of an alibi, his questionable behaviors, the cuts on his arms, Jansen's recanted confession, and now, above all, the necklace. By the end, she was near tears.

Agent Hernandez said, "It sounds like you've been through incredible emotional turmoil, Ms. Lentigo."

She wiped her eyes. "Yes, I have."

"May I ask, have you and your ex been having issues lately?"

"What?!" Hadn't this guy been listening to her? "No, that's not what this is about," she said, offended. "Until yesterday I hadn't even seen him for nineteen years."

"But it would be very understandable if you still resent him for leaving."

Susan gritted her teeth, trying to control her fury. "What's your email address?" She took out her scrap of paper and a pen. "I'll send you pictures of the two necklaces. You'll see they're the exact same."

"Ma'am, sending me pictures won't prove anything."

"But it's enough evidence that you can get Emily's necklace, right? You can get a search warrant or whatever!"

"Ms. Lentigo—"

Susan spoke in a rush. "And then you can do a DNA test on the necklace. I know it was a long time ago, but when Amy was killed, she did a lot of bleeding—"

"Look—"

"—and there's a lot of little grooves on the necklace where—"

Hernandez raised his voice and spoke extra emphatically, to stop her. "It's not uncommon for the victim's relatives to experience doubts when the perpetrator is about to be executed. It's a solemn matter to take somebody's life, even when it's completely justified—"

"I need you to reopen my daughter's case," Susan said, just as emphatically. "Right now—"

"Do you really want to live with confusion and uncertainty for *another* twenty years while this scumbag who raped and killed your daughter—"

She jumped up from the bench, unable to sit still anymore. "I'm afraid Danny's new daughter may be at risk. I didn't save Amy, but I won't let this little girl Emily get hurt!"

"Ma'am, I really do understand this is a stressful time—"

"Give me your goddamn email address!"

Susan heard Hernandez sigh. "Fine. Send me the pictures, and I'll see what I can do."

She shook her head, exasperated. "You're not gonna do anything, are you?"

He hesitated, and she knew she was right.

"Go fuck yourself," she said, and slammed down the phone.

She stood there trying to figure out her next move. Then she grabbed her suitcase and headed across town to the library.

But when she got there, she was in for a shock. The library was still closed—and it was closed all day. On a Tuesday? Tamarack must be more strapped for cash than it looked.

So how would she find Agent Pappas's phone number? She didn't know where he lived now. She wasn't even sure where he had lived back then. It was somewhere near Albany, which would have put him in the 518 area code.

Standing on the library steps, she called directory information again and discovered there were nine Robert Pappases in 518. Great, another twenty-five bucks on her phone bill. She took down all the numbers and began calling.

The first number belonged to a Robert Pappas who worked as a hospital nurse. The next number just kept ringing. The third one belonged, according to the annoyed widow who answered the phone, to a Robert Pappas who had died. He hadn't been an FBI agent when alive. By the time Susan was done, she had reached four wrong Robert Pappases, two numbers that just kept ringing, two where she left a message, and one that had been disconnected.

This wasn't working. To find the right Robert Pappas, she needed help. She needed a computer and internet access. *Where can I get that in this town?*

From Kyra.

But her flip phone didn't have email capability, so she couldn't email Kyra. And she didn't have the girl's phone number. She would have to go to the high school and find her somehow.

She checked her watch. The bus west was leaving Tamarack in twelve minutes. If she went to the high school, she'd miss it. She'd be stuck in this town one more day.

Well, fuck it. Even if she left tomorrow, she'd still make it to Hodge Hills in plenty of time, on Friday—

Her phone rang. She reached for it quickly, thinking it might be Kyra, but then remembered Kyra didn't have her number either. It was her mom.

She didn't pick up. Just thinking about Lenora made her discouraged. What if her mom was right that she was being an idiot about this whole thing?

But then she took a breath and squared her shoulders. She had to be strong. *For Amy.*

For Emily.

And shit, for Curt Jansen.

The Monster.

She walked to the high school, set her suitcase behind the same oak tree where she'd left it earlier, and went up the front steps. A security guard she hadn't seen before was standing just inside the door. She was a fit, well-muscled woman in her forties.

The guard smiled. "Good morning, how can I help you?"

Susan smiled back. "I'm here to see Kyra. It's a bit of an emergency."

The guard gave her a sympathetic look. "What's Kyra's last name?"

Susan had prepared herself for this. "Kyra Mitchell. She has a shaved head and lots of tattoos?"

The guard frowned slightly. "I know who you mean, but that would be Kyra Anderson."

"Right," Susan said, trying to act a little embarrassed but not *too* embarrassed. "Mitchell was her mother's maiden name. Anyway, I need to see her. It's important."

"What's this about? Are you a relative?"

"Yes, I'm her aunt."

"What kind of emergency is it?"

"I really shouldn't say. It's a personal matter."

The guard's frown deepened. "I'm not sure about this. Why don't you have her mother call the school?"

Oh God. "Could you at least give Kyra a message for me? It's . . ." She wanted to say, "It's a matter of life and death," but wasn't sure how the guard would take that. She gave an ingratiating smile. "I promise, it's really, really important."

Come on, I'm a middle-aged woman, don't tell me I look dangerous.

The guard bit her lip. Finally she said, "Okay, I guess we can do that."

"Thank you so much!"

Susan tore off a piece of her scrap paper, wrote down her name and phone number, and handed it to the guard. She wasn't sure if students were allowed to keep their cell phones in school, but hopefully Kyra would find a way to reach her.

Twenty minutes later, her phone rang with a number she didn't recognize. She snatched it out of her purse and said, "Hello?"

"What's up?" Kyra asked.

Susan launched right in. "The agent I told you about is retired and the FBI won't give me his information. I don't know where he lives now, but I'm guessing it's somewhere in the Northeast, or maybe Florida."

She paused for breath and was about to beg for help when Kyra cut in. "I can skip out of school at one forty-five. I'll meet you at the corner of Main and Caroline."

"I can't tell you how much—"

"Yeah, I gotta run. If I'm one minute late for math, that dickhead gives me detention."

Susan spent the next two hours calling all the Robert Pappases she hadn't gotten through to and hunting for a computer she could borrow. There were three hotels on Main Street including the one she'd been kicked out of last night, but none of them had computers in the lobby that the public could use, like the Wagon Wheel Motel back in Luzerne.

Then she went to Starbucks, found an empty cup to carry with her so she'd look like a customer, and asked an elderly man sitting in a far corner if she could borrow his phone. "My phone ran out of batteries," she explained with her warmest smile.

He gave her the phone and she googled "Robert Pappas." But there were so many Robert Pappases to wade through, and even when she tried "Robert Pappas FBI," the internet was slow, and she wasn't used to swiping on a phone screen and typing on that tiny keyboard. Then after ten minutes, the man had to leave Starbucks and take his phone back, so she wasn't able to get the information she needed.

At one forty-five, when Susan saw Kyra walking toward her at Main and Caroline, she had so much anxiety built up she didn't even say hello.

"I'm thinking if we google 'Robert Pappas FBI,' that's the best idea," Susan said. "Or we can try 'Robert Pappas Albany,' or—"

Kyra looked at her, eyebrows raised.

"What?" Susan said defensively.

"Random question: When's the last time you ate?"

"Well…"

"Don't sweat it, I'll pay. I gave up on my twenty bucks a long time ago."

They headed to a cheap, non-touristy, fast-food joint a few blocks down Caroline. Susan ordered a hamburger and fries and thought it was the most delicious thing she'd ever eaten. Even better than the Cheerios two nights ago. She scarfed it down in about three minutes.

Kyra was googling and doing whatever magic teenagers did when they were on their phones. Meanwhile she asked Susan, "What makes you so sure this Pappas guy will put his balls on the line for you? You're trying to make him look like a jerk. Like he fucked up the case and put an innocent man in prison."

Susan gulped down her last French fry and thought about Pappas. He'd always been good to her. She remembered sitting on a bench outside the courtroom one day while the trial was in recess. Danny and Lenora had gone off somewhere, and Susan was by herself, looking up at everybody passing by, and feeling so alone. None of these people knew what it felt like to lose a daughter this way. She began crying quietly, wet tears rolling down, when Agent Pappas saw her. He walked up, sat down beside her, and held her hand.

"I'm hoping he helps me anyway," Susan said. "He was a good guy."

"Couldn't have been that good if he busted the wrong dude."

Susan didn't want to argue about this. She pointed at Kyra's phone. "Any luck?"

Kyra looked up. "Is your guy widowed with two daughters?"

Susan's pulse quickened. "He was married back then, but he had two daughters, yeah."

"He lives in Vermont. There's no cell phone listed, but I got his landline. Want me to dial it for you?"

Susan swallowed. So much was riding on this call. If she couldn't convince Agent Pappas, she didn't know what she'd do.

"Okay," she said, pumping a fist to summon up courage. "Let's do this."

She drank some Coke to bring moisture into her dry, nervous mouth. Kyra dialed Agent Pappas's number and handed over the phone.

Susan waited. She heard a ring, then another one, and then a voice that sounded familiar, even all these years later. She started to speak back to it until she realized it was Agent Pappas's recorded voice.

"Hello, you've reached Robert Pappas," his voice said. "I'm on a road trip to North Dakota and I'm not picking up messages, but I'll be back next week."

North Dakota?!

The phone beeped. Susan didn't feel ready to leave a message—and why should she, if he wasn't picking them up? So she hit the red button to stop the phone call.

Then she looked up at Kyra in wonderment. "He's going to North Dakota."

Kyra raised her eyebrows. "To the execution? But if he's retired, why would he—"

"He always said Amy's murder really affected him. And it was a big deal for his career; he got promoted after that." Susan pushed her empty plate away from her and made a decision. She felt so relieved to finally have a plan. "I know what I'll do."

"What's that?"

"I'll go there, too, just like I was gonna do anyway. I'll get Agent Pappas to convince the FBI to reopen the case. I bet he still has contacts."

Kyra frowned. "Does it really work like that?"

Susan slammed her fist on the table harder than she meant to, making the dishes jump. "It *has* to. This guy is getting executed!"

Two teenage kids eating burgers a couple tables over stared at Susan. Kyra waited for them to look away, then said quietly, "I think you're gonna need more evidence than what you got."

Susan said sarcastically, "Well, yeah, if I had the actual necklace, I could just—"

Then she stopped. She got a light in her eyes.

"What?" Kyra asked.

"If I had the necklace," she said slowly, "I could give it to Agent Pappas. He could test it for Amy's DNA."

She was breathing deeply, her mind working, trying to decide if the idea she'd just come up with was smart or insane, and if she really had the courage to do it.

I have to, she thought. *I have to at least try. If I don't do this, I'll be haunted 'til I die.*

Kyra stared at her. "Jesus, now what are you thinking? I hope you're not gonna ask me to rip the necklace off Emily's neck."

Susan shook her head. "No. You should go home."

As Kyra sat there nonplussed, Susan stood up and put on her coat. "Thanks for the meal. I really appreciate it."

"Ms. Lentigo, what the fuck are you up to now?"

Susan wasn't about to tell her. "Goodbye, Kyra."

As she walked out the door, she could feel the girl's eyes boring into her. But she ignored that and didn't look back.

What Susan planned to do tonight was dangerous. She couldn't risk something bad happening to Kyra.

She would do it alone.

CHAPTER TWENTY-EIGHT

Tuesday, November 30, Present Day

AFTER HER LATE lunch with Kyra, Susan wasn't super hungry when five thirty came. But she figured it would be smart to load up, so she went back to the church for another AA meeting and another plate of noodles.

She had never been to AA before yesterday. Today was a "step meeting" where everybody was talking about the ninth step, "making amends." One woman spoke for several minutes about owing amends to her parents, who were already dead.

Susan wondered if she owed amends to Amy for not knowing Danny was a murderer. If he *was* a murderer. She started feeling sick to her stomach, either from the noodles or all this amends talk, and left the meeting early. "Keep coming back," a friendly elderly woman in the last row called to her as she walked out.

She took some deep breaths and firmly ordered herself to ignore all the confusion and anger, at both Danny and herself, swarming inside her. *Just get that necklace,* she told herself. *Get it and hand it over to Agent Pappas and let the truth land wherever it does.*

She headed back to the all-night diner, where the counterman gave her free coffee. The diner was so *normal*, and the counterman, despite his biker look and gruff manner, had turned out to be such a helpful guy that her stomach began to settle down.

But at eight o'clock she needed to leave, so she could scope out the situation at 89 Ash. She asked the counterman if he would hold onto her suitcase for a few hours.

"Why, where are you going?" he asked, one eyebrow raised.

"I'd tell you but then I'd have to kill you," Susan said, with a lot more insouciance than she felt. Really, she was terrified. If she failed tonight, she didn't have a Plan B.

Twenty minutes later, she was at 89 Ash. The sky was lit by a bright half-moon, so she had to be extra careful. She hid in the backyard this time, behind the trunk of a tall maple, so she could get a view of Emily's bedroom. She knew it was Emily's and not the ten-year-old son's, because the walls were pink and there were dozens of stuffed animals.

The bedroom was empty for a long time. Susan waited in the darkness, stamping her feet quietly to keep warm, hoping the family's large German shepherd wouldn't hear or smell her and start barking.

Finally, Emily came bouncing into the bedroom. She was in pajamas, which made Susan nervous—had she already put her necklace away somewhere? Would Susan have to go through the whole house searching for it? But then she saw it was still swinging from Emily's neck.

Then Danny came in and sat down next to Emily on the bed. He put his hands on her neck and delicately unclasped her necklace.

Susan groaned softly to herself, "Oh God."

"That's creepy, alright," a voice behind her said, and she jumped.

It was Kyra, in black coat and black jeans. How had she managed to sneak up without Susan hearing? "What are you doing here?" Susan said.

"Same as you." Kyra pointed at Danny. "He's putting it in the drawer. This'll be easy."

Susan watched as Danny put the necklace inside a drawer of Emily's bedside table. Then he closed the drawer.

She turned back to Kyra. "I can't let you help me, Kyra. You're just a kid."

"So?"

"You have too much to lose. If you get arrested, you'll have a criminal record."

"I already have a record. For cutting my mom's boyfriend when he came in my bedroom one night."

Susan wasn't sure what to say to that. Kyra turned away from her. They both watched as Danny stayed there in the bed with Emily. It seemed to Susan he was sitting way too close to her. He was her father, but were fathers supposed to act like this? Susan felt her head go wobbly.

But Kyra didn't have any of the doubts Susan had. "What a fucking creep," Kyra said. "If he doesn't leave that bedroom in five seconds, I'm going in there."

Susan pulled herself together. She had to be the grown-up here. "Nobody's going anywhere, til at least midnight. If he catches us trying to steal that necklace, he'll throw it away for sure."

"Midnight? Good thing I brought chocolate," Kyra said, and took out a Snickers bar. She tore it in two and offered half to Susan.

Susan still felt guilty about getting the girl involved. "Won't your mom wonder where you are?"

Kyra made a sound that was part snort, part laugh. "Like she even cares. She still blames me for her asshole boyfriend leaving." She looked into Emily's bedroom and frowned, upset. "Shit."

They watched as Danny kissed Emily good night.

On the lips.

Susan got an emptiness in her chest. "How could I not notice?" Her voice came out in a whisper.

"'Cause he's a sneaky fuckhead. Acts all sweet, like my mom's boyfriend did."

Danny stepped away from Emily and walked to the window. As he did, Susan saw his face straight on. A shiver of pure, unadulterated hate rolled through her. Then Danny shut the curtains, turned off the light, and left Emily's bedroom.

At least Susan thought he did.

Her adrenalin was pumping and she wanted to rush in there right now. But she forced herself to stick to her rule about midnight. By then, she and Kyra were both freezing, their teeth chattering. Clouds covered the half-moon and the sky was darker now. All the lights inside the house were off.

"You ready?" Susan asked.

"Let's go."

They moved through the yard toward Emily's bedroom. Hopefully they'd get lucky and be able to lift one of her two windows. If they were both locked, they'd try the windows in the front part of the house. And if that didn't work—

It *better* work.

Kyra stepped on a branch, and it snapped with a loud crack. "Careful!" Susan whispered hoarsely.

They made it to the bedroom. Susan watched as Kyra reached out and pushed upward on one of the windows.

It didn't move.

Kyra pushed harder, and still nothing happened.

Susan stepped to the other window and pushed as hard as she could, her muscles tightening. Nothing happened, then all at once she felt something give and the window slid up two feet!

But it made a loud, raspy grinding sound. Susan stood stock still, waiting to see if the noise woke up Emily, or if she could hear anything else inside the house.

There was only silence. So she pushed upward again. But the window was stuck now. She pushed again, shutting her eyes and giving it everything she had. No go. It would be impossible to fit her body through that small opening.

Then Kyra came toward her. Kyra put her hands on the window, gave Susan a nod, and they pushed up together. Suddenly the window came unstuck and rose two more feet. But this time it made an even worse grinding sound. Susan stopped, alarmed.

She and Kyra waited. But the house was still silent. Nobody came into Emily's room and she stayed asleep.

Susan felt along the bottom part of the screen, found the two tabs, and pulled the screen out of the window opening. She lay it quietly on the ground. Then she placed her hands on the window ledge and started to climb up onto it.

But her foot couldn't quite make it onto the window ledge on her first or second try, and she got a sharp pain in her problem leg. She was about to try again, but Kyra stopped her.

"I'll do it," Kyra said.

"No—"

But Kyra was already climbing up. Susan made a stepping-stone out of her hands, and Kyra used it to boost herself higher. She made it onto the ledge, keeping her head down so she wouldn't bang it on the windowsill above her, and dropped down onto the bedroom floor.

She landed hard.

And Emily woke up.

Looking through the open window, in the darkness, Susan saw the girl lift up her head and look at Kyra. Then, in another room, the dog barked. *Oh shit.*

Emily asked Kyra, "Who are you?"

Kyra moved toward the bedside table and said softly, "It's okay, go back to sleep."

The dog began barking more urgently. Standing at the window, Susan felt helpless. She wanted to scream at Kyra to hurry, but she knew the girl was going as fast as she could.

She watched as Kyra opened the top drawer of the bedside table and rummaged around. But her hands came out empty. *What the hell?*

"Are you looking for something?" Emily asked.

Then Kyra opened the bottom drawer of the table—and immediately her hand came out with the necklace.

Outside, Susan started to heave a sigh of relief but cut it short out of fear Emily would hear her and get even more freaked out.

"That's my necklace," Emily said.

Kyra put it in her coat pocket and headed for the window, whispering, "I'm just borrowing it."

But then Emily screamed.

From the other room, Danny shouted, "Emily?!"

"Hurry!" Susan whispered to Kyra, as she got onto the ledge.

Danny entered the room—and Susan saw he was holding a small gun.

Terrified, she held out her hand to Kyra. The girl jumped out the window and managed to land on her feet.

"Hey!" Danny yelled. He ran toward the window.

Susan and Kyra were already running away through the darkness. There were hedges on either side of them and in front of them, blocking their way to other backyards.

Behind them they heard Danny yell, "Stop!" Then they heard a crashing sound—probably he had just tumbled through the window and outside. They ran blindly toward a back hedge.

Emily yelled, "Daddy!"

Danny yelled, "Stop right there!"

And then there was a gunshot.

Holy shit!

Had Danny recognized her? Was he shooting at Susan on purpose? They kept running, crashing through the hedge.

They heard Danny yell, "Fuck!" It sounded like he'd tripped and fallen—maybe on the same branch that Kyra snapped.

But even if he got slowed down for a second, Susan knew he was still coming after them. If they kept running straight, they'd hit a street that was lit up with streetlights. She was petrified he'd catch up and see them, maybe shoot them.

Was that legal? As furious as Danny was, he might not care.

"This way!" Kyra whispered. Susan got her plan: they'd head left and slip behind the side hedge and hide there 'til he went past.

They did that, moving as quickly and quietly as they could while Danny kept yelling. He fired another shot and Susan flinched, half expecting it to hit her.

Then there was silence. Susan and Kyra were hidden behind the hedge now.

"Hey!" Danny called.

Susan moved her head slightly to the left and looked out through a thin part of the hedge. Oh God, he was so close! Maybe fifteen feet away. He was looking all around him, searching, listening.

"I see you! Come out of there before I shoot!"

He was bluffing. He didn't see them.

But then he eyed their hedge and advanced carefully toward it, gun high. Somehow he had heard or sensed they were there! Susan and Kyra held their breath, but he kept coming, closing in.

Susan was frantic. She could only think of one thing to do.

Trying not to make noise, she pulled the spray bottle her mom had given her out of her coat pocket. She opened the nozzle all the way, so the pepper spray would come out in a hard stream instead of a mist. Then she raised the bottle and put it into the thin part of the hedge.

Danny came right towards her from the other side. Maybe he'd heard her messing with the bottle. He raised his gun.

Susan aimed at his face and squeezed the lever.

Danny turned toward the sound. The stream of red pepper spray poured out of the nozzle and hit him straight in the eyes.

He screamed with pain. Clawing at his eyes, he fired wildly in the air. Then he dropped his gun so he could deal with his burning eyes.

Susan and Kyra ran like hell out of there, as Danny yelled, "You fuckheads!"

A minute later, and two blocks away, Susan and Kyra were still running when a cop car raced toward them, siren blaring. Susan froze, panicking.

Kyra said, "Just act normal, like you're my mom."

They started walking again. The cop car roared past them.

"Oh my God," Susan whispered.

"Don't worry, we're okay now. Hey, nice job with that pepper spray!"

They made it onto an intersecting street before the next cop car came, and headed back to Main. Susan felt safe—for now.

"Do you think he saw me?" she asked.

"I don't know. But what's he gonna do if he did?"

Good question. How would he play this? They made it to the all-night diner and Susan opened the door. The counterman looked up and took them both in, with their cheeks flushed from cold and excitement. "Who's your young friend?" he asked Susan.

"You never saw her," Susan said, hardly believing the easy bantering she was getting into with this man she barely knew. Her mom would be impressed.

The counterman grinned. "What's going on?"

"Nothing. We were never here."

He chuckled. "You got it."

Susan got her suitcase from the corner where the counterman had put it. Then they ordered coffee and glazed doughnuts, which Kyra paid for, and sat down in a booth. Susan took the necklace from Kyra, held it gingerly, and stared at it.

It's the same necklace, alright.

She couldn't believe she was holding Amy's necklace again after all these years. Love, sadness, and rage warred inside her chest.

This was the necklace her daughter was wearing when she was strangled to death.

Is there any other way Danny could still have it, besides—

"You okay?" Kyra asked.

Susan nodded, unable to speak. She took her purse out of the suitcase and withdrew the small plastic baggie her mom had given her. She put the necklace inside the baggie; somehow it felt safer that way.

Then she put the necklace on the table, and she and Kyra looked at it.

Finally Susan's mouth started working again. "Amy and I bought these beads together," she said. "At a little craft store in Glens Falls."

Kyra brought her head down close to the necklace and studied it. "So we're rooting for dried blood stuck in under a bead or something."

"Don't worry, those CSI people are like magicians." Susan had been an obsessive viewer of real-life forensics shows ever since Amy got killed. She picked up her coffee. "They'll find something."

"But still, it's been a long time."

She stopped drinking in mid-sip and put her coffee back down. "Amy hit her forehead on a rock that night. She bled really badly. When the killer strangled her, her necklace was still on."

Amy's body lying on that drawer in the morgue. Her bruised, bloody neck. The imprints in her blood made by this very necklace. You can see where the pink duck dug into her bloody neck when she was strangled.

"There were imprints of her necklace in the blood. If this necklace is the same one . . . If my husband killed my daughter . . ."

She touched the necklace through the plastic baggie.

"Her DNA will be here."

CHAPTER TWENTY-NINE

WEDNESDAY, DECEMBER 1, PRESENT DAY

THE COUNTERMAN WAS indeed a biker, as Susan and Kyra learned when he sat down with them a while later. His name was Mike, and he entertained them with tales of the several years he'd spent in various New York State prisons.

What would Lenora think of Susan hanging out with a biker ex-con and a teenage girl who "cut" her mom's boyfriend? No doubt she'd be amazed by all the adventures Susan was having—and also appalled. Lenora had called again tonight, but Susan just said, "I'm good, Mom, sorry, bad connection," and got off the phone fast.

Sitting there in the coffee shop, she finally told Mike the whole story of what she was up to here in Tamarack, except she didn't reveal Danny's name even after Mike asked for it more than once.

"I'll kill the sick bastard myself," he said.

"Works for me," Kyra said.

Susan wasn't totally sure Mike was kidding. She thanked him and said no—though she had to admit, it sounded awfully appealing.

But on the other hand, killing Danny wouldn't help Curt Jansen any. The date and time of his execution—just three days from now, Saturday, 5:30 p.m.—was never far from her mind.

She did take Mike up on his offer to let her sleep in the back room. There was an old sofa there, much like Molly's, and she was able to grab five hours, though they were interrupted twice by dreams about Danny that she couldn't quite remember, but they terrified her.

When she finally woke up for good, she thought again about what Danny would do. By now Emily would have told him about somebody "borrowing" the necklace. He'd know Susan was behind it, and he sure as hell wasn't gonna tell the cops his ex-wife thought he was a murderer. That was the last thing he needed.

But would he find some other way to get back at her? She sat up on the sofa and felt inside her coat pocket for the baggie containing the necklace. She would protect this necklace with her life, until she gave it to Agent Pappas.

She still could hardly believe what she and Kyra had pulled off last night. *But will it work? Will it be enough?*

It better be.

Meanwhile, Kyra slept at home, then came back in the morning to buy Susan breakfast for the road. Mike scrambled them some eggs with extra bacon.

As Susan wolfed down her food, she looked up at the clock and saw it was already after eight. She asked Kyra, "Won't you get in trouble for skipping school?"

"I might. But then again, if I ever apply for college this whole thing will make one hell of a personal essay."

They had another cup of coffee, then got up. It was time to go.

Susan said to Mike, "Your coffee saved my life the last two nights."

"Yeah, you owe me about fifty bucks," he said, and shook her hand. He wasn't the hugging type, but then again neither was she. Not with men, anyway.

Mike held the door open for them and they headed outside into the cold morning air. Kyra rolled Susan's suitcase for her down Main Street.

After their wild night, the gentle pace of small-town life was jarring. A middle-aged man was walking his white poodle. An elderly couple took a leisurely winter stroll.

Susan thought about Danny, living quietly in this little town. *At night, does he dream about hurting Emily?*

She had always wondered if the Monster intended to kill Amy from the moment he abducted her. Now she wondered, *If Danny really did kill Amy . . . did he mean to, or was he trying to do something different with her and . . .*

Susan's head started pounding and she couldn't think any further. Kyra must have been thinking along the same lines, though, because she said, "Do you think he's planning to kill Emily?"

The hairs rose on the back of Susan's neck. "If he's a psycho, maybe that's part of the thrill. Seeing if he can get away with it twice."

Ahead of them, three women tourists in expensive wool coats looked into the window of "Grandpa's House Antiques." Susan glanced in and saw a couple of big antique hunting rifles.

Kyra went on about what a disgusting creep Danny was, but Susan wasn't listening anymore. She stopped short and eyed the rifles, frowning. Something about them was tugging at her mind.

All of a sudden, she realized what it was. Her eyes opened wide as the memory came back to her:

Danny in his green and brown camo jacket, getting ready for his annual hunting trip. He kisses Susan goodbye and puts his old rifle in the trunk of his car—

Holy fucking God.

Susan choked out, "Or maybe it's more than twice."

Kyra looked at her, confused. "What?"

"Maybe it's more than twice," Susan repeated. "He went deer hunting every winter. Most years he didn't get anything." She felt the eggs and bacon rising in her throat. "Maybe he was hunting something else."

She gasped, leaned over, and threw up.

Kyra put her hand on Susan's back. After she seemed done, Kyra asked, "You okay?"

Susan nodded.

"We'll get you some water."

Susan straightened back up. The three women tourists and a couple of other people were staring at her. She looked away from them—

—and saw Danny.

He was across the street half a block away, with Emily. They were holding hands and she was skipping and laughing. They walked into a bakery, the Bread Basket. They looked so . . .

Again Kyra said out loud what Susan was thinking. "God, they look so *normal*," she said wonderingly.

Susan stared at them through the bakery window. Why wasn't Emily in school? Maybe last night had been so scary, her parents let her sleep in and pick out a morning treat. Through the window, she saw Emily pointing at the cupcake she wanted, and Danny getting it for her.

Susan's stomach clenched. "What if they *are* normal? What if I'm wrong about all this?"

"You're not wrong," Kyra said.

"My mom thinks I've lost my mind. I haven't slept well for months, thinking about this execution." She pointed at Danny and Emily, happy together. "I mean, look at them."

"Don't let him fool you again. Trust yourself."

Susan felt light-headed, her thoughts and her recent nausea making her woozy. That necklace in her pocket—what did it really prove? Maybe Danny searched the internet and found beads that were just like Amy's.

All these years Danny mourns for Amy. He keeps his sorrow buried inside, like men do. But to help him deal with the pain, he makes Emily a new necklace that looks just like the one Amy used to have—

"Let's go," Kyra said. "We don't want that prick to see us."

True, what if he tried to take the necklace back from her? Susan steadied herself and walked off down the street, away from Danny.

Five minutes later, they made it to the bus station on Main. Susan kept a wary eye out for Danny 'til the westbound bus pulled up. As soon as it came, she realized how eager she was to get the hell out of this town.

The driver stepped out—the same bored, skinny guy who had left her off here two days ago. He was wearing the same Hawaiian shirt and her nose told her he hadn't washed it since then. Not that she was a model of cleanliness herself at this point. But she'd changed her clothes and washed up in the diner bathroom again, and she'd brushed her teeth just now in the bus station, so she was feeling pretty spiffy for somebody who hadn't showered since Sunday morning.

As the driver took her suitcase and put it under the bus, Susan thought about what lay ahead. Would she really be able to pull it off? She told Kyra, "I get in to Hodge Hills on Friday morning. That only gives me one and a half days to stop the execution."

"You're gonna fucking kick ass," Kyra said.

Susan bit her lip. "I just hope I can convince Agent Pappas to test the necklace."

Kyra put a hand on Susan's arm. As Kyra's sleeve rode up, Susan noted a big flame tattoo on the girl's wrist.

"Just tell that dude everything you told me," Kyra said. "You're very persuasive."

Susan looked into Kyra's eyes. Now that she was saying goodbye to the one person in this whole world—aside from Mike the counterman—who believed her crazy story, she felt tears coming. She would be all alone again.

The driver said, "All aboard," aiming his words at Susan since she was the only passenger not on the bus yet. She wondered if he recognized her. Probably not.

She looked awkwardly at Kyra, not wanting to say goodbye. "I'll call you from North Dakota."

"You fucking better."

Then Kyra surprised Susan by stepping forward and hugging her. Susan held her tight. "Your mom's an idiot," she said.

Kyra smiled, though her eyes were wet too. "No shit."

Susan waved goodbye and got on the bus.

CHAPTER THIRTY

THE BUS HAD about twenty passengers, just like it did two days ago. Susan walked up the aisle and found the same empty seat she'd sat in then.

It was eerie: everything was the same, and yet her whole world had careened upside down.

She waved goodbye to Kyra one last time through the window, watching her disappear as the bus headed down Main Street. Then they passed Tamarack Realty, and she saw the picture of Danny in the front window. She shivered, then reached into her coat's inside pocket and felt the necklace through the baggie, reassuring herself it was still there.

The bus rumbled back onto I-90 and headed through the bare ancient hills of western New York. She felt carsick. She longed for the certainty she'd had all these years, for the simplicity of her pain. Sure, she had felt guilty about Amy's death—but she'd never experienced anything like the torrent swirling inside her now.

Did my own husband kill my daughter—and I didn't know?

She looked out the window at the trees rolling by. Then they drove toward a giant McDonald's sign. She could practically smell the French fry grease and her stomach got queasy again. An old memory came to her, incredibly vivid:

Sitting in a booth at McDonald's with Amy, the two of them eating Big Macs. Marveling at how fast her little daughter scarfs her food down.

"Honey, take your time," Susan says.

Danny walks up with his own Big Mac and smiles down at them.

"She's just a starving little carnivore," he says.

Amy asks, "Daddy, what's a carnivore?"

Danny tousles her hair. "A carnivore is you, you little munchkin."

Susan smiles. A happy family . . .

Happy.

Was it all a lie? Their seven years together?

It couldn't be.

Susan looked out the window, agitated. The McDonald's sign was out of view now. She wished she had a magazine to read, to take her mind off everything. Every minute felt endless.

After about an hour the bus came down from the rolling hills and entered an industrial wasteland. She thought she wouldn't be able to fall asleep, but weariness overtook her at last and she managed to sleep straight through the westernmost part of New York and a pie-shaped piece of Pennsylvania. Now they were all the way into northern Ohio.

Good. She was desperate to be in North Dakota already and see Agent Pappas.

They passed a used car graveyard, a tire warehouse, and vast empty parking lots. Then the bus stopped in Cleveland, where she had a two-hour layover. Kyra had given Susan her last six dollars, which brought her to six dollars and ninety cents. That was enough for a cheeseburger with a dollar forty left over.

As she ate the burger—not as good as Molly's, but not bad—she wondered how in hell she'd make it for three days on a buck forty, and where she'd sleep in Hodge Hills. She really should call Terri and ask for help.

But Terri was just as broke as she was. And more than that ... Susan wouldn't be able to talk to her without explaining what was going on. And then she'd have to listen to Terri tell her how ridiculous she was being.

If she got Agent Pappas on her side, maybe she would feel okay calling Terri then.

To get some exercise and distract herself from worrying about money, Susan walked around the bus station. She had a stroke of luck: there was a *People* magazine sitting on a chair, and she grabbed it. She'd never even seen a *People* before except in supermarkets or doctors' offices.

Her next bus rode deep into the night, through Toledo, past a rural area with endless cornfields, and into Indiana, where they stopped in Clear Lake, Sturgis, Shipshewana, and three other towns she'd never heard of. They arrived in Goshen at eleven thirty at night. The bus lights came on and she watched as the sleeping passengers woke up and rubbed their eyes.

"Goshen, Indiana. Everybody off."

Susan took her suitcase off the bus and stood there as the other passengers rode away, getting into cabs or cars driven by their loved ones. They all had places to go. She had nowhere.

The coffee shop was closed for the night, but at least the bus station was still open. There were four people inside, two men and two women, each of them looking lonelier than the next.

She found a seat in a corner near an outlet and plugged in the charger for her flip phone. She put the suitcase under her feet so people would be less likely to steal it. Then she put her phone in her lap.

She wondered why Danny hadn't called her when he realized she'd stolen the necklace. She tried to figure out if there was any way he could hurt her.

Well, he could kill me.

What if he was innocent—what would he do then?

Once again, she reached inside her coat pocket just to feel the shape of the necklace. Then she buttoned up her coat, even though the station was pretty warm, and folded her arms in front of it. If anybody tried to get into her pocket, she'd know.

She forced her eyes shut, leaned her head against the wall, and eventually drifted off into an uneasy sleep. It wasn't long before Curt Jansen appeared. Some part of her mind was still awake, and she wondered: *Should I call him the Monster, or Curt Jansen?*

He's in the courtroom, white knuckles gripping the edge of the defense table, listening as the judge reads aloud from a white sheet of paper: ". . . On the count of murder in the first degree, we the jury find the defendant . . ." He pauses. "Guilty."

Jansen's whole body goes limp.

In the gallery, with Danny sitting beside her, Susan is so relieved. She looks down at Jansen—

—and suddenly Jansen becomes Danny. The marshals walk up to Danny to put handcuffs on him.

Then, just as suddenly, Danny is back with her in the gallery again, squeezing her hand. She looks over at him. He's smiling, satisfied.

Susan's conscious mind broke into her dream. *Maybe he's too satisfied,* she thought. *He's glad he got away with it.*

The sound of the judge's voice brought her back inside the dream again. *"On the count of aggravated rape of a minor . . ."*

Somebody's crying in the gallery. She turns her eyes upward. It's Jansen's sister, Lisa, wearing another one of her conservative suits.

Susan's jaw tightens. She won't allow herself to feel bad for this woman. Damn it, her brother is—

". . . guilty," the judge says.

She stares down at Jansen again, triumphant, willing him to look up at her and meet her eyes. He does, glaring, his face filled with violent rage.

Susan's conscious mind jumps in again and she thinks, *But wouldn't I be full of rage too, if I was innocent?*

She feels a hand on her shoulder.

"Excuse me, ma'am," a man says.

What?!

"Ma'am?"

She startled awake. A security guard was standing over her, lifting his hand off her shoulder.

"We're closing up for the night," he said. "You can't sleep here. I'm sorry, ma'am."

She stared at him, disoriented, then looked around and saw everybody else at the bus station had left. Without a word, she gathered her suitcase and phone charger and walked out into the night.

A freezing wind was blowing. She pulled her coat collar up, then opened her suitcase and took out the pink and purple wool sweater she was planning to wear to the execution. It was the same sweater she'd worn to the trial; she'd been saving it, only wearing it on Amy's birthday, for twenty years. She put that on, then took out a faded blue baseball cap with the letters *RJ* on it. She couldn't remember anymore what the letters stood for. She put the cap on and looked for a place to sit or stand that would be partly protected from the wind.

The best place she found was a bench on the far side of the station. She sat down, put her hands in her armpits, and stamped her feet. For hours. She had never been so cold in her life. Her exhausted mind jitterbugged from thought to thought. She wondered what Agent Pappas looked like now, and was he really as kind as she remembered. She wondered if Danny was asleep right now, or was he awake and brooding just like she was. She wondered why she was fated to be in this situation.

Then she shook off that thought. All that mattered was getting to North Dakota and finding out the truth.

Finally, at seven o'clock, the station reopened. She walked inside and got warm at last. But her long night outside had left her desperate for food and caffeine. She got a Hershey bar for ninety-five cents, but she was still ravenous.

She decided to scavenge the coffee shop for food. She felt like a homeless woman, sitting in a corner with her old suitcase and watching people eat, hoping they'd leave behind their home fries when they stood up. But it seemed like everybody else was just as hungry as she was this morning, because they all cleaned their plates—except for one elderly man who didn't eat half of his scrambled eggs, but brought his plate up to the front counter before she could grab it. In the end, her efforts yielded only one-third of a bread roll and a half-cup of herbal tea. Making matters worse, the liquid soap dispensers in the bathroom were empty so she couldn't come close to washing up properly.

At eight thirty she was on another bus leaving Goshen behind and riding a county highway through northwestern Indiana. They stopped in Elkhart, Ligonier, Mishawka . . . She watched a mom, dad, and two rambunctious little kids with plastic wands and swords get off the bus. Was that family as happy as it looked? What would it be like to have a family like that?

Luckily she fell asleep and got a little peace, only waking up when they hit Chicago. She just had fifteen minutes 'til her next bus left, but the coffee shop here was much busier and her scavenging brought in a pretty good haul: a whole hamburger roll with mayonnaise, along with coleslaw.

Then it was on to the next bus, this one smelling of strong bleach. They went through Pingree Grove, Riley, Rockford, every mile bringing her closer to the Hodge Hills Federal Penitentiary in North Dakota, where a man she wasn't sure anymore if she hated was about to die.

They stopped at a bus station/diner in South Beloit, and she was able to get a day-old doughnut with the last forty-five cents in her purse, along with some more leftover coleslaw. A middle-aged couple saw her collecting the coleslaw and eyed her disapprovingly. Unshowered with stringy hair . . . What must she look like now?

To say nothing of how she must smell.

Night fell, and she was grateful the bus rode through the night and she wouldn't have to spend hours stamping her feet outside another bus station. They passed a "WELCOME TO WISCONSIN" sign. It was a state she had never been to, but she imagined cheese, and sure enough they began riding through dairy land. Then came "WELCOME TO MINNESOTA" and she fell asleep again.

Curt Jansen in cuffs, being taken away to prison. Susan hugs Danny. Then Agent Pappas walks up, smiling.

"We got him, Susan," he says. "We got the Monster."

She throws her arms around Agent Pappas—

Susan woke up, distressed by the dream, just in time to see a sign: "WELCOME TO NORTH DAKOTA DISCOVER THE SPIRIT!"

Holy crap, we're almost there! All of a sudden, she had a desperate need to use the bathroom and get rid of some of that coleslaw. She got up and headed down the aisle to the back of the bus.

In the bathroom, she washed her hands and face and did her best to comb the tangles out of her hair. It was a narrow space, but with a lot of maneuvering she was able to take off her coat, sweater, and shirt and wash under her arms.

When she was done, she reached into her coat pocket and took out the baggie with the necklace inside. *Yup, still there. The purple dolphin, the pink duck . . .*

The bus pulled into the station in Fargo and everybody got out. Susan would be here for an hour before she finally boarded the last bus on her journey, the one that would take her to Hodge Hills. She got her suitcase and headed into the station. It was cold, so she buttoned up her coat and put her RJ baseball cap back on.

She went straight to the coffee shop. She headed for a corner far away from the counter, so she wouldn't attract attention from the beefy security guard hanging out there. She didn't know if her scavenging was illegal, but she didn't want to find out. If anybody left any promising food on their plate, she'd use her body to block the guard from seeing her take it.

Hey, if she could break into Danny's house and steal the necklace, she could damn well outfox this guard.

From her recon spot, she saw a teenage girl stand up and abandon almost a full order of leftover home fries in the middle of the room. Susan's mouth watered just looking at them. She hurried over there with her suitcase.

But then a busboy swooped in and took the plate away.

She was crestfallen.

She felt a little nutty focusing so much on food when her whole world had just been ripped apart. But hell, it beat thinking about other stuff. Maybe all the stress was making her extra hungry. She searched the room for targets and lasered in on a table where somebody had left two whole pieces of toast, along with jelly. *That'll work.* She headed toward there. But just as she picked up the slightly burned toast, she heard a woman say, "Excuse me."

Susan jumped, startled, her face instantly reddening at having been caught in the act. She thought some waitress would ask her to leave, maybe call the guard over.

But when she turned and looked, it was another customer speaking to her, a woman in her fifties with curly gray hair and a wide face. There was a grilled cheese sandwich in front of her.

"Would you like half my sandwich?" the woman asked.

Susan stuttered, "That's okay, I—"

"Please, I ordered too much, I can't eat it all."

The woman had big warm eyes, and the sandwich did look good, oozing yellow cheese out the sides. She took half the sandwich off her plate and held it out to Susan.

"Thanks," Susan said, as she stepped forward and took it.

"Would you like some water?" the woman asked, moving her glass toward Susan. "I'm just drinking coffee."

"Thanks," Susan said again. "I'm not usually like this. Somebody stole all my money a couple days ago."

"Oh my God, that's horrible." The woman gestured toward the seat across from her. "Sit down. Do you know who stole it?"

She sat down, wondering if this woman was lonely like her or just very friendly. "I think somebody at another bus station took it when I fell asleep."

The woman shook her head, and once again Susan admired her curly gray hair. "There sure are some terrible people in this world," the woman said.

Susan was afraid the woman would ask her more questions about herself, and she wasn't in the mood to share her whole frantic confusion about who had killed her daughter. All she really wanted to do was eat this delectable-looking half-sandwich. So she steered the conversation away from herself.

"So where are you heading?" she asked, as she lifted the half-sandwich to her mouth.

"Hodge Hills," the woman said.

With the food still in midair, Susan stopped and stared at the woman, at her open, attractive face and curly gray hair.

Oh my God.

The courtroom, twenty years ago. An attractive woman in her thirties, with curly black hair, sitting in the gallery. Moaning with pain when the judge says, "Guilty."

Curt Jansen's younger sister, Lisa.

And now here she was: the same woman, twenty years older.

CHAPTER THIRTY-ONE

Susan was so stunned she could barely hear the words coming out of Lisa's mouth. But then her mind cleared up enough that she could make out Lisa saying, "I flew in to Fargo, but after that it's either rent a car or take a bus, and this is cheaper."

Susan realized her mouth was wide open and made an effort to close it.

"What about you?" Lisa asked. "Where are you going?"

Susan wanted to lie, but she'd be taking the same bus with this woman. "I'm going to Hodge Hills too."

Lisa raised her eyebrows and smiled. "Really. What for?"

Susan put her hand to her baseball cap and pulled it down a little lower to hide her face. She wore glasses now, her face was heavier, and she wasn't dying her hair blonde anymore; but still, she was terrified that at any moment Lisa would recognize her. What would Susan say? *I'm thinking maybe you were right all along and your brother's been wrongly imprisoned for twenty years. But I'm not really sure.*

Out loud, Susan said, "Family stuff," and shrugged. She lifted the glass of water to her lips, hiding the bottom part of her face with it.

Lisa gave a short laugh. "Yeah, me too, in a way. What kind of family stuff?"

Without even thinking, Susan said, "A wedding."

"God, I wish I was going to a wedding." Lisa had a gulp of coffee, and Susan saw for the first time that her movements were a little jittery, like she was on edge. Her next words were proof of that. "I'm such a mess. I'm going to an execution tomorrow."

Susan wished she were anywhere but here. "Really."

Lisa nodded. "That's why I'm too tense to eat." Putting down her coffee cup, she leaned forward and said confidentially, "It's my brother. He's getting executed for killing somebody."

"I'm sorry," Susan said.

"Yeah." Lisa rubbed her cheek, looking suddenly tired. "It happened twenty years ago, but I still can't believe he did it."

Susan eyed Lisa and blinked, trying to figure out what she meant by that. *Does she still think her brother's innocent—or did she change her mind?*

She leaned closer to Lisa. "Do you think he really did do it?"

Lisa looked at the coffee in her cup and swirled it around, as if searching for wisdom in the coffee waves. "He confessed to the FBI. But then he took it back."

Susan felt guilty for trying to trick Lisa into talking. When Lisa saw her at the prison tomorrow and recognized her, what would Susan say?

But she was desperate to know if Lisa had some kind of proof her brother was guilty. So she asked, "What did he say to you about it?"

Lisa waved her hand, looking self-conscious. "You don't really want to hear all my troubles."

"I'm interested."

Lisa had a sip of her coffee, then looked up at Susan. "My brother was a real troubled kid," she said. "Dyslexia *and* ADD. Couldn't read, couldn't sit still. Now they have treatments for that, but back then . . ." She shook her head before continuing. "He acted out. Got caught stealing when he was sixteen, went to juvie and never looked back." She gave Susan a beseeching look. "But he was a real sweet big brother, you know? When our parents were out getting drunk or whatever, he would always cook my favorite meal, spaghetti and meatballs. So I couldn't believe he'd ever hurt a girl like that."

Lisa frowned, bewilderment crossing her face. "But I guess he did. He did kind of confess to me."

What the hell does that mean? Susan felt a jolt of excitement, and realized she was desperately hoping Curt was guilty after all and Danny was innocent. "He *kind* of confessed?"

Lisa nodded. "It was three years ago. I was visiting him in prison and crying about how unfair it all was, and he told me to let it go. He said he deserved it. Deserved the death penalty. So I guess he really did it."

Susan was afraid to look into Lisa's eyes, because that might help Lisa recognize her, but she had to understand what this woman was really thinking. So she gazed directly at her and said, "You don't sound too sure."

"Really I think Curt was just trying to make me feel better," Lisa said. "Like if I believe he's guilty, then it's not so horrible him being put to death like a dog."

She looked down at her coffee again. "I guess I'll never know the truth. He'll die tomorrow and that'll be it."

Then she raised her eyes to Susan. "Sorry to lay all this on you. I guess I needed to talk."

Susan nodded awkwardly, feeling like a shit. "It's no problem."

Lisa peered more closely at Susan, at her face beneath the baseball cap. "You look kinda familiar. Where are you from?"

Susan's mouth opened. She had a sudden powerful urge to tell Lisa everything.

But what if she couldn't prove Curt Jansen was innocent? *What if he's actually guilty?* It would be incredibly cruel to get Lisa's hopes up, and then have her brother get executed anyway.

Susan couldn't do that to her.

"I'm from Boston," she said.

"Never been there. Always wanted to go."

Susan was afraid Lisa would ask for details about Boston, a city she had never been to either. But luckily a voice came over the loud-speaker. "Bus for Jamestown, Bismarck, Hodge Hills, and points west ready for boarding."

"Shall we?" Lisa said. She pointed down at Susan's half-sandwich, which lay on a napkin, mostly uneaten. Susan had been so hungry before, but now her appetite had disappeared. "Don't forget to bring that."

The two of them got up and rolled their suitcases to the loading area, where they got onto a local Dakota Northern bus that looked way more rickety than the Greyhound and Trailways buses Susan had been riding. But for the first time in this entire trip, her bus was packed. In addition to the usual random passengers, there were thirty or so ladies in their sixties boarding the bus too, maybe some church group going to a convention, or a social group going to a casino. So there were no two empty seats together. Susan was relieved; it meant she wouldn't have to sit with Lisa and keep lying to her. She took an aisle seat next to a quiet-looking young woman, and Lisa sat a couple rows back.

But then Lisa stood up again and stepped forward. "You want to sit together?"

Susan couldn't figure out how to say no, and before she knew it, Lisa and the quiet woman were switching places. *Great.*

Susan moved over to the window seat and Lisa sat down next to her. "How come you're not eating your sandwich?" she said.

Susan forced herself to eat it, even though it seemed tasteless to her now.

Lisa put her purse in her lap and said, "You know, the truth is, I always kind of thought it was the father."

Susan didn't understand at first. "What?"

"The girl who got raped and killed. I thought her father did it."

Susan gagged on the bread and started coughing.

"You okay? Can I get you a cough drop?"

"I'm fine. What made you think it was her father?"

"It's usually somebody the victim knows. And he seemed kinda creepy."

"How did he . . . seem creepy?"

"Well, there was a lot of really disgusting stuff in the trial. Testimony about his daughter's rape and all these gross pictures. Sometimes I'd look at him, and he didn't seem as upset as he should've been. I mean, he had a frown on his face, but somehow he almost looked intrigued, you know?"

Susan made herself nod. *How could I be so stupid that I didn't know about Danny, when this woman figured it out right away?*

But then she thought, *How could I have known?* Danny was a football star in high school, clean cut, a popular guy. He was the only man she had ever made love to. The schoolgirl uniform thing seemed a little odd, sure, but she just figured it was probably . . . well, a normal fantasy for a lot of guys. And what did she know about men?

She had been so glad Danny was such a loving dad, from the very beginning. He wasn't like other men, who wouldn't change their baby's diapers—

Oh God, I can't go there, I can't. She felt about to vomit and began coughing uncontrollably.

"You sure you're okay?" Lisa said. Susan doubled over a little, and Lisa put a hand on her back.

"I'm fine," Susan said again, straightening up, but then she coughed even harder.

Lisa brought out her cough drops and made Susan take one, and finally her fit subsided. She told Lisa she needed to sleep for a while.

Anything to avoid talking.

She shut her eyes and pretended to fall asleep. The bus was freezing, the lousy shock absorbers made her feel every bounce in her bones, and she was sitting next to a woman whose brother she might have wronged beyond belief. This bus ride to hell would last four hours, but it would feel like forever.

But then she heard Lisa's breathing grow steadier, and she cracked her eyes open to check on her. Sure enough, Lisa was sleeping. At least now Susan wouldn't have to pretend to be asleep herself.

She gazed out the window. The bus was riding up into the raw, primitive badlands of North Dakota. The steeply sloping rocks and the array of colors were unlike anything Susan had ever seen. But she couldn't enjoy them. Lisa shifted restlessly, perhaps sensing her seatmate was awake, and Susan froze, not wanting to wake her. Then Lisa's head fell onto Susan's shoulder and rested there.

This was torture. It got even worse when the thirty elderly ladies sang *"A Hundred Bottles of Beer on the Wall"* for the next half hour.

When they were down to four bottles of beer, the bus crested a rocky hill. Outside the window, Susan saw three rows of twenty-foot-high barbed wire. Behind them was a complex of squat, windowless, concrete buildings, accompanied by several tall watchtowers. In the nearest tower, a man in a gray uniform had his rifle laid out in front of him in the turret.

The bus came to a driveway with a brown metal sign: "Hodge Hills Federal Penitentiary." *This is where I'm coming tomorrow,* Susan thought. *Somewhere inside one of these buildings, Curt Jansen is counting down the hours.*

Just at that moment, she felt the pressure on her shoulder lighten as Lisa woke up and lifted her head.

Susan watched Lisa gazing out the window at the prison. A tear formed in Lisa's right eye and slid down her cheek.

Susan was relieved when the bus drove on and left the prison in the distance, and Lisa dried her eye. "So who's getting married?" Lisa asked.

Susan blanked for a second, then remembered her lie. Once again she had an impulse to tell Lisa everything, but repressed it. "My cousin," she said.

"Oh, what's his or her name?"

"Molly," Susan said, and changed the subject, asking Lisa questions about herself. She learned that Lisa taught fourth grade in western Pennsylvania and liked to bake gingerbread cookies for her class. She was divorced with two grown daughters in California.

Susan hoped Lisa would forgive her tomorrow for lying. *If I save her brother, she'll definitely forgive me.*

As they rode past a couple oil derricks into the town of Hodge Hills, population 7,362 according to the road sign, Lisa started talking about the execution again. Her two girls barely knew their Uncle Curt. They'd only visited him in prison once, and it upset them so much she never brought them again. They offered to come to the execution to support her, but she said no.

"I *have* to come," Lisa said. "I don't have a choice. But there's no reason they should be traumatized for the rest of their lives by the sight of Curt dying."

Susan thought about how eager she'd been to see him die, how hard she'd pushed the judge to give him the death penalty.

The bus went over the Sasquit River, which was more of a stream, and arrived at Main Street. Hodge Hills seemed a little better off than Luzerne, maybe because of prison jobs, or the oil. The trailers they passed looked mostly well kept. There was a cheerful-looking tattoo parlor called Loved N Hated and a couple of Chinese restaurants. They stopped in front of a bus station that was painted bright blue and looked like an old '50s diner.

Susan and Lisa got out along with several other passengers. As they took their suitcases from the luggage compartment, Susan looked around and wondered again where she would stay tonight.

"Is your cousin picking you up?" Lisa asked.

"Yeah, she's always late, I'm sure she'll be here soon."

Lisa pulled down the hood of her parka against the wind. "I guess I'll hit the hotel and see if they let me in before check-in. I got a nice rate with Triple A."

Susan needed to be rid of Lisa so she could get to work finding Agent Pappas already. "Good luck," she said.

But Lisa didn't leave; she kept on talking. Maybe she wasn't ready to be alone yet. "I get a contact visit with Curt tomorrow. It's been years since I've hugged him."

Susan just nodded.

"They don't let you bring in homemade cookies, but I got him a box of really good chocolate macadamia cookies made in Hawaii."

Susan couldn't take any more. She put her hand on Lisa's shoulder and said, "I know this sounds weird, but if there's anything I can do to help you and your brother, I'll do it."

Lisa looked at her. "Unless you can get a pardon from the president, forget about it."

A rusty gray cab came around the corner and Lisa hailed it. "It's just a half-mile to the motel, but I'm gonna treat myself. You sure you don't want a lift somewhere?"

"I'm good. Take care."

"Thanks. You're a sweetheart."

Lisa hugged Susan. Then she got in the cab and drove off, waving goodbye through the window.

Susan took a deep breath, relieved to finally be alone. She brought out her phone and the worn piece of paper from her back pocket. Blowing hot air onto her fingers to warm them, she made a call.

The phone rang twice and then a woman with a cheerful, young-sounding voice picked up. "Hi, this is Public Relations. May I help you?"

"Yes. Is this . . ." They had spoken on the phone before, but she'd forgotten the woman's name, so she checked her paper. "Pam Arnold?"

"Yes, it is. How can I help you?"

"This is Susan Lentigo."

"Ms. Lentigo!" Pam said joyfully, as if Susan were a long-lost pal. "I'm so glad you called. Where are you?"

"I just got into Hodge Hills."

"Terrific. I hope you had a nice trip?"

"Yes, I did, thanks." She was about to say more when Pam—Susan pictured her in her late twenties, bubbly, a little plump—broke in.

"Ms. Lentigo, I want you to know. Tomorrow is a big day for all of us. It always feels extra special to send a child killer on his way."

Susan shut her eyes, feeling a headache coming. "I wanted to ask you something—"

"Just so you know, everything is going nice and smooth."

"I'm sure it is—"

"We got the Pavulon shipped in this morning. That's the most effective drug on the market—it causes muscle paralysis and respiratory arrest. So now we're all locked and loaded."

Susan rubbed her forehead, pained. No human being should be allowed to be as chipper as this Pam Arnold person. "Who else is coming to see the execution?"

"Well, for the condemned man it's just his sister. And the chaplain, of course. But for you? You'll have lots of company in *your* viewing room. I'll be there, along with the warden, two ADAs, *and,* there's a special guest. You'll never guess who it is."

"Robert Pappas?"

"Oh my goodness! You smashed it right on the nose!"

Susan said, "I'd like to thank him for coming. Do you have his cell phone number?"

For the first time, Pam's relentless effervescence fizzed out. "I'm sorry, I'm not really allowed to give that out."

Shit, now what do I do? Susan thought. *Hunt for him in all the motels? I don't have time. Curt Jansen gets executed tomorrow!*

Trying to sound casual, she said, "I just want to thank him for everything he's done for me."

She pulled at her hair, waiting for Pam to respond. The seconds went by. Finally she heard a loud theatrical sigh over the phone, and Pam said, "Well, seeing as it's you, I'm sure he won't mind. 518-403-3653."

"Thank you so much," Susan said, writing it down.

Pam's bubbliness returned. "Let me know when you're coming tomorrow. I'll meet you on the front steps of the admin building, so you can talk to the media."

"Sure." Susan just wanted to get off the phone.

"There's always lots of TV reporters at an execution, especially for a really horrible crime like this one. You'll be the star tomorrow."

That was the absolute last thing Susan was interested in. "Okay. Thanks."

She hit the *off* button and shut her phone. Then she picked up her suitcase and turned around.

Danny was standing right there.

CHAPTER THIRTY-TWO

Susan gasped, too terrified to scream.

Danny said, "Hi, Susan."

She got a sudden fear he'd kill her. But they were on a main street in the middle of the day with a lot of people around.

Maybe he'd grab the necklace and run off. Her coat was loose so she couldn't feel the necklace against her body, but it was in there, in her inside pocket. *What if he reaches in and snatches it?*

But how would he know it was there? Maybe he'd think it was in her suitcase—

"You okay?" he asked with a smile. "I didn't mean to scare you."

Was that an amused smile or was he angry underneath it? His eyes were shiny, but she couldn't tell what they were saying. She let go of the suitcase and buttoned her coat up tight, then got scared he'd guess from that where the necklace was.

"What are you doing here?" she said.

Danny lifted his shoulders. "Thought you might be on that bus. Figured I'd offer you a ride."

Was he making fun of her? He held up his hands in apology. "Sorry, I shouldn't mess with you." He paused. "Even if you did break into my daughter's bedroom and steal her necklace."

He smiled again. She blinked, even more confused. She couldn't read him. Maybe she never could. Behind him the bus pulled away. The freezing wind was picking up and driving people inside, and she realized the street was growing deserted. She took a step back from him.

His smile disappeared and his eyes aimed at hers like lasers. "Susan, what on earth were you thinking? You scared the shit out of me. I thought you were a fucking pedophile trying to kidnap Emily, just like Curt Jansen—" He stopped and shook his head, horrified. "For God's sake, I could've killed you. I was *shooting* at you. How could I ever have lived with that?"

"I'm sorry," Susan said, and then thought: *Why am I apologizing? How do I know he's telling the truth? Maybe he saw it was me and shot at me on purpose!*

"Why'd you do it? Did you think that was *Amy's necklace?*" His eyes widened in disbelief. "Do you think I had something to do with her death?"

She froze, unable to speak. His hands came away from his sides and his fingers stretched out like he was about to grab her and shake her. "Answer me, Susan!"

The nearest pedestrian was a woman in a Post Office uniform carrying a satchel, a full block away and headed in the other direction. Susan took another step back and felt the heel of her boot almost coming off the sidewalk. Her leg wobbled.

But then she thought, *Amy would want me to be strong.* She steadied herself and stared directly at Danny's face. "Where did you get that necklace?"

He glared at her, but took a breath to control himself and dropped his hands. "I made it."

Now Susan was the one giving a disbelieving look. "You *made* it?"

"*Yes,*" Danny snapped. "It's not so hard, you just put beads together on a string."

"But where did you find the beads? They were the exact same as Amy's."

"How can you even ask me these questions? For God's sake, look at me." He held his arms up, as if submitting himself to being searched. "I'm Danny. Your childhood sweetheart. Regular guy. You've known me most of your life!"

He's not answering me. She stood firm, her hands balling into fists. "You have to admit it's weird. Finding the exact same beads twenty years later?"

"Yeah, well there's this thing called the internet, okay? You google 'dolphin bead' and you find ten thousand different kinds. And if they don't have the right one, you go on eBay and Etsy."

Maybe he was right; she had googled "duck tea cosy" once and been amazed at all the different varieties. But... "But why would you do it?"

Danny shook his head again. "*Why?*"

"I mean, you wanted to forget Amy. Why would you—"

"*I never forgot Amy,*" Danny said. "How could I? You know how much I loved our baby." He stopped and swallowed, like he was trying to pull himself together. "I named my daughter Emily 'cause it sounded like Amy. And now she's almost seven, and she reminds me so much of our girl... just before she died. Every time I look at Emily ..." His voice caught. "I wanted to honor Amy's memory somehow. So I got that old photograph of her wearing the necklace and I spent two months looking for beads that were just like it. And then I gave the necklace to Emily."

Susan thought, *That's gotta be bullshit.*

But then she looked at Danny, at the pain in his eyes, the mute appeal in his sad, drooping lips, and thought: *Maybe the man I married, the father of my child, isn't a rapist and killer after all.*

She felt a sudden warmth flooding through her.

Maybe I don't have to feel so guilty.

But as much as she wanted to believe him . . . "Emily said you found it."

"Yeah, I told her that 'cause I didn't want her to know she had a half-sister who got murdered. Don't you think that's too scary for a little kid?"

Susan could imagine feeling the same way if she was Emily's mom. "But why did you tell her you found it? Why not just say you made it for her as a gift?"

"'Cause I didn't want to have to answer a million questions about why I chose which beads." He pulled his dark leather coat tighter against the wind. "Look, Susan, I'll answer any questions you have, but honestly . . ." His mouth opened wide, then shut and opened again before he spoke, like he was struggling to form words. "How can you think I would . . . do all those horrible things to our daughter? That's insane."

He's right, Susan thought suddenly. *I'm insane.*

I'm fucking insane. This whole thing is just . . .

She needed to apologize to Danny for being such an idiot. She should reach into her pocket and give him that necklace right now.

She said, "Danny . . ."

He shook his head, exasperated. He clearly didn't realize she was about to give in, and his jaw jutted out and his eyes hardened. "What?"

She looked at his angry face and thought: *But what if I'm not insane?*

"I need to go," she said. She grabbed her suitcase and started off down the sidewalk.

He followed her. "What are you gonna do with the necklace?"

His voice had gotten cold and hard. Lunchtime must be over, because now the street was empty for two blocks in each direction. Susan got hit by a fresh wave of fear, her breathing turning fast and shallow. "I'm sorry, I really need to go."

He stayed right beside her. "You're not gonna give it to the police, are you?"

Was she right to be scared? "Please, quit following me."

"Stop being such a drama queen."

She sped up. "I'm not kidding. You better leave right now or I'll scream." But would anyone hear her? There was a bank on the far corner. She'd leave her suitcase behind and run toward there—

Danny put up his hands. "Hey, I'm just trying to keep you from making a fool of yourself. That's the whole reason I came out here."

Now Susan's fear gave way to rage. *He must think I'm stupid, telling me such a bald-faced lie.* She stopped hurrying away and faced him dead on. "That's total bullshit."

"What's bullshit?"

"You don't give a fuck if I make a fool of myself. I don't know the reason you came here, but that's not it."

Danny blinked, and his eyes opened wide. "Susan . . . don't you understand?" His lips trembled. "I never stopped caring about you."

A jolt of long-forgotten emotion rushed through her. She tried to shut it down, but he kept talking in that same gentle voice. "After everything we went through together, how could I not have feelings for you?" He touched his chest. "They're still here."

Susan's mouth opened. His eyes, his mouth, the lines on his face, they all looked hurt, and vulnerable. She so wanted to believe him.

"You were right," he said softly, "what you said to me in Tamarack. I need closure on Amy—and on you too. And I won't get it sitting in my damn office."

This was what Susan had hoped for. She wanted to fall into his arms.

"Susan, you were my first love. I've never felt about anybody the way I felt about you."

Her lips parted. She was breathing so deeply now it was making her shoulders heave. It was like something was melting inside her that had been frozen for twenty years.

He put out his hand and touched her hair. It felt like he was touching her heart. "Susan," he said, and then, tears in his eyes, he hugged her.

She started to yield to him and return the hug.

But then she remembered the necklace in that inside pocket. She went rigid. *What if Danny feels it through my coat? He might take it!* She held her body away from his and broke off the embrace.

Up close, she saw his lips tighten with irritation and his eyes go half-shut. That look seemed familiar, and then she remembered where she'd seen it before. He would look that way when something at work had aggravated him, like when a sale fell through.

That's what's going on in his head, Susan thought. *I'm a sale that just fell through.*

Now he had a look of concern on his face as he asked, "Are you okay?"

But she could see through it now. This whole "I never stopped caring about you" routine was bogus.

Wasn't it?

And what about everything else he said?

Is he really a killer?

I need to find Agent Pappas.

She said, "I'll see you later."

Danny nodded, disappointed, and wiped his eyes. Then he looked down at her suitcase. "Is it my imagination, or did we buy that in Albany about twenty-five years ago?"

Susan forced a smile. She didn't want to antagonize him even more, though why she cared about that she didn't know. "It's lasted pretty well."

Danny smiled back. She watched him. Much as she was desperate to leave, she was still having trouble breaking away. She wished she could rip open his heart and find out what was inside.

He said, "Listen, before you go, how do I get on the list to view the execution? I just got in this morning, and I wasn't sure who to call."

Why ask her this? Maybe he was still hoping she would promise not to go to the police and interfere with the execution.

He was still selling.

She didn't want to argue anymore; she needed to get out of here already and escape his spell. So she just said, "You can call the prison's public relations office. The woman's name is Pam Arnold. She's very"—Susan rolled her eyes—"enthusiastic."

Danny pointed toward Susan's face and grinned. "I remember that look."

Again warmth flooded through her, taking her by surprise. That grin . . .

Danny scoring the winning touchdown, then running up to the stands and giving her the game ball, flashing her that same grin with the whole school watching . . .

It's the moment they become an official couple.

For the next nineteen years.

"Sure you don't want a ride?" he asked. "That's my rental right there." He took out his key fob and beeped a car parked nearby at the curb. It was a Chevy Malibu and reminded her of Danny's parents' Malibu. When she and Danny first went out, they spent a lot of time in the back seat of that car.

Don't think about that. Don't get sidetracked.

"I'm sure. But thanks for coming," she said, and almost meant it for a moment.

He put out his hand and touched her. Once again, she felt that jolt. "Susan, I have to tell you something. I didn't come here only because I wanted closure."

She tensed. What was he about to confess to?

"I've tried so hard to protect my family from all this," Danny said. "I didn't even tell my children where I was going this week. But if you go to the cops with this crazy thing, it'll go public. Think what that'll do to my kids. All their classmates and friends will start teasing them and whispering about them and making fun of them behind their backs. Emily's life will be shattered. She's a very sensitive girl."

Susan felt bad for a moment. But then she studied his eyes, the way they flickered and narrowed a little, and felt like there was something else going on behind there. She believed she finally understood why he had come to North Dakota.

Danny wasn't really afraid about how this would affect his family. Well, maybe he was. But mainly he was scared she'd hurt his reputation—and his real estate sales.

Even if he was innocent, he'd be terrified of that.

And if he's guilty . . .

She said, "Danny, I'll for sure keep that in mind, okay? I promise." She gave him a sweet-little-girl look with her face tilted down and her lips pouting slightly, and she instantly remembered this look as something she had used to defuse his anger back when they were married.

A look of frustration crossed his face, and she sensed he was searching for one more way to sell her. But at last he gave her an accepting nod, as if he realized he'd gotten all he could right now. "Okay. Take care of yourself, Susan."

He got in his car and drove off with a wave. She waved back, her shoulders heaving with relief. Then she took out her phone and piece of paper and made a call.

A man with a deep voice picked up on the other end after the first ring. "Hello?"

Her breathing sped up. "Hi, is this Agent Pappas?"

"Yes. Who's calling, please?"

"Susan Lentigo."

There was a brief pause, then Agent Pappas said, "Ms. Lentigo. Where are you?"

"I'm in Hodge Hills. How about you?"

"I'm here too. You want to get together?"

She sure did.

CHAPTER THIRTY-THREE

Susan walked into the bathroom of a Sunoco station, where she took off her baseball cap and took another shot at combing her knotted hair. She would have taken off her coat, sweater, and shirt and washed under her arms again, but she didn't want to be late to meet Agent Pappas.

She came out of the bathroom and headed for the motel five blocks away where Agent Pappas was staying. Actually, it was called a hotel— "Econo Lodge Hotel." She had never understood the difference between hotels and motels.

The Econo Lodge was pretty ugly, five stories of brown concrete with tiny windows. But there weren't a lot of other places for people to stay in this town.

As she rolled her suitcase up the driveway, she saw the front door open and a man come out. It was Agent Pappas. He gave her a wave hello and walked quickly toward her.

His hair had turned gray and his hairline was receding, and as they got closer, she could see the age on his face. Like her, he wore glasses now. But he still had the same erect posture she remembered and the same softness in his eyes. Looking at him, she could almost feel the hugs he gave her in the courtroom twenty years ago.

But they were on the same side then. How would he treat her now when she basically accused him of fucking up, like Kyra had put it?

"Hi Susan, it's great to see you," he said.

"It's great to see you too, Agent Pappas."

They looked at each other. Susan felt like they were old warriors who had fought together in a long-ago war. She didn't know whether to shake hands or hug, and it looked like he didn't either. After a moment they shook hands. Maybe it was because Susan felt uncomfortable, knowing what lay ahead of them.

"I'm just plain Robert now. Retired a year ago."

She didn't want to let him know yet that she had already found this out, and she'd been thinking about him for two days. "Congratulations."

He gave a self-deprecatory smile. "Yeah, it's a mixed blessing. Shall we have coffee in the hotel?"

"Sure." Despite everything else on her mind, she was hoping she'd get more than coffee out of this. A burger and Coke would go down real smooth right about now.

Agent Pappas—Robert—took her suitcase and said, "Let me get that for you." He carried it toward the hotel, didn't even bother rolling it. *In his sixties but still strong,* she thought. Good—she needed that.

"Where are you staying?" he asked.

"I'll figure that out later," she said, not wanting to tell him she was dead broke.

He turned somber. "I want you to know, I've never forgotten about your daughter. I think about her more than anyone else it's ever been my honor to find justice for."

She hated what she was going to have to say to him in a little while. She felt ungrateful. "I truly appreciate that."

He held the door open and they headed inside. She could see the coffee shop on the other end of the lobby, could even smell the hamburgers cooking.

"I live near my daughter and grandkids now. My wife died a couple years ago."

"I'm sorry."

He nodded. "Anyway, they live out in the country near the Vermont border. It's just a few miles up the river from where Amy was found."

Suddenly Susan saw a woman with curly hair at the concierge desk—Lisa. *What if she turns around and sees me with the FBI agent who busted her brother? She'll figure out who I am!* "Oh God," Susan said.

Not hearing her, or not understanding her, Robert continued, "So every time I drive up there—"

"We have to get out of here."

Susan turned and hurried back out the door. Robert followed, bewildered, carrying her suitcase.

Once outside she walked fast, making it halfway to the street before she let Robert catch up to her. "What's going on?" he asked.

"We can't eat there."

His forehead crinkled with confusion, then cleared up as though he finally understood. "You're concerned about the media, aren't you? There's definitely a lot of reporters staying there."

"It's not that," Susan said, as they kept walking away from the hotel. "The woman at the desk, I met her on the bus. She's Curt Jansen's sister."

"Oh shit," he said. "Pardon my language. That must have been unpleasant. How did she treat you?"

"I didn't tell her who I was."

She was embarrassed by her cowardice, but Robert nodded like she'd done the right thing. "Good thinking. I remember her. She was in total denial about her brother being a killer. Pretty standard reaction for families."

Susan took a deep breath. "Agent Pap—Robert—we need to talk."

"Sure, how about this pizza joint right here?"

She let her dreams of a hamburger die. She wasn't about to get picky right now. "Sure, that sounds great."

They walked in and ordered two pepperoni pizza slices apiece from a friendly young man in his early twenties. Robert offered to pay and Susan didn't protest.

"You here for the execution?" the young man asked.

"Yes, we are," Robert said.

"Well, have a nice time."

"Thank you."

Susan and Robert carried their slices and diet Cokes to a booth in the back of the pizzeria. There were couples on either side of them. As they slid into their seats, Robert asked, "So what did you want to talk about?"

How to begin? She looked into his brown eyes and asked, "Why did Amy's murder stick with you all these years? Were you ever afraid that maybe we got it wrong?"

He frowned, puzzled. "Got what wrong? Who killed your daughter?"

"Yeah."

"No, of course not. But my two girls were about the same age as Amy. And seeing you in that courtroom every day . . ."

Susan bit her lip. *Here goes.* "I've been wondering if Curt Jansen is really guilty."

Robert stared at her. "Susan, are you shitting me? Curt Jansen confessed."

"Could you tell me about the confession?"

She sensed he was trying to be sympathetic, but he was pissed off. "What's there to tell? You know what he said. You read the transcript."

The four pizza slices sat between them, uneaten. "Robert, I am so grateful for everything you've done for my family. But I gotta ask: since you felt so deeply about Amy's murder—"

He gave her an incredulous look. "Did I beat a confession out of him?"

She kept going, determined. "Well, yeah. Or at least—"

"No fucking way. I would never do something like that. Is that what the sister told you?"

"You questioned him for ten hours without a break."

"I didn't do a single damn thing out of the ordinary. It was just good solid interrogation technique."

Despite his anger, Susan forced herself to press on without apologies. "You told him you'd found his fingerprints."

"It's perfectly legal to lie during an interrogation."

"But I mean, people do make fake confessions, right?"

Robert picked up his fork. "All I said to him was, if he told us the truth, we'd give him a break. And let me tell *you* something." He pointed his fork at her. "After that man confessed, he slept like a baby. Put his head right down on the table and passed out. 'Cause that's what guilty people do. Soon as they give it up, their whole body relaxes. Curt Jansen killed your daughter. There's not a single doubt in my mind. In my twenty-five years with the FBI, I never once arrested a man I thought might be innocent."

Susan held up her hands placatingly. "I understand you being pissed off at me—"

"I'm not," he said, though he obviously was. "I just don't want you to have some crazy delusion that—"

She took the baggie with the necklace out of her coat pocket. She set it on the table next to the pizza slices.

He stopped dead. She could tell he recognized the necklace immediately.

He stared at it. Then he touched the necklace through the plastic, as if proving to himself it was real. Neither of them said anything for about ten seconds.

Then he asked, "Where the hell did you get this?"

"I made a surprise visit to my ex-husband in western New York. He has a new six-year-old daughter now, Emily. She was wearing this necklace."

She took the photo of Amy out of her wallet and held it up. She named the beads on Amy's necklace, in order. "Purple dolphin, pink duck, yellow, green, an orange cat . . ."

He took the photo from her, holding it next to Emily's necklace and comparing the two.

"Same pattern in both," Susan said.

Robert ran his hand through his hair, then looked up at her. "Maybe your ex-husband had a new one made."

"That's what he said. But it's not what Emily told me. She said, 'My daddy found it.'"

Robert's eyes opened wide. "You're shitting me."

"Her exact words. I'm scared for her."

Robert put the photo down and stood up. He looked like he wanted to run away. But his eyes kept getting pulled back to that necklace sitting on the table.

He said, "Do you have any other reason to suspect him, or just this?"

Susan looked down. Shame washed through her, but she had to overcome it. She had to convince Robert.

She had to tell him—and herself—the truth.

"There's so many things about Danny I tried to ignore all these years. But now they're coming back to me."

Robert sat back down. "What kinds of things?"

"He had a terrible temper." She looked up at Robert with appeal in her eyes. "He'd scream at me for no reason. If I overcooked his eggs."

Robert gave her a frown. "That doesn't exactly make him a child rapist and murderer."

Before she even knew what she was saying, she said, "He looked up her dress."

Robert's mouth fell open. Susan felt horrible she'd never told this before to anybody, not even the cops who investigated Amy's murder. "I wanted to believe I imagined it. So I told myself I never really saw it. I convinced myself."

She felt tears starting up but kept going. "When we made love, he'd want me to wear these little-girl outfits. And talk really cutesy."

Lying in bed in that stupid schoolgirl uniform. Danny on top of her pulling up the pink plaid skirt. Susan looking away, waiting for it to be over . . .

God, it was so sick! But she'd tell Robert everything, goddamn it, she'd spare herself nothing.

She wiped her eyes with her hand and said, "And the way he acted toward Amy sometimes. Like when she was taking a bath . . ."

Amy at age five, taking a bubble bath. Danny sits in a chair by the tub, rubbing her little tush with a washrag. Susan watches from the doorway, wondering if this is okay.

"I thought I was just being stupid. That I should be happy Danny and Amy were so close . . ."

She couldn't hold it back anymore and started to sob. Through her tears she looked at Robert. "I'm so ashamed—"

But he wasn't looking at her; he was staring at something behind her. "Shh!"

"What?" she said, bewildered. She was about to turn and look at whatever had drawn his eyes, but then he startled her by sweeping the baggie with the necklace off the table and out of sight. It was in his lap now, she thought. Why had he—

"Agent Pappas," she heard Danny say. He was walking up from behind her and coming to their table.

Robert didn't stand up to greet him, no doubt because of the necklace in his lap. He looked up at Danny with a welcoming smile. "Mr. Lentigo."

The men shook hands. Robert was acting so friendly to Danny. Did that mean he didn't believe her story?

But he has to believe it.

Robert said, "It's great to see you again." He'd used those exact same words with her, and she wondered if she could really trust this man. She saw his right arm move and sensed he was putting the necklace away inside one of his pants pockets. *He wouldn't steal it from me, would he? That's crazy thinking, isn't it?*

Danny said, "Agent Pappas, thank you so much for coming. It means the world to us, doesn't it, Susan?"

Us? Susan thought. But she said, "Yes, it does." Still trying to figure out what was going on between the three of them, she wiped her tears with her napkin.

Danny said sympathetically, "You want another napkin?"

"No thanks," she said, her voice tight.

Danny turned to Robert. "Susan's been pretty emotional lately. Not that I blame her, with the execution tomorrow."

He's telling Robert I'm a stupid hormonal woman and he shouldn't take me seriously. She watched Robert, willing him to resist Danny. But Robert just nodded pleasantly and said, "Susan was telling me you live in western New York now."

Danny sat down next to Susan in the booth, as if Robert had invited him. She felt trapped. She smelled Danny's aftershave—God, it smelled like the same kind she and Amy had bought him!—and wanted to scream.

Danny said, "Yeah, I moved a few hours from Lake Luzerne. I had to get away."

Robert rubbed his chin thoughtfully. "I can understand that. Get a whole new life, huh?"

Susan sensed he was trying to figure Danny out. Danny sensed it too. He looked straight at Robert's eyes. "So what else have you and Susan been talking about?"

"Different things," Robert said.

Danny scrutinized Robert for a couple moments, then gave a huge sigh and rolled his eyes. "Oh God, she told you, didn't she? She told you her crazy theory."

Susan held her breath. Robert said, "Yes, she told me."

Danny slapped his hand on the table. "I can't believe this crap. Jansen confessed. He confessed to *you*."

Robert nodded again. "It's true."

His face was so bland. Susan couldn't tell whose side he was on. Were FBI agents trained to act like this?

She felt like she should say something, but didn't know what. Danny said, "You've got to convince her to stop this nonsense."

Robert cocked his head, studying Danny. "Why?"

"What do you mean, *why*? That monster killed my daughter! I want him to die and I want it to be over." Danny turned to Susan. "Haven't we suffered enough?"

"How did you make that necklace anyway?" Robert asked casually, like it was just something he was kind of curious about, not something of earth-shattering importance.

Relief poured through Susan as she realized at last that Robert really was taking her seriously.

Danny realized it too. "Oh for chrissake," he said. "Get on the internet. You'll be able to find the same beads yourself."

"Is that the kind of thing you do?" Robert asked. "Have you ever made anything crafty before?"

"None of your damn business," Danny snapped.

Susan hoped that Danny losing his temper made him seem more suspicious to Robert. But Robert's face still gave nothing away. He nodded solemnly, then picked up his two mostly uneaten slices of pizza and stood up. He said to Danny, "If you'll excuse me, I need to go take care of some things. I'll see you tomorrow."

Susan stood too, eager to get away from Danny. But he said, "Look, Agent Pappas," and started to get up—

Robert put a hand on Danny's shoulder. It was a seemingly friendly hand, but it kept Danny stuck to his seat. "No, you just got here. You should stay and try the pepperoni."

Then he leaned down and spoke quietly into Danny's ear. "It's delicious."

Susan was startled by the menace Robert had managed to put into those two words. She could see Danny was taken aback too.

But then he recovered. He pointed his finger at Robert's head.

"You don't get it," Danny said. "Susan is mentally ill. I love her, but she's been like that for twenty years. If she fools you into believing her delusions, when you *know* what happened to Amy, then you're an idiot. You deserve everything that happens to you."

Robert gave Danny a nod and walked out.

Susan started to follow him, then turned and took one last look at Danny. The anger on his face softened to compassion. "Susan, you need help. You gotta start therapy or something. If Prozac didn't help, try something else."

Danny always knew how to throw her off balance. Her mouth opened, but no words came out, and then she turned and left.

She joined Robert on the sidewalk. As they headed down the street, he said, "If I didn't know better, I'd say that guy is scared shitless."

Susan thought Robert was on her side now—but how far would he go to help her? She said, "That's why he came—he's trying to stop me."

The walk light turned red just when they got to the corner. Robert said, "But we still don't know, what's he scared of? Did he really . . . kill Amy?" Susan noticed he had trouble saying that out loud, just like she did. "Maybe he's just afraid the real killer will get another trial and the execution will be postponed. And Danny will have to deal will all these media people falsely accusing him of murder."

The light turned green again and they started walking. What if Robert backed down and refused to get involved? What would she do then?

"You have to help me," she said. "They're killing a man who may be innocent. And I'm afraid Danny will do the same thing to Emily that he did to Amy."

Robert shook his head. There was a bewildered anger in his eyes. "Curt Jansen was a fucking scumbag. And he *told* me he did it. Right to my face. He said he raped your daughter."

Susan looked closely at him. "But you're not sure anymore."

He didn't speak for a moment. She continued, "And you have the evidence right there in your pocket."

Robert breathed out heavily and his jaw tightened. Finally he said, "Well, let's go see if you're right." He checked his watch. "If we leave now, we can make it to Williston by four."

Susan frowned, confused. "What's in Williston?"

"Hopefully," Robert said, "that's where we'll learn the truth."

CHAPTER THIRTY-FOUR

<small>Friday, December 3, Present Day</small>

Five minutes later, Susan was riding out of town in Robert's rented gray compact. He said, "I don't know when they close for the weekend. You okay if I go eighty?"

"No problem," Susan said. They were headed toward the FBI's North Dakota field office in Williston, a hundred forty miles away.

"If the cops stop us, I'll flash my old FBI badge." Robert gave her a mischievous grin. "I told them I lost it, so I still have it."

Susan said, "I don't know how to thank you."

"Hey, I'm doing this for me too. You think I want to be responsible for killing an innocent man?" He added, "If that's what he is."

They climbed up into the rocky hills, practically the only ones on the road. The car was warm, and Susan realized she felt comfortable with Robert driving. Maybe her feelings about Danny were a mess, but she'd read Robert right: he was a kind person. She tried to remember the last time she had been alone in a car with a man. Well, not including the choir director of her church—

"So what have you been up to for the past twenty years?" Robert asked.

She gave a nervous laugh. "Kind of a big question."

"You still live in Lake Luzerne?"

"Yeah. Same house, even."

Robert didn't say anything, and Susan realized how sad that must sound. She said defensively, "I got it in the divorce and it's paid off. It would be expensive to move."

"Sure. So are you working or . . ."

"Yup, I'm still at Molly's Diner. She died though. Her daughter Tina owns it now."

"Wow, you really are a Steady Eddie."

She looked at him, confused.

"Sorry. When I was a kid, that's what we called people who were, you know, steady."

She nodded ruefully. "You mean boring."

"No, reliable. If you were boring, you never would've stolen that necklace."

He snuck a glance at her, and she figured out what he was up to. She raised an eyebrow at him. "Are you trying to ask me something?"

He smiled. "Fine, I'll just be direct. How'd you get the necklace, did you steal it?"

"Yup."

He laughed at the simplicity of her answer. She looked over at him, liking that she had made him laugh.

He asked, "How'd you steal it?"

"You gonna arrest me?"

"Only if you had to kill somebody to do it."

"Didn't kill him. Did squirt homemade pepper spray in his face though."

Robert looked over at her to see if she was kidding. "Homemade pepper spray?"

"My mom's special recipe. Rubbing alcohol and cayenne pepper."

"Okay, you *have* to tell me this story."

She did, and made him laugh a couple more times. Maybe she wasn't quite as boring as she thought.

She was grateful he wasn't making her talk more about Danny. The necklace would do the talking.

The FBI office in Williston was a two-story brick building, located next to a shopping mall a mile outside town. They made it there at 4:05. As they got out of the car, Robert said, "I hope these guys don't leave early on Fridays."

They went inside and went up to the front desk. The receptionist was a man in his thirties who looked Native American and wore his hair in a long braid. Susan was surprised a guy with that kind of hair would work for the FBI, but maybe they had different rules up here in North Dakota.

"Good afternoon," Robert said briskly. He held open his old FBI badge. "I'm retired Special Agent Robert Pappas from the New York Division. I need to speak to the director of this office."

The receptionist checked the badge, then looked Robert and Susan over. He didn't seem impressed. "Do you have an appointment?"

"No. But I have evidence that the man who's scheduled to be executed tomorrow at Hodge Hills may not be guilty."

The receptionist blinked, scratched his unshaven cheek, and twenty minutes later Susan and Robert were sitting in an upstairs conference room across the table from Stan Williams, Director of the North Dakota Division of the FBI, along with three special agents in their thirties and forties. Susan had been told their names, but she'd forgotten them. Director Williams was clearly the man they had to impress.

"So what do you got?" Williams said in a tired voice, like he was eager to get to his weekend already.

Susan and Robert launched into their story for the next ten minutes, him talking about the original case and her talking about everything she'd discovered and remembered in the past several days. Williams held an unlit pipe in his hand. From time to time he'd fiddle with it, or smell it, or tap it against the table. His lips were curled in a sardonic expression that barely changed even when Robert dramatically produced the baggie with the necklace and laid it on the table in front of him.

The three special agents were pretty stone-faced too, but Susan got the feeling they were intrigued yet hiding it in case their boss felt differently. She hoped that Williams's cynical look was just a mask and he was intrigued too.

Robert finished with, "So as you can see, we need you to order immediate DNA testing on this necklace."

Williams nodded thoughtfully—a good sign, she felt—and tapped his pipe on the table twice.

"Do you know the expression *folie à deux*?" he said.

Robert attempted a little levity. "Sorry, my French is a bit rusty."

"It means, a folly shared by two people." He pointed his pipe at Robert and Susan, making clear who those two people were. "This guy was tried and convicted. He filed about . . ." Williams checked a printout on the table in front of him. "*Fifteen* appeals over a period of twenty years, and every single one of them was shot down."

"But now we have new evidence that may be exculpatory," Robert said.

Williams rolled his eyes. "Right. A stolen necklace."

Susan watched Robert as he sat up even straighter, holding his ground. "That doesn't matter. As long as it wasn't stolen by a cop during the course of an investigation, it's admissible."

Williams waved his pipe dismissively at Susan. "We'd have to take her word on where she got it from."

Susan said, "The individual I stole it with would back me up."

"You do realize you'd be opening yourself up to criminal prosecution."

"Do you think I care about that?"

Robert broke in, "Sir, I'm not saying her ex-husband is definitely guilty, but don't you think this evidence merits looking into?"

Williams regarded Susan, using his free hand, the one that didn't hold the pipe, to stroke his chin. "Why are you doing this? Are you trying to get back at your ex for some reason?"

Susan's jaw dropped. *What an asshole!* "Yeah. He may have killed my daughter."

"Are you still mad at him for divorcing you?" Williams pressed.

Susan was speechless. Robert said, "That's no way to talk to her."

Williams folded his arms. "I'm sorry for this woman's loss, and sorry she got you snookered somehow, but I won't let her wreak havoc on the entire criminal justice system just because—"

Susan stood up, outraged, her chair tumbling to the floor behind her. "I am trying to save an innocent man and protect a six-year-old girl who's in danger."

Williams waved his pipe. "You don't know that—"

She reached out and slapped his pipe away. It fell to the floor. Williams' eyes opened wide, startled, unable to believe somebody would do that to him. Susan could hardly believe it either, but she wasn't about to let this shithead stop her. She leaned her face in so it was only a couple feet from his. "If you don't test this necklace for DNA, immediately, I will stand in front of all the TV cameras at the prison tomorrow and I will say: I'm the victim's mother, and the man who's being executed did not kill my daughter. And I will tell everybody *you're* the man responsible for this sick tragedy. What was your name again—Williams?"

Robert said to Susan, "That's right—Stanley Williams. I know some national reporters you can talk to. This'll be way bigger than just North Dakota."

Williams was furious. "Did you put her up to this? It's unconscionable. It fits the legal definition of blackmail."

"Call it what you want, Mr. Williams," Susan said. "If my ex-husband killed my daughter, he's going to pay for it."

Williams said, "This is preposterous. It would be literally impossible to get that necklace analyzed by tomorrow. We don't even have the victim's DNA to compare it to."

"Yes, we do," Robert said. "It's in the case file."

He held out a thick file folder to Williams. But Williams didn't take it. "Even with that," he said, "it would take weeks to analyze the DNA."

"Not if you send the necklace to the lab in Minneapolis on the very next plane and pay them triple-time to get it done overnight."

Williams snapped, "I'm not letting some retired agent tell me how to do my job."

He went over to where his pipe lay on the floor. But Robert reached down and grabbed it. He took the pipe in both his hands and snapped it in two, splitting the stem from the bowl.

Williams stared at his busted pipe, then at Robert, seething. Robert said, "Williams, don't be a fucking idiot. Think what a hero you'll be, saving an innocent man from execution at the eleventh hour and putting the real killer in prison. Susan and I will sing your praises to the sky, won't we, Susan?"

Susan put her hand to her heart and said to Williams in a high breathy voice, "You're the best, sir."

Williams looked back and forth between the two of them, and his eyes looked lost, like he didn't know which end was up anymore. In that moment, Susan knew they had won.

Finally Williams said, "Whatever. *Fine.*"

Susan said, "Thank you," trying to let Williams lose with grace. Then she sat and listened as Williams and the three special agents, who were still sitting in the room even though they hadn't spoken the entire time, discussed the details of who would travel with the necklace to Minneapolis, and who Williams should contact at the lab.

Five minutes later, Susan and Robert headed down the hallway to the elevator, trying not to exult too loudly in their victory. But as soon as the elevator door closed behind them, leaving them alone, they both broke into smiles. Robert put up his hand and gave her a big high five.

"'You're the best, sir,'" he said, imitating Susan's voice.

She laughed, then asked, "Do you think Williams will get it analyzed properly or will he just pretend?"

"Are you kidding? You think he wants the two of us coming after his ass again?"

Soon they were on the highway riding back to Hodge Hills, still punchy from their success. Again, they seemed to have signed some sort of pact not to talk about Danny or Amy for a while. Robert told her some FBI war stories, like the time he was working undercover and had six months' work go down the drain when his younger daughter called one night and asked, "Daddy, are you still working undercover?" so loud the bad guys heard it. Another time he solved a bank robbery when he noticed on the video that the robber sneezed. They were able to recover his DNA from the window he sneezed on.

"That'll teach him to cover his nose next time," Susan said.

Robert smiled. "In his defense, he was holding a gun at the time."

Then he asked about her life in the past twenty years, and she managed to find her own funny stories to tell. About John Walker, or as everyone called him Walker John, a ninety-year-old customer at the diner who liked to put his bony hand on her elbow and offer her "sexual healing"; about her choir director, who always referred to God as "You Know Who" and never scheduled practices on the 13th of the month because that was unlucky; and of course about Lenora and her complicated love life.

"Your mother is an inspiration," Robert said.

Outside the sky grew dark. Susan began to feel weird about having a good time when a man's life was at stake, and she might be about to discover her ex-husband had killed her daughter.

Next to her, Robert heaved a sigh. She looked at his profile as he drove. She found herself gazing at the lines next to his right eye and remembering when she first met him and was obsessed with his dark irises.

He seemed to be feeling contemplative too, because he said, "Times like now, I kinda miss being an agent." Then his face twisted a little. "Don't miss fuckwads like Williams, though."

Susan looked out the window. In the darkness, she made out an abandoned barn on top of a hill.

She said, "After all this, they better find something on that necklace."

"I've gotten DNA off of objects a lot older than that." He drove around a lumber truck that was doing forty. "I counted six places on the necklace that were likely reservoirs for DNA. In fact, there was material in a crevice under the dolphin's flippers that definitely looked like it could be dried blood."

Susan shook her head and said, "Fuck."

"What's wrong?"

She chewed at her thumbnail. "He was my childhood sweetheart. Now I'm trying to prove he's a psychopath who raped and killed my baby."

Robert nodded. "I'm trying to prove I got a false confession and put an innocent man on death row for twenty years. This was my biggest case, you know. The one I was most proud of."

As they passed a billboard for a restaurant that advertised split pea soup, of all things, Susan said, "I so appreciate you doing this. It took a lot of courage."

Robert looked at her, and something about his look made her skin tingle. "Talk about courage," he said. "For you to do this, you're the bravest person I've ever met."

She looked away, embarrassed.

"Are there any good bars in Hodge Hills?" she asked.

"One," he said.

They headed toward it. When they got there, a country band was playing and the Friday night crowd was already out in force. The place was called The Tipsy Cow and reminded Susan of the Crow Bar back home in Luzerne. A dozen or so people danced while others clapped along to a song about cowboy boots and red skirts that she recognized from the radio.

They made their way to a booth and got the menu. Then she thought of something. "Robert, I feel like I should buy you dinner, because you're doing so much for me—"

"No worries."

"I just feel like I should explain," she said, and went on to tell him the story of how her money was stolen.

"I'm so sorry," he said. "Order double of whatever you want. You deserve it."

"That's why I haven't been able to take a shower all week," she said. "I'm sure you've noticed it, even though you're too nice a guy to say anything."

She listened to herself and thought, *Oh my God, am I flirting?* She thought she'd forgotten how.

Robert smiled and said, "I haven't noticed. But then again, I have a lousy sense of smell."

The waitress came, and Susan ordered the hamburger she'd been craving all day. Robert got a burger too. Then he started tapping his feet to the music and she was afraid he'd ask her to dance. Not only was she rusty at dancing but her leg was feeling a little off. But luckily, he seemed content to talk, or listen to the music when it got too loud for that.

The burgers came and she dived right into hers, eating it in about eight bites. It was amazing. "This is absolutely the best hamburger I've ever had," she said.

"It's not half bad," he agreed. "And wait 'til you try the fries."

They each had a beer, and after dinner they ordered more. The Tipsy Cow didn't mess around; their beers came in big thick mugs with good heads of foam.

Susan said, "I just want to sit here and drink in this bar for the rest of my life."

Robert lifted his mug and toasted her. "To justice. However delayed."

They clinked glasses and were about to drink when Susan saw Lisa Jansen staring at them from across the bar. Susan froze, drink in hand, as Lisa stormed up.

"You fucking bitch," she said to Susan.

CHAPTER THIRTY-FIVE

SUSAN AND ROBERT put down their drinks, startled.

Lisa stood over Susan. "The second I saw you with this asshole" —she pointed at Pappas—"I figured out who you really are. Why did you lie to me?"

Susan's throat tightened and she felt like she couldn't breathe. She wanted to tell Lisa everything. But she couldn't, not yet. What if the necklace came back negative for Amy's DNA? How could she tell Lisa there was a chance her brother might be freed, and then have it not happen? That would be sheer torture for Lisa.

"I'm sorry," Susan mumbled.

Lisa's eyes narrowed with disgust. "*Sorry?* What the hell were you up to yesterday?"

Robert tried to interrupt. "Ms. Jansen—"

Lisa turned on him, furious. "You shut up. You're the scumbag who forced a false confession from my brother." Then she turned back to Susan. "In the coffee shop. Why were you asking me all those questions? It was like you were interrogating me."

Susan shook her head, unable to think of what to say.

"It's because you have doubts about my brother's guilt. Don't you?"

Susan still didn't answer. She wasn't ready. She pictured the whole mess she'd be causing if she said yes right now. Lisa would tell the reporters. She'd tell lawyers. Who knew what would happen then?

She needed solid proof Danny had committed murder before she accused him to the whole world. Because what if he was innocent?

"You have to tell the cops!" Lisa said, pleading now. "Curt is gonna die!"

All around them people were watching. The band was taking a break, so Susan and Lisa were the entertainment now.

"I'm sorry, Lisa," Susan said.

Lisa's eyes bored into her. "You just don't give a shit, do you? Fuck you." She turned to Pappas. "And fuck you too."

With one quick motion she swept their two mugs of beer off the table. They crashed to the floor, glass breaking and beer flying.

Robert jumped up to protect Susan, but Lisa walked away. At the front door of the bar she looked back at them with loathing. Then she stalked out.

Robert asked Susan, "You okay?"

Susan looked at the messy floor. Robert sat back down. "You didn't want to tell her?"

"What if it all turns out to be a big nothing?" Susan said. "What if they don't find any DNA? Or they find Curt's DNA."

Robert frowned. "You think Curt and Danny were in on it together somehow?"

Susan grabbed at her hair. "I don't know what I think!"

Their waitress came over with a busboy, who carried a mop and broom. "Had a little excitement here, huh? We'll clean that up for ya."

As the busboy started mopping, Susan said to Robert, "Let's just get the DNA results. Then we'll know what to do."

The bar no longer felt like a safe, warm place, so Robert paid up and they walked out. "Now where?" he said.

She had been dreading this moment. She'd have to go sleep in the bus station—if it was open. No way she would ask Robert to pay for a hotel room for her.

"I should get my suitcase out of your trunk."

"Where will you sleep?"

"I'll find somewhere. No worries."

"Don't be silly. I'll get you a room."

"You really don't have to do that—"

He waved off her protest. "You can pay me back later. We'll go back to the Econo Lodge. Now that Lisa knows who you are, there's no point in hiding from her."

They headed for the hotel, where they walked up to the front desk. They didn't see Lisa, but there were several people nearby in their thirties and forties—men in khakis and women in business suits—who looked like out-of-town media people. Susan hoped they wouldn't recognize her.

"Hi, I'm looking for a room for my friend here," Robert told the desk clerk, a middle-aged woman with a worried expression.

"I'm afraid we don't have any vacancies," the clerk said.

"You must have a room somewhere," Robert cajoled. He gestured toward Susan and said quietly, "This is Susan Lentigo. She's the mother of the little girl who was killed."

Susan looked around, afraid some reporter had heard and would start asking her questions.

The clerk's brow furrowed and she looked even more worried. "I'm sorry, but between all the reporters and TV people and protesters—"

"Ms. Lentigo has had a very difficult week. She needs a good night's sleep before the execution."

"I'd like to help you. I just can't."

Robert shook his head, frustrated. "Fine. What's the name of that other hotel, on Clark Street?"

"The Clark Street Hotel." Susan wondered if the clerk was messing with Robert, but decided this woman was too nervous to be telling jokes. "But they're booked up too."

"Okay, what other hotels should we try?"

"There's only two others in town, and they're both full." She tugged at her ear. "You could maybe look for an Airbnb, but it's kind of late."

Robert and Susan walked away from the desk. She sensed what he would say next even before he said it. She felt her shoulders bunch up with anxiety. But she also felt a thrill in her chest that she hadn't felt for a long, long time.

He said, "You know, you could stay in my room. There's an extra twin bed."

"Okay, thanks," she said, before she even knew she was going to say it.

His room was up on the third floor. He offered her the bathroom first.

"You may regret that," she said. "I plan on spending about two hours in the shower."

"Consider me warned."

As soon as the water hit her body, Susan felt her whole self relax. She washed her hair three different times with the hotel's two little bottles of shampoo and threw on every ounce of conditioner too. She scrubbed herself vigorously with something called "body wash," which she hoped would work as well as regular soap.

It wasn't until she was toweling herself off afterwards that reality hit her again. She might be clean and fresh-smelling, but there was still a good chance tomorrow would be one of the worst days of her life.

Not including twenty years ago.

She had brought along a flannel nightgown, but she didn't want to wear it tonight. It felt too personal, wearing a nightgown while sleeping in the same room with a man she barely knew. So she put on fresh jeans and a T-shirt. After that she took off the ring she'd worn all these years and stashed it in the bottom of a suitcase pocket. She'd decide later if she wanted to sell it or throw it away. Then she came out of the bathroom.

"You were right. That *was* about two hours," Robert said.

"Told you so."

He went in the bathroom and closed the door behind him, just as Susan's phone rang. She picked it up. It was her mother.

She thought about not answering, but she knew her mom would be upset. And she'd call back another ten times until Susan finally answered. So she hit the talk button and said, "Hi, Mom."

"Susan, where are you?"

For a second she thought about telling her mom she was in a man's bedroom, just to see how she'd react. "I'm in Hodge Hills. Everything's good."

"You're not having any more crazy thoughts about Danny, are you?"

"No more crazy thoughts, no."

"Good." Susan heard her mom sigh with relief. "You're too sensible for that."

"I'm sensible, alright. How's Rumples doing? Does he miss me?"

"He meowed half the night last night. You sure you're okay?"

"I'm fine, Mom."

"Did you find a nice hotel room?"

"Yeah, it's comfortable."

"How much did it cost?"

"It was pretty cheap, actually."

"Good." There was a pause, then her mom said, "I was thinking. You know how people always say, 'Give so-and-so my love'?"

"Sure."

"Well, if you get a chance to talk to Curt Jansen, please give him my hate."

"Will do," Susan said.

She finally got off the phone. She wanted to get into bed, but there was one more call she had to make. To the only other person besides Robert that she trusted.

She dialed the number and almost immediately Kyra came on the line, like she'd been waiting for this call. "What's up?" she said.

"Agent Pappas is on board."

"Fuck yes! I knew you could do it."

"We're supposed to hear from the lab around noon."

"And they're planning to kill the guy at five thirty, right?"

"Right, so that should give us enough time."

"Damn. You're like a superhero, you know that?"

Susan laughed. "Thanks, Kyra."

Just then Robert opened the door from the bathroom and came back in. He was wearing blue flannel pajamas. She couldn't remember the last time she'd seen a man in pajamas. He had a little pot belly, but it wasn't too bad—

Kyra broke in. "Promise you'll tell me as soon as you hear."

"You got it, Kyra."

"Okay, cool. Break a leg."

"Thanks."

Susan hung up the phone. Robert was shutting the window curtains. "Who was that, your crime partner?" he asked.

"I'll never tell."

"You know, you guys are lucky Danny didn't kill you."

"He's lucky I didn't kill *him*. I sure as hell wanted to."

"He deserved it."

She looked up at him from the bed. "So you really think he did it?"

He pursed his lips. "If I had to bet, I'd say yeah."

Susan felt the darkness descend on her again. She said, "It always comes down to the same thing."

"What's that?"

She closed her eyes and took a deep breath. "How could I not have known?" She opened them again. "How did I not know?"

Robert sat down on the bed beside her. He said softly, "What Danny did to Amy . . . It's not your fault."

She wasn't so sure she believed him. She bowed her head in pain.

He said, "Look, I'm supposed to be a hotshot FBI agent, but he fooled me too, just like he fooled you. Now we're doing everything we can to stop him. That's all that matters."

Susan found herself fighting back tears. She felt so terrible, but she also felt the warmth of this man's body through his pajamas. It was bewildering.

Then Robert put his arm around her, and everything inside her froze solid.

She looked over at him. His face was so close. His whole body was so close.

She said haltingly, "I'm not really up for anything."

Robert's face reddened with confusion and embarrassment. Instantly she was pretty sure she'd misjudged his intentions, and she got embarrassed herself.

He moved his arm away and stood up, giving her a forced smile. "Just being friendly, ma'am. I'm not up for anything either."

"I'm sorry, I thought—"

"It's all good." He got into the other bed.

She said, "I'm not used to men touching me just to be friendly. Danny never used to do that."

As soon as she said it, she felt pathetic. Why was she being so open with this man?

And it wasn't really true that Danny never touched her. She remembered how he used to comfort her after Amy went missing.

But maybe that was just to hide the truth about what he'd done.

"Good night," Robert said from the other bed as he pulled up the blanket.

"Good night," Susan said, still embarrassed. He turned off the light, and she lay in bed and looked at the dark ceiling.

She felt stupid that she had never made love with anybody in her whole life besides Danny. For so many years now, she'd hardly ever even touched a man, aside from handshakes or bodies accidentally brushing against each other. What had she missed?

She had loved being the object of Danny's desire. She enjoyed the feeling of him on top of her, his urgency increasing until he exploded.

But she had never really felt that same explosion herself. Not when she was with him anyway. She only felt it when she took care of herself, which she used to do when she was a teenager but less frequently after she got married. She felt like she was cheating on Danny when she did it.

After Danny left, when men got interested in her, she had been flattered but never really went for it. She put it down to just being older, or not being built that way anymore, or still grieving for her old life.

But now, after everything she had learned and remembered during these past few days, she wondered if her inability to feel attracted to men had a different cause.

Maybe Danny had been a psychopath and on some level she knew it. So she was just too scared to trust any man at all.

She listened to Robert's breathing. It was so strange, the two of them together but in separate beds, listening to each other. Then his breathing changed and she sensed he was asleep.

Lying there, she tried to quiet her thoughts. She badly needed a good night's sleep herself. She hadn't had one for a week, and tomorrow she'd need every last bit of strength.

But images kept running through her head, ruthless and unstoppable:

Lisa offering half of her sandwich.

A photograph Susan saw on the internet once, of a man strapped down in the execution chamber about to die.

Danny playing basketball with Amy and lifting her high.

Having sex with Danny and looking up at him.

Thinking about Danny, her heart started thumping so badly she worried she might be having a heart attack. Then, out of nowhere, she had an image of Robert. *Sitting beside her on the bed, putting his arm around her . . .*

She focused on the feeling of Robert's arm and his reassuring tone of voice, and she started to calm down. Her breathing slowed.

Eventually, she found herself in an apple orchard, on an autumn morning. The trees were full of red and yellow leaves and the apples were fat and luscious. Then she saw Amy through the trees.

Amy running toward her, laughing, holding up a shiny red apple with a big crease in the middle, like two apples joined together. "Mommy, look!" she calls. "Doesn't this look like a heart?"

Susan smiles and holds her arms open wide for her daughter.

Amy runs closer. Still laughing, but coming slower now, slower . . . Her body jerks. Her joyful smile twists and turns creepy. She pitches forward and drops the apple. It bursts open, spilling thick liquid the color of blood. The redness covers her terrified face and neck—

Susan woke up and jerked upright in bed, gasping.

"Fuck," she said, and was taken aback to realize she'd said it out loud. She listened; Robert was still asleep, his breathing unchanged.

She was so jealous. She felt like she'd never get back to sleep. *How am I gonna make it through tonight alone?*

Then she stood up. She walked over to Robert's bed and looked down at him. *Am I really going to do this?*

It was a single bed, but he was lying on the other side of it. That made it easier for her. She gently lowered herself onto the bed and, lying on her side, put her head on his chest.

She immediately felt incredibly self-conscious. *Oh God, what if he pushes me away?*

She felt a change in his breathing and sensed he was awake now. She was terrified.

He shifted his body a little. Then she felt his arm come around her shoulder and hold her.

Her fear left her, and before she knew it, within seconds maybe, she was asleep.

The next morning, they were both still lying in that same position when a loud, harsh ring from the hotel phone woke them up.

CHAPTER THIRTY-SIX

THE FIRST THING Susan noticed was that loud ringing. The second thing she noticed was, there was some kind of weight on top of her.

She panicked and lifted herself up. To get leverage, she pushed down on something that confused her at first—but then she realized it was Robert's leg. "Sorry!" she said, scuttling backwards off the bed. The weight on top of her had been Robert's arm. Now she remembered everything that had happened last night, and how she'd wound up in bed with this man.

Robert grunted "Good morning," looking only barely awake.

"I'm sorry," Susan repeated as the phone rang again. Robert sat up in bed and looked at her. She touched her hair, flustered. Maybe he thought she was way too aggressive, coming into his bed last night. But he must understand she hadn't wanted sex, just comfort—

The phone rang again. It was sitting on the bedside table. *Could the DNA results be in already?!*

Robert picked it up. "Yeah," he said in a deep morning voice.

Susan stepped close to him so she could hear too. Oh God, was she being overaggressive again? Well, screw it, she had to hear this.

"Is this Robert Pappas?" a man's voice said.

"Who's calling, please?" Robert said.

Through the phone, Susan heard the commotion of other voices. The man said, "This is Zack Dietz from KMOT-TV. Actually, I'm looking for Susan Lentigo. I understand she's with you."

Who told him, the desk clerk? Susan thought. Or maybe somebody else in the lobby saw them go upstairs. *Great.* Her day of media had just begun.

Then it hit her: Would the reporters say on TV that she and Robert were sharing a room? They did that nowadays, didn't they—they put in every possible piece of gossip. What would people think?

Hell, her mom would be thrilled. Despite everything, Susan smiled.

Robert said, "I don't know where she is."

The man— Zack Dietz—said, "What is her response to Lisa Jansen's allegations?"

Susan's smile faded. *Oh shit, how do I deal with this?*

"What allegations?" Robert said.

"Come on down to the lobby and find out," Dietz said. "She's holding a little press conference."

Robert hung up the phone. Susan grabbed the TV remote control. "What channel is KMOT?"

"Don't know."

When the TV came on it was a different station, but it didn't matter. They were showing Lisa Jansen too. She was standing by the fake fireplace in the middle of the hotel lobby, talking to reporters. A chyron at the bottom of the screen said: NEW QUESTIONS ABOUT CONDEMNED MAN'S GUILT.

Lisa's curly hair framed her freshly made-up cheeks, and Susan thought her angry passion made her beautiful. She held her arms wide as she declared, "Amy Lentigo's own mother now believes Curt may be innocent. If you don't believe me, ask her."

Susan said to Robert, "What do we do? Do we tell them the truth?"

On TV, Lisa said, "Maybe she'll have the guts to admit it. Or you can ask Agent Pappas."

Robert said, "We could, but there'll be a serious shitstorm—"

Somebody knocked on their hotel room door. It hadn't taken the reporters long to find them.

Robert said, "No comment."

A man in the hallway called, "Agent Pappas!"

"No comment!"

The man knocked louder. "This is Director Williams. Open up!"

Susan froze. The DNA results must be in!

Robert got up and opened the door.

Williams entered, carrying a manila folder. Susan tried to read his face, but it looked blank, with empty eyes, like he was staying expressionless on purpose.

He took a good long look at Susan, here in Robert's hotel room. Then he turned back to Robert. "Nice pajamas," he said.

Robert said, "What's going on?"

Williams tapped the folder against the palm of his hand. "I wanted to give you these results in person, so there'd be no mistake."

Susan thought, *Please God, please God,* then realized she was praying her ex-husband would be proven a child killer.

Williams reached into his folder and pulled out a two-page, stapled report. He handed it to Robert wordlessly.

Susan came and stood next to Robert, reading over his shoulder. But there were so many words she didn't know: "histological," "RNA," "nucleotides." She glanced at Robert and tried to read what he was feeling as he studied the report.

Williams said, "Mr. Pappas, in case you've gotten a little rusty on your forensics, the necklace you gave me has no DNA that matches Amy Lentigo's DNA."

Susan's heart sank. She stood there with her mouth open, devastated.

Robert said, "What about these samples that have insufficient markers? That could be cross-contamination. You need to run a statistical—"

"We did. Thanks to your brilliant blackmail maneuver yesterday, I made sure the lab gave it the gold-star treatment. There's no match."

Susan thought, *But I know that was Amy's necklace! I know it!*

Somehow, even though the DNA results had come up empty, she was even more positive than ever now that Danny had raped and killed Amy. It was like the results had made clear to her, once and for all, what she truly believed in her heart.

And what she believed was: *Danny did it. That sonufabitch did it. These FBI agents must have missed something.*

She asked, "Did you check every single crevice?"

"We did."

She looked to Robert for support, but he just frowned down at the report, obviously not seeing anything there he liked.

Susan was desperate. "He must have washed the DNA off the necklace! Danny's not stupid. I'm sure he studied all the CSI books to figure out what he had to do!"

Williams folded his arms. "Ms. Lentigo—"

"There must be some other way to prove it was Amy's necklace! I know it was hers!"

Williams took another piece of paper out of his folder. This one didn't have any complex words on it, or any words at all. It had nothing but a big, blown-up photograph of the pink duck bead that Susan remembered so well. It was the very first bead she and Amy had bought that day at Soave Faire in Glens Falls.

Except the photo didn't show the top side of the duck, it showed the underside. There was a logo there that Susan had never noticed before: a tiny, darker pink capital "A" with a double hoop around it.

Williams said, "We ran this logo through the U.S. Patent and Trademark Office database. It was trademarked by the Adirondack Bead Company in 2014. Before then, this logo did not exist. Which means this bead did not exist."

Susan stared down at the paper, stunned. *2014?*

Williams said, "Your daughter was killed in 2001. So there is absolutely no way she ever wore this necklace. Understood?"

She was numb, still staring at the paper. *Danny is innocent? He's actually innocent?*

She looked at Robert. He was eyeing the logo too and seemed to be feeling the same way she did.

Williams said, "This ridiculous exercise in futility has cost the Bureau eight thousand dollars, and now we have a huge public relations mess with the killer's sister that needs to be cleaned up. Mr. Pappas, if you were still an active agent, I'd suspend you." He pointed a disdainful finger at Susan. "You were unduly influenced by your closeness with this woman. Why didn't you tell me you were sleeping with her?"

Susan's cheeks burned. She was relieved that at least she had worn her clothes to bed. She couldn't imagine confronting Williams in her nightgown right now.

Actually she couldn't confront him, period. She had to get out of here. She moved swiftly to the hotel room door, where she had left her boots, and put them on as fast as she could.

"Where are you going?"

Susan didn't know, so she didn't answer, just threw on her coat. Williams said, "Hey," and grabbed her arm.

"Get off me," she snapped, wrenching her arm away and reaching for the doorknob. But Williams, with his sturdy six-foot-two frame, blocked her way.

"Watch yourself," Robert told Williams.

Williams ignored Robert. He told Susan, "You need to go downstairs and tell the media you have total faith Curt Jansen is the killer. You owe it to your daughter to do that. And not just her. You owe it to everybody in the FBI and elsewhere who worked so hard to get justice for Amy." He gestured toward Robert. "Including this man here who you dragged into your insane conspiracy theory."

Susan looked at Robert. He must hate her now. She felt so terrible about what she'd put him through, and all for nothing.

Danny, innocent? Is that possible?!

She felt short of breath. If she stayed in this room with Williams and Robert for one more second, she would pass out. "Get out of my way," she told Williams.

"No. Not until you—"

She shoved him, hard, and knocked him back just enough that she was able to open the door and make it through. She started running.

From the hotel room, Robert called, "Susan! Where are you going?"

She ran down the hall to an exit sign. Shit, that was the elevators; she needed stairs. She kept running.

Behind her, she could hear Williams, and maybe Robert too, chasing her. They were getting closer. Williams yelled, "Stop! What are you gonna tell them?"

She found the stairs and ran down, getting a sharp pain in her right knee. She heard the men behind her, coming fast, maybe one landing above her. Robert was calling, "Susan, wait!" and Williams was shouting, "Stop right now!"

She made it to the first floor and burst through the stairwell door. She slammed it open with such force it banged against a wall. Meanwhile Williams shouted, "Don't be fucking stupid!"

The racket made everybody in the lobby turn toward them. Thirty feet away, by the fireplace, Lisa was still holding forth to about twenty newspaper and TV reporters and cameramen.

Lisa pointed at Susan. "That's her! That's Susan Lentigo!"

Susan stopped short. All the media people started coming at her. Behind her, she heard Robert and Williams. What the hell should she do?

She ran. Ignoring the pain in her leg, she raced through the lobby.

Reporters, cameramen, and anchorpeople got in her way, thrusting video equipment and their own bodies at her. Their questions ratatat-ted like machine-gun blasts: "Ms. Lentigo, do you agree with Curt Jansen's sister!" "Do you still believe Jansen killed your daughter?" "Do you support the execution?"

She dodged her interrogators like a running back, dashing to the right, then switching back left, and finding a gap between two anchor-people. She raced out the front door.

"What are you running from, Susan?" she heard Lisa calling. From outside, she took one last look into the lobby and saw Robert and Williams still chasing after her. But the media people had recognized Robert, and sensed Williams was important somehow, so they were blocking the two of them and asking questions.

Susan knew Robert wouldn't be coming outside to chase her, not for long anyway, since he was still in pajamas and bare feet. She cringed when she thought about how he would look on TV. She hoped he wouldn't be too upset.

But Williams might come after her, to say nothing of Lisa. And three media people were coming out the front door right now.

So she turned and ran. She heard people shouting her name and picked up her pace. The adrenalin killed the throbbing in her knee. She ran down the street and zigzagged through three side streets before she finally turned around again.

Her pursuers were gone.

Now what?

She was standing in an empty lot next to a hardware store. She took her flip phone out of her pocket and dialed a number she had committed to memory by now.

Danny answered on the first ring. "Hello?"

"We need to talk," Susan said.

CHAPTER THIRTY-SEVEN

"The FBI checked the necklace for DNA," Susan said. "They didn't find any traces of Amy."

She was with Danny, in the front seat of his rented Malibu, in a church parking lot on the main street. She sat as far away from him as possible, with her hand close to the door handle. She hadn't been eager to meet with him in his car, but it was too cold to meet outside and she didn't want to be in a coffee shop or some place where the media might recognize her. Here on the main street she felt she could jump out of the car and run if things between her and Danny got weird or scary.

"Of course they didn't," Danny said. "It wasn't Amy's necklace."

"And the duck bead on the necklace didn't even exist until seven years ago. It looked the same as Amy's bead, but it was a different manufacturer."

"Okay, good," Danny said. He looked at Susan. "So we're all done with this then."

Their eyes locked. That's why she'd come here. She wanted to just look him in the eyes. She thought maybe that would convince her once and for all that Danny had nothing to do with Amy's death.

His face softened. "Look, I'm not mad at you. I'm just freaked out and hurt that you would think this of me."

He paused, waiting. She realized she was supposed to apologize to him.

But it felt like her lips had been locked up. She couldn't speak.

Danny said, "But I get the pressure you're under. That we're both under. We'll feel better tonight after it's all over."

Susan thought about what would happen in just a few hours: Curt Jansen's execution. She realized what was stopping her from apologizing. *I'm still not sure about Danny. Even after everything Williams said, I'm still not sure.*

She had been silent for so long that Danny asked, "Susan? You okay?"

She bit her bottom lip, so hard it hurt. Somehow the pain unlocked her and she was able to speak again—even challenge him, the way she wanted to. "You have to admit, you had some weird . . ." She stopped, looking for the right words. ". . . sexual things."

He raised his eyebrows, incredulous. "What the hell are you talking about?"

She pushed on. "Wanting me to dress like a little girl."

Danny sputtered angrily, "I liked fantasy role playing, so that makes me some kind of fucking evil pervert? What the hell is wrong with you? Do you *still* think I killed Amy?"

Susan couldn't stop now. "You liked to give her baths."

"Jesus Christ, I did that when you were tired coming home from the diner! What has gotten into you?"

"You were so cold after she died."

"Are you kidding? I spent a year taking care of you!"

"But you never cried about Amy."

"Sure I did!"

"Not after that first week. Not after they arrested Curt Jansen and you stopped being a suspect."

"What, you think I was *faking* being upset?" Danny banged the steering wheel in frustration. She was afraid he was about to punch her, something she had to admit he'd never done; he had just shaken her hard, that one time. She braced herself, though he didn't seem to notice. "Susan, that whole first year I was just trying to hold it together. I cried a thousand times, just not when I was with you. You were falling apart. You needed somebody to be strong for you."

"*Strong?* You left me."

Danny sighed heavily. "I'm truly sorry." He started to reach out his hand toward her, to touch her shoulder or something. But then he pulled back like he wasn't sure how she'd respond.

She wasn't sure either. She'd either run screaming from the car or cry in his arms.

He said softly, "Susan, we both know, most couples break up when their child gets killed. People mourn in different ways. I couldn't just sit there and talk about my feelings like you did. I needed to get up and *do* something. I had to get outta that town. I needed to . . ." He stopped. "I needed to forget about Amy, at least for a while. Or at least that's what I thought I needed. I was dying, Susan. Every day I thought about jumping off that bridge in Corinth. Every single day."

Then Danny started to cry. Heavy, heaving sobs, the kind she had never seen from him that whole year.

Susan sat there, not sure what to do. She was tempted to leave the car but couldn't bring herself to. Instead, she moved closer to him in the front seat and held him. He buried his face in her shoulder.

At last he opened his eyes and sat up again. "Thank you," he said.

She nodded. She felt so . . . She didn't know what she felt. Her head was pounding. So was her heart. "I need to go." She reached for the door handle.

"Susan, I want things to be right between us." She paused with her hand gripping the handle and looked back at him. His eyes were wet and red-rimmed, pleading. "We don't know if we'll ever see each other again after tonight. Let's go out for a drink afterwards, or just drive around like we used to when we were first together. When we were in high school, before . . . Before everything."

She had loved this man once. She wondered if some part of her still did. "I'll see you later," she said, and got out of the car.

As she walked out of the church parking lot, her phone rang. It was her mom, so she didn't pick up.

Then Kyra called. Susan couldn't bear to talk to her either.

The noontime sky was dark gray. Susan walked away from the center of town, pulling her coat closed against the brutal North Dakota wind. She found herself on a bridge, looking down at the thin river she and Robert had driven over. In two or three weeks, four at the most, this river would be ice.

She gazed up at the barren hills looming above the edge of town. They looked menacing today, all their solemn anger aimed straight at her. In the distance was an oil derrick, all alone.

It's not the same necklace. For the hundredth time in the past hour, she wondered: *Does this mean I was wrong about all the rest of it too?*

Her phone rang again. She figured it was her mom or Kyra calling back, so she almost didn't look at the display. Then she saw it was Robert.

She hoped he didn't hate her. She hit the talk button and said, "Hi."

"Are you okay? Where are you?" Robert said.

He didn't sound mad. But then again, he was a nice guy, polite, like they probably taught you at FBI school. Who knew how he really felt toward her?

"I guess it's time to deal with reality," Susan said.

"Where are you?" he repeated.

She told him, and a little later he drove up. She got in his car. "Thanks for picking me up," she said, still trying to gauge his feelings.

"You ran out of the hotel so fast. I was worried about you."

"I just wanted to get away."

Robert nodded. "I don't blame you." He gave her a little smile, and she felt a lot better.

He asked, "What are you thinking? Do you still want to go to the execution?"

Susan wanted to just run away again. She couldn't imagine she'd get any grim pleasure out of the execution as she'd once expected.

But she couldn't imagine staying away from it. So she said, "Yes, let's go."

They headed back up into the hills. Susan would be so glad to get the hell out of North Dakota.

Though how she'd get back home with no money, she had no idea. There were limits on what she could ask from Robert. Maybe she would finally call Terri tonight.

Robert rubbed his forehead as he drove. "After this morning, that prison will be crawling with reporters."

Susan said, "I am so sorry I dragged you into this mess."

He gave her that little smile again. "You didn't drag me. I believed the evidence you brought."

"What do you think now?"

He took a moment to answer her. "I'm guessing Williams and his people did a solid job analyzing the necklace. So I believe them that it's not the same necklace Amy wore. And that was the only real evidence we had."

She slapped the dashboard with her hand. "This is so fucked up."

"It always is."

Was he teasing her somehow? "What do you mean?"

He shrugged. "I've been to four executions. There's always something screwed up that goes on. Executions just make people crazy."

"Then why do you go?"

"Because if it's one of my cases and I *don't* go, it doesn't feel right. If somebody's getting killed because of work that I did, I should be there and accept the responsibility for what's happening to him."

She gave a faint smile. "Wow, you're a pretty deep guy."

"I wouldn't go that far."

She looked out the window. "I wish I had a cigarette. I haven't had a cigarette in thirty years. Since before Amy was born."

"Are you hungry?"

"Not really. I feel kind of sick."

"The execution's not 'til five thirty. And I've made it a rule: never go to an execution on an empty stomach."

Susan couldn't tell if he was joking, but she decided to take his advice. They got off the highway at the next exit and found a Burger King, and she discovered she was ravenous.

As they left the restaurant and headed back to the car, Robert said, "So what are you going to tell the reporters?"

"What should I tell them?"

"What you believe."

If only I knew what that was, Susan thought.

An hour later, they reached the penitentiary gate.

CHAPTER THIRTY-EIGHT

Two groups about thirty people strong stood on opposite sides of the gate, carrying homemade signs. Susan eyed them warily as she and Robert drove toward them.

They ranged from kids to the elderly. One group held up signs with messages like "Don't Kill for Me" and "Execute Justice Not People." The other group's signs proclaimed "An Eye for an Eye is Just" and "Death for Child Killers."

But despite being polar opposites, the two groups were noncombative and seemed respectful of each other. Nobody was shouting and they all seemed to be honoring the solemnity of the occasion. Maybe it was just too cold out here to get in a big fight.

The one thing Susan found disturbing was that several of the pro-death-penalty people had huge, blown-up pictures of Amy wearing the necklace.

Robert and Susan rode up to the gate, which blocked their way. A corrections officer with a red, puffy face and a beer belly stood at the opening of the small guardhouse, holding a clipboard.

Robert rolled down his window and handed over their drivers' licenses. "We're here for the execution. We're on the witness list."

The CO checked their licenses, then leaned down and peered into the car at Susan.

"Susan Lentigo," he said, his beady black eyes narrowing. "You're not really backing the scumbag that killed your daughter, are you?"

Susan was too taken aback to speak, but luckily Robert stepped in. "Officer, that's not your business, is it?"

The CO glared at Robert menacingly. "If she's coming in here to cause trouble, then hell yes it's my business."

Robert stared straight back. "Why don't you shut the fuck up and let the lady through?"

Susan was stunned, but apparently Robert had read the situation right. Although the CO's eyes flared with anger, he didn't do anything. He just handed the IDs back to Robert and opened the gate.

"Thanks," Susan said to Robert, as they headed up the long driveway to the main administrative building.

He gave a dry smile. "No worries. That guy's a bully, but he wasn't about to mess with the mother of the victim. Not in any way that could get him in trouble."

As they came around a small hill and approached the building, Susan saw the big parking lot was close to full and there were six or seven TV vans with cable dishes. Robert parked at the edge of the lot. By the front steps, about fifty reporters, anchorpeople, and cameramen were waiting, loosely guarded by two or three corrections officers. They were probably waiting for Susan, but they hadn't spotted her yet.

"God, there's a lot of them," Susan said. "Guess Lisa got them all excited."

Robert looked at her. "We can stay in the car for a while if you want."

"That won't make it any easier."

Susan's right leg was bothering her again, but she was determined to ignore it. They headed for the front steps of the building. As soon as the media people saw her, they raced up with their microphones and cameras. Susan knew what their questions would be even before they started shouting at them.

"Susan, how do you feel?"

"Did Curt Jansen kill your daughter?"

"Are they executing the wrong man?"

Robert stepped in front of her, blocking the media and trying to clear a path so they could make it to the steps. "Give us room, please. Step back."

But the questions kept coming: "Susan, who do you think killed your daughter?" "Is Lisa Jansen telling the truth about you?"

Robert said, "Let us through, please. Let us through—"

"Susan, look this way."

"Susan, are they killing an innocent man?"

Despite Robert's efforts, the crush was overwhelming Susan. Why weren't the COs trying harder to control these people? Maybe they were slacking because they were pissed off at her, just like the CO at the front gate.

Following closely behind Robert, she managed to make it halfway up the steps. Then a woman in her mid-thirties, well dressed but a little plump, came down the steps toward them. She seemed somehow different from the media people, with a different kind of worry on what looked like a usually cheerful face. She said loudly, so Susan could hear her over the reporters, "Susan, I'm Pam Arnold from Public Relations. You don't have to talk to them. Come on inside."

Pam tried to pull her up the final steps into the prison. But when Susan made it to the top step, she said, "Hang on a second."

The media were still yelling questions, even more aggressively now that their quarry was about to escape inside the prison where they couldn't follow. A twenty-something man shoved a microphone into Susan's cheek so hard it rattled her teeth.

Robert pushed the man backwards. He fell into an anchorwoman, who stumbled and almost fell herself, which led to a brief interruption to the questions. Robert took quick advantage of that. He raised his hands and said, "If you'll all be quiet for a moment, Ms. Lentigo has a brief statement she'd like to make."

Susan stepped up next to Robert.

On the other side of her, Pam said, "Susan, are you sure this is a good idea?"

Susan ignored her. Below her on the steps, everybody with a microphone or a camera jostled for better position. She waited for them to quit pushing each other, and for her own heart to stop beating so fast.

But her heart kept pounding, and she quit hoping that would change. She needed to speak, right now. *Just do it.*

"I'd like to say," she started, and then stopped. Her voice sounded both squeaky and hollow. It didn't feel right, like it was coming from another person.

She began again. "I'd like to say that . . ." She paused again, still disconcerted by the strange sound of her voice, then plunged on. "Curt Jansen's sister seems like a very kind woman, and she's been through a lot. I'm sorry she misunderstood me."

Her throat caught for a second, like there was a big lump stuck in there. Then she continued. "I am confident that Curt Jansen is the man who killed my daughter."

The lump grew, but she was able to get out, "That's really all I have to say."

Then Susan turned and went inside, as the media yelled questions and Robert and Pam followed her.

CHAPTER THIRTY-NINE

THE REPORTERS' SHOUTS faded as the door closed behind Susan, Robert, and Pam.

"Well done, Susan," Pam said enthusiastically. "I shoulda known all those rumors about you taking the killer's side were nuts."

"Thanks," Susan said.

Robert sensed her discomfort and changed the subject. He pointed to the metal detector and told Susan, "Okay, they have super-sensitive metal detectors at prisons, so get rid of anything you can think of."

Pam said, "Absolutely. Cell phones, loose change, anything."

"Okay," Susan said, and began emptying her pockets.

Pam said, "I'm so glad Agent Pappas is here to protect you from all those rabid reporters. And now your ex-husband is coming too? That's wonderful! At times like these, families should be together."

Susan was already sick of this woman. "Should I take off my belt?"

"Yes, please. Like I told your ex on the phone, if you don't set off the metal detector, we won't have to pat you down. I hope you took my advice about the . . ." Pam pointed delicately toward her own chest. ". . . undergarments?"

Susan had indeed made sure to pack only wireless bras. "I did."

"Perfect."

Susan and Robert made it through the metal detector without incident. Then they started walking through the prison. Pam chattered away about how big it was, when it was built, how many inmates there were, but Susan quit hearing her. This place was terrifying. She had never been in a prison before. Every time a door was opened or shut, there was a deafening clang. First a CO would open a door for them, steering them into a small enclosed space. Then the CO would clang that door shut, and the door in front of them would clang open, they'd walk through, and then that door would clang shut with a huge echoing sound. The echoes all got trapped in the long hallways.

Susan felt trapped too.

She passed several inmates, white, black, and brown. They all wore dark green prison uniforms and looked at her stone-faced. She wondered: Did they hate her? Did they know one of their fellow inmates would be killed tonight and she had demanded it?

Were these men murderers? Rapists? Or just drug users? Were they all guilty, or were some of them innocent?

Nothing on their faces gave them away.

Pam's endless patter— "This is a federal prison, so we get folks from all over. Last year we even had two Samoans. Boy, were they huge!" —started to scratch on Susan's ears like sandpaper. Luckily, they seemed to have the same effect on Robert, because he interrupted her.

"How did the run-through go?" he asked.

"Bing bang boom," Pam said cheerily. "We have the A team today. They've all done at least three executions. The nurse has done ten of them."

A nurse at an execution? What for?

Pam continued, "So we won't have to worry about the condemned man herking and jerking and the needle coming out and chemicals spraying everywhere. That's no fun."

Susan winced, imagining the herking and jerking. She asked, "Is Curt's sister here?"

"She's with the inmate now. Don't worry, you won't see her. We keep the families of the condemned man and the victim totally separate." Yet another door clanged behind them, and they left the administration building and entered a hallway that led to a cellblock building. "Would you like to visit the execution chamber? Some family members do and some don't. It's your choice."

Susan hesitated, then turned to Robert. "What do you think?"

Robert said, "It's probably a good idea. You'll feel more prepared."

"Okay," Susan said, turning back to Pam. "Let's go."

"You got it. You'll even get a chance to see Death Row. It's on the way."

Great, Susan thought.

When they made it through two more clanging doors into the cellblock building, things got more crowded. They acquired two COs who accompanied them for protection. Inmates and COs were everywhere, some surly, some laughing. The smell of bleach got stronger. It felt like a college dorm, except for the uniforms and the fact most of the men were older than college-age. Susan was self-conscious, wondering how often these men saw women in person. Not that she was a hot young chick or anything, but still. She looked furtively into the eyes of the men passing her and wondered how many of them would hurt her if given a chance.

They came to another thick metal door and waited for their two COs to open it. "Okay," Pam said, "we're coming to the Row."

The two COs, one of them a muscular guy who looked like he spent his off hours at the gym and the other one tall and wiry, opened the door and shut it behind them. Susan immediately smelled something that felt a little off, then realized it was human shit.

They turned a corner and came to Death Row. *So this is where Curt Jansen has spent his last twenty years,* Susan thought.

As if reading her thoughts, Pam stopped in front of the very first cell. "This is Jansen's cell. Or should I say, it was."

Susan looked through the metal bars at the tiny six-by-nine room. Against the back wall was a skinny bed with a thin blanket. A metal toilet with no seat occupied one corner. Two books lay on the floor by the bed: a biography of Ted Williams, who Susan remembered used to play for the Boston Red Sox; and a book called *You Can Have Heaven on Earth.*

Must be some kind of self-help book, Susan thought. But so what? No doubt killers and rapists read self-help books too. It didn't mean anything.

"Seen enough?" Pam said.

Susan nodded. She looked at Robert, standing there silently beside her. His eyes looked so soft. She just wanted to cry in his arms.

They headed down "the Row." On either side of them, inmates looked up from their books, push-ups, and solo chess games. Their faces sullen, they watched the visitors pass by. Pam was saying, "So after the inmate eats his final meal—Curt Jansen asked for a T-bone steak and chocolate ice cream, by the way, what you might expect— anyway, then he sees the chaplain if he wants—"

To their right, an elderly inmate with missing front teeth came to the bars of his cell and looked straight at Susan. "Hey, honey. Curt says your daughter had a real tight pussy!"

That did it. All the other inmates started whooping and shouting. "Oh yeah!" "Shove that dick in there, baby!" "Fuck me, sweetheart, suck my dick!"

The muscular CO yelled, "Y'all better shut up right now, or you're going in the hole!"

The inmates got even louder. "I'll give you my dick too, asshole!" "Mothafucka, I'll carve you up!"

Susan, Pam, and Robert walked faster down the Row, not saying anything anymore. The COs' clenched jaws showed they wanted to go into those cells and bash a few heads, but instead they followed the three visitors.

At the very last cell on the Row, just before they could make it into an adjoining hallway and get out of there, a young inmate wearing thick, black-rimmed glasses lunged forward to the bars of his cell. As Susan turned toward him, he lifted his lips and spit at her. She felt wetness on the back of her hand and screamed.

As she frantically wiped her hand on her coat, all the other inmates on the Row laughed and shouted insults. The tall, wiry CO snapped at the young inmate, "You just got five months in the hole, dipshit."

But the inmate shouted at Susan, "Fuck you, Curt didn't do it! He's innocent!"

"Come on, let's go," Pam said, and they got the hell out of there.

CHAPTER FORTY

They made it to the adjoining hallway, another windowless cement corridor painted dull green, with the inmates' yells still in their ears. Pam said, "Sorry about that. The natives always get a little restless on Execution Day."

"We'll deal with that guy who spit at you later," the muscular CO said.

"It's okay," Susan said, because she knew she was supposed to say something.

"I hope we don't have to go through there again when we leave," Robert said.

Pam said, "No, there's another way, it just takes a little longer."

"Wish we'd taken that way coming in," Robert said.

"You're probably right," Pam said cheerily. "Live and learn!"

Geez, what an idiot, thought Susan.

Pam continued, "So when the time comes, the condemned man will walk down this hallway with at least four officers escorting him. Some of them fight like monsters with superhuman strength. Some of them drag their bodies on the floor like dead weights and scream the whole way." She shrugged. "And then some of them just walk in and sit right down at the chair like they're getting a haircut. You never know."

The tall CO opened the metal door into the execution chamber, and Susan walked in with the others.

The room was painted the same dull green as the hallways outside. In the center of the room was a large, wooden reclining chair. It had thick black straps attached. Nearby was a medical cart with three plastic bags containing liquids. It reminded Susan of the cart in her mom's hospital room when she had pneumonia.

Facing the death chair were two thick-looking windows. On the other side of the windows were two rooms, which she figured were the viewing rooms for people to watch the execution. They were both painted tan, with gray folding chairs set out.

The COs shut the door behind them in the execution chamber. *Clang!* Susan's chest tightened, like there wasn't enough air in here. She put her hand on her chest and tried to breathe. Having Robert beside her wasn't enough to calm her.

Pam sat down in the death chair, looking like this was her favorite part of the tour. "Once they're in the chair, they're tied down with these straps," she said, as she laid the straps over her body. "Then they're given a chance to say some final words." She gave an amused chuckle. "Last guy we had in here just said 'F you, f you, f you' a couple hundred times 'til they finally put a gag on him."

"Will we be able to hear what he says?" Susan asked.

"This room is soundproof, but when the time comes, we'll turn on the intercom so we can hear him but he can't hear us. Who knows, maybe we'll get a deathbed confession."

God, I hope so, Susan thought.

Pam picked up a black hood. "After they finish talking, if they want, we cover their heads with this. And then . . ." She pointed to the three bags of liquids, one by one. "Drug number one puts 'em to sleep. Drug number two stops their breathing, and that's really enough to kill 'em. But just for good measure, drug number three stops their heart." She paused. "Pardon the dark humor, but drug number three is like beating a dead horse." Her face tilted up into a half-smile, and she looked disappointed when Susan and Robert didn't smile along with her.

Susan turned around and looked at the viewing rooms again. "Will he be able to see us?"

"If he doesn't wear the hood, sure." Pam pointed at the viewing room on the left. "The sister and the chaplain will be in that room." Then she pointed at the room on the right. "You and your people will be in there."

Robert turned to Susan. "The viewing rooms are soundproof too, so we won't hear Curt's sister."

Susan imagined herself sitting in one of those gray folding chairs, watching Curt Jansen die. She had been so eager to be the last person Curt saw while he was taking his final breath. She wondered, would the judge have given Curt the death penalty if she hadn't demanded it?

"Any other questions?" Pam asked.

"I feel like I'm gonna throw up."

Pam took a barf bag out of a drawer of the medical cart. "We got you covered," she said, her voice sounding extra cheerful, if anything.

Robert placed his hand on Susan's shoulder. He asked Pam, "You don't happen to have any cigarettes, do you?"

Pam said sternly, "Cigarettes are illegal in this facility."

Then she gave Susan a wink. "If you get caught."

The two COs opened the door again, and after multiple clangs and more interminable chatter from Pam, Susan found herself with a pack of Pam's old-school Newports inside a women's restroom on the second floor of the administration building. Pam had to go deal with the media, so Robert was in the bathroom with Susan while the two COs waited in the hallway. She stood by the open window and breathed out a hefty lungful of smoke through the open bars into the icy outside air.

Much as Pam annoyed her, she had to admit these cigarettes were a lifesaver. Smoking was just as good as she remembered. She didn't even cough once—it was like she'd never stopped. As she inhaled the smoke, she wondered why the hell she ever quit. Then she remembered: she was pregnant, and she didn't want to risk hurting the baby.

Well, she didn't have to worry about that now. She wondered if she would start smoking again. And then she thought: *Who cares?*

She breathed out some more smoke through the bars. Robert leaned against a sink, watching her. "Feeling better?" he said.

Her phone buzzed. She'd been avoiding calls from her mom all day. She looked at her phone and groaned. It was Kyra. In some ways that was even worse.

But she picked up. She owed it to Kyra. "Hi," she said.

She heard Kyra's aggrieved voice. "I saw on the news. You said Danny didn't do it."

"It looks that way. It wasn't the same necklace after all. Emily's necklace was new."

"What do you mean?!"

Susan explained about the absence of any DNA from Amy, and the pink duck bead that had been manufactured in 2014 or later. "So that means we've got no evidence against Danny."

"Fuck the evidence!" Kyra said. "Listen to your gut. This guy has a six-year-old daughter!"

Susan felt a stab of pain in her chest. "Look, there's nothing I can do."

"You'll let her get hurt, just like Amy? We both know Danny did it! Stand up and fight, for fuck's sake! You can do it!"

"I'm sorry, Kyra," Susan said, and shut her phone. She felt crushed.

"Your cigarette," Robert said, pointing, and she saw it was burning her finger. She dropped it to the floor and stubbed it out. She could smell her burning flesh.

"Let's pour some cold water on that," Robert said.

"I'm fine," she said. At least the pain in her finger distracted her. She looked at Robert. "Curt Jansen had better be fucking guilty."

He nodded.

"Let's go," she said.

Robert held out another cigarette. "We still got another five minutes."

Susan shook her head. "No, let's just go," she said, and led the way out of the bathroom.

CHAPTER FORTY-ONE

The two COs led Susan and Robert on a roundabout route to their viewing room, avoiding Death Row this time. As the doors clanged around them, Susan listened to her footsteps echoing down the hollow hallways. She felt like she was walking to her own execution.

They reached the hallway that had doors to the two viewing rooms. They were about to enter the room for the victim's family when Susan heard footsteps heading toward them and looked up.

Lisa Jansen was coming her way. She was flanked by a CO and a sandy-haired, gentle-faced man who Susan figured was the chaplain.

Lisa saw Susan and stopped, glaring with hatred and disgust. But Susan forced herself to look Lisa right in the eye. She wouldn't back down. *Goddamn it, I'm not doing anything wrong!*

"Look, your brother confessed," she said. Her voice sounded harsh to her, harsher than she felt, but she kept going. "He said he killed my daughter."

Lisa's lips curled. "Don't try to make yourself feel better."

"You would've done the exact same thing if it was one of *your* little girls."

Lisa stepped up close to her, so close she could smell coffee on Lisa's breath.

"My brother is not a killer," Lisa said. "But you are."

Then she turned and walked off to her viewing room, followed by the chaplain and the CO.

Susan stood there frozen for a moment, watching Lisa go. Then Robert took her arm and led her into the other viewing room. When she entered, she saw Danny sitting on one of the folding chairs. He looked up and gave her a welcoming smile.

She looked down at him and swallowed, unable to figure out how she felt.

There were other people in the room too: Pam, Director Williams, and two men and one woman in suits. Pam rose immediately to greet her.

"Here you are, just in time," Pam said, beaming. "Susan and Agent Pappas, meet our warden, the amazing Jim Tomey; Assistant District Attorney David Johnstone; ADA Karina Navarro; and Director Williams of the FBI I believe you know."

Williams said sarcastically, "Thought I'd stick around and make sure nothing else screws up."

Warden Tomey graciously ignored that and shook Susan's hand. "Ms. Lentigo, we'll try to make this as positive an experience for you as possible."

But it was Danny that Susan was focused on. He looked so *normal*, in his new blue jeans, black wool coat, and Timberlake boots. His face had just the right combination of somberness and concern for Susan, along with a bit of gentle humor.

"For a second there I thought you weren't coming," he said. "I saved you a seat."

He can't be a rapist and murderer. He just can't.

It made sense that the two parents would sit next to each other, so she did what she was supposed to and sat in the folding chair next to Danny. Robert sat on her other side.

As soon as she sat down, she wished she and Robert could switch chairs. She hated being this close to Danny.

What if he is the killer?

She wished she and Robert were back at that bar, drinking pitchers of beer, listening to country music.

Director Williams eyed her with his permanently irritated expression. She wanted to give him a defiant stare but couldn't summon the energy. She looked through the window into the execution chamber and was just in time to see the door from the hallway open.

Curt Jansen walked into the execution chamber. Behind him came four COs.

Because of the soundproofing, Susan couldn't hear anything from inside there. But Curt wasn't dragging or screaming, he walked with his head held high. He looked a little grayish from lack of sun, but he had a haircut and was freshly shaved. Also, somebody—his sister, no doubt—had given him a suit to wear to his death. He looked sort of . . . *distinguished.*

"Show time," Pam said brightly. Robert and the woman lawyer gave her an annoyed look, but nobody said anything.

Susan watched Curt. She thought, *This is the moment I've been dreaming of for twenty years. I helped make it happen.* He was looking up at the two windows facing him, and his eyes caught something in the other window. The way his face softened and he smiled, Susan guessed he was seeing his sister. He gave her a wave.

Then Curt looked through the window into Susan's viewing room. His eyes roamed the small crowd until he found Susan.

He looked at her steadily, unblinking.

She found herself unable to look away. She couldn't read him, had no idea what he was thinking.

She flashed back to how his face looked twenty years ago when she spoke at his sentencing. She remembered her exact words: "*I hope you get raped in prison. But life in prison isn't enough for this man. I demand that he be sentenced to death!*" The fury in his eyes had been so powerful, it felt like a physical attack.

Now his eyes looked . . . intense, like he was boring a hole into her heart.

One of the COs in the execution chamber said something Susan couldn't hear, and pointed Curt toward the death chair. Curt sat down and stretched out his legs, getting comfortable. The COs buzzed around him, strapping him in. They blocked his eyes from Susan's, which she was grateful for.

A prim-looking woman in her forties, dressed in a white uniform, came into the chamber. Pam leaned down to Susan and Danny and explained, "That's the nurse."

"Thanks, I was wondering," Danny said. "This whole thing is so professional."

"We do our best," said Warden Tomey.

God, these people are all acting so laid back, thought Susan. *Especially Danny.* She couldn't understand why he wasn't more emotional, witnessing the death of the man who had killed his daughter.

Warden Tomey stood up and said, "Excuse me, folks."

He walked out of the viewing room, carrying a piece of paper with an official-looking seal on it. Pam said, "Shall I turn on the volume? Like I said, we'll hear them, but they won't hear us."

She hit a wall switch, and now Susan could hear what was going on in the execution chamber. Mainly it was rustling and clicks, as the COs finished with the straps and the nurse went over to the medical cart and took instruments out of a drawer. Curt, his face still hidden by the officers' bodies, was silent.

Warden Tomey entered the chamber from the hallway and nodded solemnly to Curt and the COs. The officers stepped back, and Susan was able to see Curt's expressionless face as Tomey began reading from his document.

"In accordance with the sentence arrived at in Federal Docket #10347, the defendant Curtis Jansen . . ." Here Curt closed his eyes, and Susan wondered if he was praying or just in fear about what was going to happen minutes from now. ". . . having been found guilty of aggravated kidnap across state lines, aggravated rape of a minor, and homicide in the first degree with special circumstances, will now serve his sentence, which is: death."

Tomey lowered the document and turned to Curt. "Mr. Jansen, do you have any final words?"

Curt opened his eyes. "I do."

Susan watched as Curt turned to the other viewing room and took a deep breath.

"Chaplain Davis," Curt said, "I want to thank you for everything. You're the best thing about this place. Your wise words and your kindness have really helped me a lot." He paused, then said, "And go Red Sox! We'll win it all next year!"

Susan watched, spellbound, as Curt moved his head and eyes and found his sister.

"Lisa," he said, "you're my rock. I love you. I never would've made it this far without you. Please, promise me you won't be bitter." He gave his sister a soft smile, then said, "I'll see you on the other side, Lisa."

Now came the moment Susan had been hoping for, and dreading. Curt turned and looked straight at her. *What the hell is he thinking?*

"Ms. Lentigo," he began, "I do want to say, I didn't kill your daughter."

Susan's heart sank, and she realized how deeply she had been hoping that he would finally, for the second time, confess to her daughter's murder.

Curt continued, "But there's no hatred in my heart for you. I think you're a good person who's gone through incredible pain. I know you really believe I killed her, and that's why you're doing this. So that's okay." Susan thought she could see Curt shrugging his shoulders under his straps, to emphasize it truly was okay.

Then Curt said, "I did hate you for a long time, but now I love you." He smiled at Susan, but then his brow furrowed. "And I'm sorry for your loss. If you ever find out the truth about what happened to Amy, don't blame yourself for what happened to me. You truly thought you were doing the right thing. I forgive you, and I'll see you on the other side too."

Susan could barely breathe.

CHAPTER FORTY-TWO

Curt leaned back in his chair, still watching Susan. The same soft smile he had given his sister now played on his face.

"What a crock of shit," Danny said. "This asshole doesn't have the decency to admit it even when he's about to die."

Susan eyed Danny. He looked disgusted, but his face was red with some emotion she couldn't place. *Excitement*, she thought.

Then she heard Warden Tomey, down in the execution chamber, ask, "Do you want the hood?"

"No thank you," Curt said.

"God be with you," Tomey said, and stepped out of the room.

Danny turned to Susan. "God will fucking send him to hell."

In the execution chamber, Curt gazed up at his sister. He made a kissing gesture with his lips. His hands were tied down, but Susan saw him wave to Lisa with his fingers.

Then Curt looked back at Susan, and once again she felt overwhelmed.

She felt her left hand being held, and started to recoil until she realized it was Robert holding it. He squeezed her hand.

Susan couldn't stand it. *How am I supposed to feel?*

She stared down at Curt Jansen and tried to picture this man hurting Amy. She had to remember Curt looked very different back then, twenty years ago. He was thick-lipped and surly, in the mugshots at least, his face swollen from too much drinking.

She shut her eyes and pictured Curt sitting in his car on that last Friday afternoon, while Amy came out of school wearing her necklace.

Amy skipping out of school, saying goodbye to her friends, looking around for her grandma's yellow car with the red stripe. Curt sits in his old Ford across the street—

No, Susan corrected herself, *on the same side of the street, close enough to see the necklace.*

He's unshaven, half drunk, his hands down his pants—

Oh God, so gross. He's been here twenty minutes, watching kids. He recognizes Amy, from seeing her play basketball in her pink dress. Maybe he even heard me call her name to come inside. Suddenly, on an impulse, no thought, he pulls up in front of her. He opens his mouth and smiles. Yellow teeth. "Hi Amy, get in the car. Your mom sent me."

Amy is confused, pouts her lips. "But my grandma's picking me up."

"Your grandma's working. I'm supposed to take you to her house. Come on, she's got ice cream."

He opens the door.

Amy gets in . . .

Maybe, thought Susan. That could be what happened. But her mind kept churning.

Amy skips out of school, saying goodbye to her friends and looking around.

Danny sits in his Honda, drinking beer and waiting. He sees Amy and waves.

She runs to him. "I thought Grandma was picking me up."

"No, it's me today. Hop in."

He opens the door. Amy gets in. Danny looks all around, makes sure nobody's paying attention to them . . . and drives off.

And then—

"If you wanna see this, you gotta open your eyes," Danny said into her ear.

His voice was jarring. She looked at him like he was a stranger, then watched the nurse preparing the IV line. Curt was watching the nurse too, and Susan could feel the panic rising in him.

She couldn't take this. They were about to kill this man! Was he really guilty? She closed her eyes again.

Late afternoon. The woods. Curt holds Amy's hand firmly as they walk toward the river. Nobody else around.

Amy whines, "I want to go home."

It felt right to Susan. But then again:

Danny holds Amy's hand as they walk toward the river.

"Daddy, I'm cold. I want to go home."

Then what? Oh God, the lean-to.

Curt shoves Amy to the wooden floor—

Danny shoves Amy—

Susan shook her head violently. No, she couldn't go there.

On her left, Robert squeezed her hand again. She ignored him.

Amy runs from the lean-to, Curt chasing. She looks behind her, trips, falls headlong into that sharp rock. Her forehead bleeding, dizzy, she rolls and gets up. But Curt grabs her.

She screams. Curt yells, "Shut up!" Or it's Danny. Danny grabs her by her bloody necklace and she screams louder. Danny puts his hands around her neck and Amy gasps. Then she stops screaming. Stops moving. Danny takes off Amy's necklace—

"Susan," Danny said. She opened her eyes again. "You're not gonna fall asleep, are ya?"

She forced herself to look at Danny, at the small black pupils in the middle of his bright, wide-open eyes . . . This execution had him all keyed up.

She looked at Curt, biting his lip as the IV needle went into his immobilized arm, just inside his elbow. A little blood flowed around the edges of the needle.

Curt runs back to his car carrying the bloody necklace . . . The necklace swinging in Danny's hand . . . The necklace . . .

Now Susan saw the individual beads in the necklace, close up. *The necklace, in the plastic bag . . . The necklace, in Amy's photograph . . . The necklace, around Emily's neck . . .*

The necklace . . .

Fuck! Something about the necklace! What was it?

Pam said, "Looks like they got the IV in okay."

The nurse stepped away from Curt and attached the IV to one of the three clear liquids. She pressed a button on the cart and the liquid began dripping into his arm.

Watching Curt, Susan sensed his fear of death hitting him all at once. He gulped and his chest heaved. She could hear his breath, deep and nervously quick.

Pam kept playing tour guide. "Now they're pumping in the sodium thiopental. He'll be out of it in about fifteen seconds, but they'll let it go another three minutes before they give him the lethal drugs."

Curt looked over at the other window and gave a weak smile to Lisa and the chaplain. Then he looked back at Susan.

He gave her the same smile as he held his eyes on hers.

She looked back at him, and slowly his eyes drooped and then closed.

She kept staring at him. Three minutes and it would all be over.

The necklace. The fucking necklace.

Emily outside her school, wearing the necklace.

The photo of Amy, wearing the necklace.

The photo of Amy . . .

Susan was panicky, trying to think. Robert said something to her, but she didn't hear it.

The photo of Amy with the necklace.

Emily outside her school, turning to go inside, and there's her necklace . . . The back of her necklace . . .

The back of her necklace.

Susan's eyes flew open. That was it!

The back of Emily's necklace, inside the baggie. Black, yellow, blue, red, and orange beads, in order. The blue bead is a unicorn.

Amy at the kitchen table stringing the beads with Susan. Black, yellow, blue unicorn, red, and orange. In order.

The exact same pattern of beads—on the back of the necklace.

"Oh my God," Susan said.

"Bye bye, Curt," Danny said, with that same oddly excited look in his eyes. He turned to Pam. "Do they soil their pants when they die?"

Susan was unable to sit down anymore. She jumped up and asked Danny, "How did you copy the whole necklace so perfectly?"

Danny looked up at her, his face turning bewildered. "What?"

"You heard me," Susan said. "You said you copied it off that picture of Amy, right?"

Danny shrugged. "Sure."

Susan felt Robert and everybody else in the room watching her as she quickly reached in her wallet and took out the picture of Amy wearing the necklace.

She showed it to Danny. "But the picture only shows half the necklace. How did you copy the part behind her neck that you can't see?"

Danny opened his mouth trying to come up with an answer, but he was stuck.

Susan said quietly, "You killed her. You killed her, Danny."

"Oh, come on." Danny gave a laugh that came out sounding sickly, at least to Susan. "I remembered what the necklace looked like."

No more quietness. Susan yelled, "Every single fucking bead? Even the ones that were always hidden by her hair?"

She turned to Tomey. "Warden, you have to stop this execution!"

Tomey held his hands up. "Ms. Lentigo, calm down—"

How much time was left—two minutes? One? She yelled into the execution chamber, "Stop it! Stop the execution!"

Pam said, "They can't hear you, Susan."

She banged on the window with both fists. The two COs who were still in the execution chamber could hear that, and they looked up at her confused.

"He's innocent!" she yelled, hoping that if they couldn't hear her, they could at least read her lips.

"Don't be ridiculous," Danny said.

She banged the window again. "He's innocent!"

Director Williams stepped toward her. "You need to stop this. You're hysterical—"

"How did Danny make a perfect copy of Amy's necklace? The only way he could do that is if he still has it!"

Danny said, "Jesus, what the hell is the matter with you?"

Director Williams told Susan, "We only have your word that it's a perfect copy."

"I remember every bead! Amy and I made that necklace! You have to stop the execution! He's innocent!"

Down in the execution chamber, the two COs and the nurse were looking up at the viewing room, wondering what was going on. Susan watched as Warden Tomey motioned for them to keep going. The nurse gave him a nod in response.

Susan was horrified. "What are you doing?!"

Tomey said, "It's too late, Susan. If you don't calm down, I'll have to ask the officers to escort you out of here."

"Fine, I'll go down there myself and rip that thing out of his arm!"

She headed for the door, but Williams grabbed her.

She yelled, "Get off me!" and tried to break free, but then the muscular CO got between her and the door.

She looked to the two ADAs, the man and the woman, who had barely said a word this whole time. "Help me! They're killing this man!"

They both looked shell-shocked. She could tell even before they said anything, they'd be worthless.

But they never got a chance to speak, because Robert stepped toward Danny and said, "Danny—"

Susan begged Tomey, "Please, listen to me—"

Robert held up his hand to Susan. "Wait." Then he turned back to Danny. "Pam said you called her. *You asked her if you would be patted down.*"

Danny blinked, then tried to shrug it off. "Yeah, why?"

Robert turned to Pam. "Has anybody ever asked you that before?"

Pam looked confused, like she had no idea where Robert was going with this. But Susan started to get it. She watched, desperately hopeful, as he tried to work his magic.

Pam said, "Not really. It *was* kind of an odd question."

Robert said, "Yes it was." He advanced on Danny. "*I know where the original necklace is. The one Amy wore.*"

Danny's eyes widened with alarm.

"You brought it in here, didn't you?" Robert said.

Danny shook his head. "Why would I do a stupid thing like that?"

"Because you get off on danger and you're fucking sick. You were probably sitting here playing with the necklace and jerking off."

"Oh, come on—"

Robert looked closely at Danny's right pocket. Susan followed his eyes there.

"What's that in your pocket?" Robert said. And now Susan saw it too: tiny little lumps several inches below his waist, where the bottom of his pocket would be. "Looks like keys, but I don't think it is."

As Robert moved even closer, Danny pushed his chair backwards. But Robert grabbed Danny's arms and held them behind his back.

Susan broke away from Williams and the COs. She leaped forward and reached into Danny's pocket. She dug deep—and there it was.

She pulled the necklace out of Danny's pocket and held it up.

Director Williams and everybody else stared in shock.

Susan said to Danny, "You piece of shit."

Then she looked at the execution chamber. The three minutes was up, and the nurse was now attaching Curt's IV to the first lethal drug, Pavulon. She was getting set to release it.

Susan said to Warden Tomey, "Stop the fucking execution!"

Tomey looked paralyzed. Williams said to him quickly, "You need to stop it."

"Now!" Susan yelled.

Finally, Warden Tomey jumped into action. He ran out of the room.

In the execution chamber, the nurse was about to hit the button on the medical cart that would release the Pavulon into Curt's bloodstream when Tomey rushed in. He yelled: "Don't touch that!"

The nurse was totally bewildered—but she moved her hand away from the lethal button.

Still holding the necklace, Susan collapsed against a wall, gasping with relief.

Robert was gripping Danny's arms. He turned to the two COs. "Officers, could you please take custody of the suspect?"

Danny was struck dumb, terrified, as the COs grabbed hold of him.

Susan looked down at Danny with hot fury.

Robert put his hand on Susan's arm. "Let's get the hell out of here."

Williams said, "I'll need that necklace as evidence."

Susan looked to Robert, who nodded. She took one last look at the necklace . . . the purple dolphin, the pink duck, the blue unicorn . . . and handed it over.

She thought, *It's a beautiful necklace. It caught my daughter's killer.*

She took one last look at Danny, fiercely triumphant. Then she walked out the door with Robert and Pam.

They made it out into the hallway just as Lisa stepped out of the other viewing room, escorted by the chaplain. Lisa looked totally wrung out, her hair a scraggly mess and her makeup running. Her eyes were uncertain, like she knew her brother had just gotten a reprieve for some reason, but she didn't understand what had happened. She stared at Susan, her eyes begging for clarification.

Susan said, "Your brother's innocent. My husband killed Amy. He's going to prison."

Lisa blinked, then started to weep. Susan walked toward her, and the two women fell into each other's arms.

CHAPTER FORTY-THREE

THE SKY WAS already dark when Susan came out onto the front steps of the prison, along with Warden Tomey, Director Williams, Pam, Robert, and Lisa. The media jostled for position and shouted out questions about the rumor the condemned man hadn't been executed yet. Warden Tomey straightened his sport jacket and got up in front of the microphone.

"Good evening. I'll get right to it," the warden said. "I've ordered a stay in the execution of Curtis Jansen. New evidence has surfaced that strongly calls his guilt into question."

The whole place went instantly silent. The media was too stunned to shout more questions. The only sound Susan could hear was the rushing wind.

The warden continued, "Now I'll turn these proceedings over to Stanley Williams, the director of the North Dakota Division of the FBI."

Williams stepped up to the mic and cleared his throat. "The North Dakota Division recently commenced an investigation based on an alternate scenario for Amy Lentigo's murder. The investigation reached fruition this afternoon, and the FBI has now arrested a new suspect. That suspect is Amy's father, Daniel Lentigo."

It sounded to Susan like everybody in the entire crowd gasped at once.

She was annoyed at Williams for making it seem like the FBI was responsible for catching her husband. She had done it. It was her.

But what did that really matter? As long as Danny was in prison. Forever.

Williams went on about how the FBI never gave up on a case. Susan was too lost in her thoughts to hear it all. But after a minute or two he was finished, and Pam motioned for her to come up to the mic.

As she stepped up, she looked at Robert, standing to her right, and Lisa, on her left. Then she looked out at the crowd.

Everybody was waiting for her. She had to say something. But what? She felt so scared. Would the world judge her for not knowing what a monster her husband really was?

Well fuck it. She shook her head to shake away her fears. She'd start talking and whatever came out, came out.

"I just want to thank Agent Pappas," she began, and nodded to Robert. "When I told him I thought Curt Jansen was innocent, he didn't fight me. He didn't care if it might make him look bad. He understood, we all make mistakes." She paused. "My mistake cost Amy her life."

She took a breath, as the truth of that sunk into her, before she continued. "But now I've done everything I can to make up for it. And so has Agent Pappas."

She looked directly into one of the cameras. "Curt, when you see this video, I just want you to know, I am so sorry. Because of me, you lost twenty years of your life and suffered who knows what kind of horror. The fact that you don't hate me now . . ." She felt her eyes getting wet, but fought to keep going. "You are the best man I have ever met."

She turned to Lisa. "And I want to apologize to you too. I was so wrong about your brother."

Lisa broke into fresh tears and hugged Susan, hard.

*   *   *

As Susan continued speaking, the entire country began to tune in.

At the Crow Bar in Lake Luzerne, Lenora had dropped in for a couple beers to kick off her Saturday night. Now she sat there, eyes wide, staring at the old TV above the bar along with the bartender, waitresses, and other customers.

"I'm just glad we saved an innocent man's life," Susan said on the TV screen.

Lenora was so utterly stunned, her glass of beer fell out of her hands and crashed to the floor.

*   *   *

Three hundred miles west, in Tamarack, Emily was in her backyard at 89 Ash Street throwing tennis balls to the family dog. But Emily's mom was in the living room watching TV in shock. Susan was saying, "And we stopped my ex-husband from hurting any more innocent children."

On the other side of town, Kyra was in her room, sitting cross-legged in bed. On her phone screen, she watched as Susan said, "Thanks to Agent Pappas, and a brave young woman in Tamarack, New York, named Kyra Anderson . . ."

Kyra put her hand to her heart.

Meanwhile, in North Dakota, standing on the prison steps, Susan looked out at the TV cameras and reporters and said, ". . . my beloved daughter, Amy, can rest in peace at last."

EPILOGUE

New Year's Day

Four weeks later, on New Year's Day, snow fell on the Hodge Hills Federal Penitentiary.

The barbed-wire fences and barren hills were covered in white. A foot of snow lay on the roofs of the buildings and watchtowers. It was four o'clock, time for the afternoon count, so all the inmates were back in their cells. Outside, it was quiet.

Then a side door of the administration building opened and Curt Jansen came outside, followed by Warden Tomey. Curt was dressed in civilian clothes—blue jeans and a thin green parka. He carried a small suitcase, not much bigger than a backpack, with all the belongings he was taking with him. He'd left most of his stuff behind for the other guys on the Row.

He blinked up at the sky, at the first freedom he had known in twenty years. He put down his suitcase and reached out his hands to feel the snowflakes.

Then he saw his sister, Lisa, running toward him.

Curt held out his arms.

*   *   *

In upstate New York, the snow was falling, too, as Susan and Robert headed toward the cemetery.

Robert was staying for a week or so at the Wagon Wheel Motel on 9-N. Last night they had walked along the Hudson for hours, talking about so many things, way back to their childhoods. When they got to the bridge over the waterfall, they kissed. It was wonderful, except she burst out crying and couldn't stop. She was so scared he'd be frightened away. But he just stood there holding her, and at last she calmed down, and then they kissed again, and it was even sweeter.

They weren't going any further than that, not yet anyway. She was still reeling. Since coming home from North Dakota, she'd made an appointment with a therapist in Glens Falls that Terri recommended. And she'd been going to see Parson Parsons at the church a couple times a week. Last Sunday night, they sat together in the dark church for almost an hour, not speaking, just breathing.

Susan's mom, of course, was eager for her and Robert to close the deal already. Lenora kept whispering to Susan, "Oh my, he's so *handsome*."

Now, as Susan and Robert rode to the cemetery together, Lenora was in the back seat. She asked, "Did you hear Rumples this morning? He was purring so loud I thought it was a car motor."

Kyra, sitting next to Lenora, answered, "Yeah, for a fourteen-year-old cat, he's pretty kickass."

Lenora laughed. Kyra was spending Christmas vacation in Luzerne, and Lenora had fallen in love with her, seeing her as a kindred free spirit. She was even threatening to get a flame tattoo just like Kyra's.

The first night Kyra was there, just before she went to sleep, Susan had changed the dusty old sheets that had been on Amy's bed for twenty years. She'd moved Amy's stuffed bunnies off the pillow and onto the windowsill.

Susan was beginning to get used to the changes. Last night at two a.m., when she came home, she stood in the doorway of Amy's room, just listening to Kyra's light snore.

As the car curved right and crested a hill, the cemetery came into view and they all fell silent. Robert drove through the gate and parked.

They got out of the car and walked through the snowy quiet to Amy's grave. Her headstone read, *"Amy Lentigo Beloved Daughter 1994–2001."*

Susan placed the pink roses she had bought this morning in front of the stone.

Kyra asked, "Can I give her my necklace?"

"Of course," Susan said.

Kyra took off her dreamcatcher necklace and laid it next to the roses. Susan thought it looked perfect there.

"She was a happy kid," Lenora said. "Had that big wide smile."

Susan smiled too, remembering. She whispered, "I loooooooooooove you more than the moon loooooooooooooves the stars."

Robert put his arm around Susan, and Kyra linked her arm through Lenora's. They stood still for a while as the white snow fell all around them.

AUTHOR'S NOTE

NINE YEARS AGO, I read an article in the *Glens Falls Post-Star* about a woman from a small town in upstate New York who was holding a fundraising event at a local bar. She needed money to travel to the upcoming execution of the man who had raped and murdered her young daughter twenty-two years before.

Everything about this story stuck with me: not only the tragic death, but also the woman's dire circumstances and her quest to find justice and closure two decades later.

For years I wanted to write a novel about this, but I didn't know what the story would be. Then one day I was having coffee with a writer friend, John Henry Davis, and he suggested: "What if the guy who's being executed maybe didn't do it?"

And that's how *The Necklace* was born.

After I wrote the novel, I discovered something amazing. There is a woman in Idaho named Carol Dodge who devoted her life to proving that Christopher Tapp, the man imprisoned for raping and killing her daughter Angie many years earlier, was innocent. Thanks to Carol's relentless efforts, Tapp was finally set free and the real killer, Brian Leigh Dripps, was arrested.

Talk about life imitating art!

The Necklace is not only the story of an incredibly courageous woman, it's a story about life in the foothills of the Adirondacks, where I've spent a lot of time for the past thirty-five years, including living there for ten. The area has struggled in this new century, with factories and mills shutting down and tourism not quite filling the economic gap. And yet people continue to cobble livings together, raise their families, and work for a better future.

Susan, the diner waitress who's the heroine of *The Necklace,* is a composite of several women I've known in the Adirondacks. The relationship between her and her mom—the good part, not the guilt-ridden part!—is inspired by my wife's relationship with her mother.

Other characters are inspired by real-life people too. FBI agent Robert Pappas is based on my friend Paul Bishop, a writer who was an LAPD sex crimes detective for seventeen years. I used to teach playwriting at the Hudson Correctional Facility in Coxsackie, New York, and Curt Jansen is inspired by one of my students there, a dignified man in his thirties who had been in prison for murder for fifteen years and preferred to be called Mr. Smith instead of by his first name.

As for Kyra, the rebellious teenage girl in the novel—I'm not really sure who she's based on. I think maybe she's based on me!